CHRISTMAS CANDY CORPSE

I slipped my phone from my pocket. I'd felt a text come through during our conversation. I tapped the screen to bring it to life. Eric answered my text about Kinzy with shock and grief, then ended the message with a stern warning to stay out of the murder investigation.

How could I? Kinzy was a coworker and I feared Shannon would be considered a person of interest. Why wouldn't she? She'd argued with Kinzy and was angry enough that she said she'd kill her if she made another crack about her weight. Then Kinzy made a second remark. My heart dropped. When Shannon reported to the set late after lunch, I thought it looked like she'd been napping. Maybe not. A struggle with someone fighting for their life would rumple your clothing, mess up your hair and smear your makeup. Her hair and makeup had been fixed. Her wardrobe hadn't. I felt certain Sheriff Perry would notice.

I didn't believe Shannon murdered Kinzy. She'd stuck by me with unwavering faith and I planned to return the favor.

Who else might want Kinzy dead? Maybe Leon?

After their vicious argument this morning, then Kinzy ignoring his text, had Leon come to our set and confronted her?

Had they argued again, and it escalated to murder?

Books by Rosemarie Ross

COBBLERED TO DEATH

FINISHED OFF IN FONDANT

CHRISTMAS CANDY CORPSE

Published by Kensington Publishing Corp.

Christmas Candy Corpse

ROSEMARIE ROSS

KENSINGTON
PUBLISHING CORP.

www.kensingtonbooks.com

CHAPTER ONE

"Merry Christmas, Courtney!" Quintin Shepherd, the producer of *The American Baking Battle*, greeted me with outstretched arms. "Welcome to the kickoff mixer for the Christmas show."

I hesitated a moment at his out-of-character welcome. He stood between me and the entry to the grand ballroom in Coal Castle Resort, once a private home built in the Gilded Age by a coal magnate. I leaned toward him. Without making body contact, I air kissed his cheek. He dropped his arms and followed my lead. Our lack of physical contact had little to do with him being my boss and everything to do with me being camera ready. We both knew wrinkled clothes and smudged makeup didn't make for good filming.

"You look fantastic and festive."

"Thank you." I heard the surprise in my voice and quickly returned Quintin's smile.

The skirt of my evergreen sheath grazed the top of my knee. The sequined neckline and my metallic pointed-toe pumps shimmered in the chandelier lighting. I'd tucked my straightened hair behind my ears to show off the emerald studs adorning my lobes.

I studied his face. The lines around his eyes and mouth seemed softer. Did he seem happier because he landed a Christmas special for the baking competition? Or something else? I realized the silence had stretched to an awkward level, so I said, "You do too." The Christmas red cummerbund and bow tie against his black tux created a striking ensemble.

He sobered. "Thank you for being flexible and rearranging your schedule."

This time I checked my disbelief before it showed on my face. An astute businessman, Quintin worried about the bottom line. I'd never received a compliment or thank you from him. He'd hired the talent and expected us to fulfill our contract duties. I wanted to ask if I or anyone else had a choice. A clause in our contracts stated that when the show was ready to film, the talent reported to set. It's one of the reasons I had to tape few episodes of my weekly show, *Cooking with the Farmer's Daughter,* on location in the past. In those instances, we'd had plenty of time to prepare and adjust our normal schedules. Not this time.

The call came on the Monday before Thanksgiving with instructions to arrive by late afternoon on Black Friday. My eat-and-run Thanksgiving dinner left my cousin Caroline alone for the remainder of the holiday. Both single lonely-onlys with busy parents, we celebrated holidays together. She insisted she understood, yet I saw the disappointment on her face.

"My securing a Christmas special for this year took you away from something important?" Quintin interrupted my thoughts.

I nodded. "Not only did it shorten my Thanksgiving holiday, it leaves my cousin Caroline on her own to kick off a hospital toy drive." A registered nurse, she'd worked extra emergency room shifts to get the four-day holiday weekend off so we could organize the fundraiser like we did every year. Illness doesn't take a holiday and the hospital ensures Santa makes a stop in each child's room on Christmas Eve. I'd promised I'd pull double duty on my fundraising efforts when I returned to Chicago.

"Well." Quintin smiled. "I want to make it up to you and Caroline. The show will pay for a spa weekend whenever it works in your schedule and we'll make a generous donation to your organization. Okay?"

What? Had I stepped into a Dickens novel? Had Quintin been visited by three ghosts? Like Scrooge, Quintin was a penny-pincher. His expectant expression told me I needed to reply, I grabbed his hand and squeezed. "Yes! The donation's enough."

"Nonsense. We'll cover both. I'll have my accounting manager contact you."

The door to the ballroom opened. "There you are." Kinzy Hummel, assistant director for the show, poked her head out looking first at Quintin, then at me. "Since Courtney has arrived, are we ready to start the party? Should I have them bring in the contestants?"

"Yes," Quintin said.

Kinzy pushed the door wider to allow me to enter.

"Wow!" I stopped short and looked around the room.

Christmas had arrived at Coal Castle Resort. I'd thought the lobby decorations were beautiful. They'd gone all out on the ballroom. A floor-to-ceiling Christmas tree stood in front of double doors that, I guessed, led to a balcony with a spectacular view of the Pocono Mountains. Old-fashioned bubble lights lit the floor-to-ceiling long-needled pine. Artificial red poinsettia blooms decorated the branches. A white ribbon flecked with gold started at the illuminated starburst tree topper and wound the circumference of the tree, giving it a polished finish.

Evergreen swags, twisted with multicolored lights, bordered the walls in scallops. Starched red cloths covered the tables. Matching bows tied pristine white slipcovers to the chairs. On the stage a small string quartet softly played carols and popular songs of the season.

A mahogany bar was tucked into a far corner of the room with a large mirror, edged in stained glass, mounted behind it. Cocktail tables dotted the area around the bar. Shannon Collins, a judge on the baking competition, stood beside one and sipped an amber liquid from a clear mug. Bourbon, I presumed.

I swallowed hard, remembering the burn of the alcohol the one and only time I drank it. It was my penance for misleading my new friend. Shannon, like my viewers, had thought I was really a farmer's daughter. Thank goodness, my network allowed me to clear the air on that myth.

It'd only been eight weeks since I'd seen Shannon, but I'd missed her. Text messages and emails weren't the same. Shannon and I became fast friends during the taping of the first show.

"Shannon!" I couldn't wait to share her excitement.

The show was featuring her new line of aprons. What a boon for sales!

She looked up and waved. I hurried over. We wrapped each other in a loose hug. When I pulled free, I checked my surprise. Shannon had gained some weight. Stretched to the limits, her black form-fitting cocktail dress flattened her breasts. When she tugged at the fabric, I flicked my gaze to her face.

Pretending I didn't notice her weight gain, I asked, "Are you over the moon to have your aprons featured on the show?" I laid my evening clutch on the table beside her drink.

"I guess." She lifted her mug.

Her voice lacked the enthusiasm I'd expected.

"Wait." I touched her hand. "Let's toast your apron line." I cranked my neck looking for a waiter carrying drinks with plans to wave them over.

"No one's serving. If you want a drink, you must go to the bar. Quintin's so cheap. He didn't spring for servers. It's the least he could do since we had to disrupt our lives to film this special." Her words hissed out in a catty tone I'd never heard her use before.

Momentarily taken aback, I shook it off. "Give me a quick second." I made a mental note to keep Quintin's offer of a spa weekend for Caroline and me a secret as I made my way to the bar. I ordered a mulled wine for me and a bourbon for Shannon.

She was sipping from her mug when I got back to the table. She cast a glance my way. My disappointment must have shown. "We can still do a toast," she said.

"I know. I bought you a bourbon."

Shannon looked at the glass and licked her lips.

"Thanks." She took the drink, set it on the table, then lifted her cup. "I'll just toast with my apple cider."

Her snippy response didn't encourage me to do a celebratory toast, yet I'd suggested it, so I needed to make the toast. "To product lines!" I clinked my glass to her mug and pushed a smile to my lips.

"Here, here!" Shannon said, sounding like her old self. "Any update on your knives?"

"Yes. The company's working on a prototype of the eight-piece set. I hope sometime next year we'll be toasting my product line." I sipped my spiced wine. Wait. Did Shannon say she was drinking apple cider and not a cocktail? "When did you become a teetotaler . . . ?"

"Is it hot in here?" Shannon interrupted. She tugged at her sleeveless dress.

"I'm comfortable."

"I'm going to find someone to adjust the heat." Shannon drained her mug and took off with a determined stride, which caused the blond curls cascading down her back to bounce.

I stood beside the cocktail table and watched her brush past Harrison Canfield, a renowned chef and judge on the show, and Skylar Daily, my cohost, with barely a greeting before she zoned in on a waiter preparing a banquet table.

"What's with her?" Skylar asked, joining me at the cocktail table.

"She thinks it's warm in here."

Harrison shrugged. "I'm comfortable."

"Me too. We're both dressed warmer than the ladies in their lovely party dresses," Skylar said, laying on his charm. It's the reason he was on the baking competition. He was popular and handsome.

Harrison wore his standard three-piece designer suit. His choice of a silver-gray necktie with the black suit and shirt made a vivid statement. Skylar sported a brown and green tweed jacket over a green Oxford shirt, open at the neckline, with khaki-colored trousers. It tickled me that the judges and cohosts unknowingly twinned their counterpart without the assistance of wardrobe.

"Everyone!" The familiar clap of our director Brenden Hall's hands followed his voice. Cast and crew stopped talking and gathered around him near the stage. He signaled the quartet to stop playing. "Before we bring in the contestants, I want to cover changes in filming regarding the Christmas special."

"First, I'd like to thank everyone for rearranging their schedules to accommodate filming," Quintin interrupted.

"Yes." Brenden nodded. "We appreciate it. And thank you to Quintin for his stellar negotiations to get us a Christmas special airing *this* year."

Everyone, except Shannon, clapped. Quintin gave a slight bow.

"Now," Brenden said. "Things are a little different for this show. We have seven days to film the special. The Christmas show is culled down to three two-hour specials showcasing six bakers. The first episode will have a one-person elimination, the second a double elimination." Brenden paused when the crowd murmured their surprise. "The third segment is the finale where the remaining three contestants compete for the top prize of fifty thousand dollars."

"Wow!" Harrison called out.

"Well, it's Christmas!" Quintin's response coaxed others to voice their surprise.

The buzz of conversation grew loud until Skylar whistled loudly to quiet them. "Was there anything else, Brenden?" Skylar asked.

"Yes. We've just finalized themes. Each episode will have three competitions based on past, present and future recipes. The first day is for Christmas candy. The second day is Christmas cookies. The finale is Christmas desserts. Tonight, for the meet and mingle, we've planned a fun activity to break the ice with the contestants. The talent will stand by a cocktail table. There's a basket of small gifts. The contestants will choose a present and open it. It will have a surprise kitchen utensil for them and a conversation starter question. It's going to be a great way to get them over being starstruck or nervous. We're filming the entire evening for use to advertise the show. I think we're ready to meet the contestants. Could someone signal . . ."

"You can't go in there." A deep voice carried through the door when it burst open.

Everyone's attention turned toward the door. A woman, tall and sturdy, stood in the frame of the doorway. Her posture, designer clothing and trendy asymmetrical bob screamed chic and sophisticated. Her platinum hair sparkled under the lights, giving her a haloed effect. Her gaze searched the room and landed on Brenden. She stepped further into the ballroom, letting the door close on the warning from the guard from Nolan Security, a private security company hired by the show.

"Surprise!" With her eyes riveted on Brenden, she lifted her arms to the air and smiled.

"Mother?" Brenden hurried to her. "What are you doing here?"

They clasped hands and held each other at arm's length.

"I came to watch you work and spend some time with my only child. It's the holiday season when family should be together." She released his hands.

"Yes, well . . ." Brenden turned. He seemed more flustered than surprised. "Everyone, this is my mother, Victoria Hall. Please introduce yourselves after the meet and mingle with the contestants. Harrison, Shannon, Courtney and Skylar, please take your place by the table. Kinzy has briefed the contestants. Mother, let's get you a drink." Brenden escorted Victoria to the bar.

Once we were in place, Quintin opened the door and Kinzy led the group of contestants into the ballroom.

I flashed my most welcoming smile and it hooked an older woman who'd make an excellent Mrs. Claus except for her flaming red hair. She walked straight to my table.

"Hello." I extended my hand.

"Nice to meet you." She grabbed my hand and shook. "I'm Carol Thlunaut. I'm part Tlingit and run a candy company in North Pole, Alaska. I watch your show all the time back home." She started to rummage through the basket of colorfully wrapped boxes.

I didn't think this woman needed a conversation starter.

"What kind of candy do you make?"

"Chocolates of all kinds, caramel filled, vanilla nougat, mint, cherry, molded in Christmas images, Santa, reindeer, snowmen. Tourists eat them up." She grinned and winked.

"I bet they do. Do you have a website?" I might have found my stocking stuffers.

"Yes." She looked over her shoulder. "I'm not allowed to give it out."

"Of course." Certain I could find it via an internet search, I asked, "What was in the gift?"

"A carving knife." A young man hovered nearby so she moved on to Skylar.

"Dylan Smyth," the twenty-something-year-old contestant introduced himself. "My mom and I make and distribute frozen cookie dough. It's a regional company." He focused on unwrapping his gift, held up a melon baller, then read the question. "Ask Courtney what her favorite Christmas candy is."

"Coconut brittle. What's yours?"

He pushed thick plastic-framed glasses up the bridge of his nose. "I never thought about it. Candy cane?" With a wave, he was off.

"Mya Brooklyn." A young woman extended her hand. "I take my food seriously."

"Me too," I said as we shook hands. Tall and slender, Mya appeared to share the same generation as I. Her light brown hair, cut into a classic bob, framed a girl-next-door face. Her hazel eyes sparkled with kindness.

She drew out and opened a gift. "A citrus zester." She held it up for me to see, then read the note inside. Looking up, she asked, "Who's your favorite chef?"

"Tough question. I'll say Chef Russo. He runs a small Italian restaurant in Chicago. His eggplant parm is to die for. Do you have a favorite chef?"

Her olive skin darkened with a flush. "It's you."

"Thank you."

Nodding, she said, "You're welcome. I'd better go."

"Good luck," I called, realizing she never gave me her baking or cooking background. Something I'd have to find out in the course of filming.

"Tim Scott." A beefy man with dark skin and a shaved

head stepped to the table. "I don't need a conversation starter. I'm not the starstruck kind."

"Nice to meet you. You still get a gift."

He chose a slender package, unwrapped and revealed a small offset spatula. He read the question to himself then grunted. "Do you really want to tell me what your favorite holiday side dish is?"

"I don't mind."

"I don't care. Here's what you need to know. I'm a baker who specializes in infusing liquor into my baked goods," he said, then walked away.

Lucky for me, I only had two to go. I saw Shannon had finished meeting the contestants. I hoped she'd been pleasant.

"Hi. I'm Marley Weaver."

I pulled my gaze to the man standing in front of the table. He wore a tie-dyed T-shirt. He'd pulled his long salt-and-pepper hair into a ponytail. He looked at me through thick-lensed round wire rim glasses.

He lifted his fingers into a peace sign, then chose a gift. He smiled when he held up tweezers. "Perfect for sitting pearls on my cookies." He pinched the ends together repeatedly. "I work part-time in a grocery store bakery. I want to start my own cookie company."

"Wonderful." I waited for him to read the paper and ask the question.

"Cool." He stared at me a few minutes then turned and walked away.

Focused on watching his abrupt departure without asking the question, I didn't see Skylar loop behind me. He whispered, "Yep, the old hippie did the same thing to me."

I giggled and playfully slapped his arm. "I'm sure he's just starstruck or nervous."

Skylar winked. "I know."

"Excuse me." A meek voice drew my attention back to my duties.

"Hello. I'm sorry for that interruption."

"Don't be." The young woman, in her early twenties at best, watched Skylar walk away. Appreciation shone in her baby blues. She flipped her dark hair over her shoulder. "I'm Brystol Olivette. I specialize in cheesecakes. I have a good business and need to expand out of my small kitchen space. I'm so glad I was chosen as a contestant."

"Nice to meet you. Sorry, you're stuck with the last gift."

"It's okay."

Intent on watching Brystol tear the paper from the box, my body jerked when the door to the ballroom burst open and knocked against the wall.

My gaze flew to the door. Sheriff Perry stalked into the room, followed by Drake Nolan, Head of Security, along with a man I didn't know. Sheriff Perry cranked his neck from side to side.

Quintin stepped in front of him. "Can I help you, Sheriff?"

"Yes, we need to speak with Kinzy Hummel."

"Who's we?"

"I see her," the stranger said. He pushed through Quintin and Sheriff Perry and stomped toward Kinzy. "Miss Hummel," his voice roared through the room. "Don't you care that your grandfather's dead?"

CHAPTER TWO

"That attorney really put a damper on last night's festivities." I took the to-go cup of coffee Skylar offered me. Shannon, Harrison, Skylar and I sat in our makeup chairs waiting for our stylists to arrive.

"I'll say. He went for drama with his announcement." Skylar swiveled his chair with his toe.

"Or humiliation," I said. I sipped the coffee. Skylar had had the forethought to hit Castle Grounds, the resort's coffee shop, before our ride arrived, and had bought us all peppermint mochas. As yummy as the mocha tasted, it didn't hit the spot like my normal hazelnut latte.

With the approach of winter, the brisk air and darkness made it a risk for the talent to walk to the workshop where we were filming, so the show provided six-seater electric carts to transport us, though the carts' hard tops did little to protect us from the elements. We'd had strict orders from Kinzy to catch our lift at the main door of the resort at exactly six forty-five for our seven o'clock call time. Obviously, since our stylists were nowhere to be found, they weren't on the same transport schedule. Or maybe they had to walk?

"I think Kinzy should've decked him." Shannon spat out the words. "Who delivers bad news in the manner he did? Blurting out in front of everyone that her grandpa died. He should be ashamed. I was heartbroken when my Pawpaw passed away."

"I agree. I found the whole scene odd and upsetting, like he had an agenda. Did anyone find out his name?" Harrison asked.

"Yes, it's Leon Chapski. I'm telling you. He gives cowboys a bad name."

Shannon's cowboy reference pertained to Leon's attire, a Western-cut brown suit complete with bolo tie, leather boots and a brown Stetson. Given Shannon's mood, I refrained from saying his choice of clothing didn't really make him a cowboy. Once Sheriff Perry ushered Leon and Kinzy out of the ballroom, we'd learned from Drake that he was an attorney from Montana.

"He ruined the party vibe," Skylar said. "I feel bad for the contestants. The show throws those shindigs to help them relax. They're nervous enough about the competition. I'm sure the shocking scene last night ramped up their edginess."

"I agree." I took another sip of my coffee.

"Say, I bought the peppermint mochas for us to make a toast to the Christmas special and holidays in general." Skylar held his cup out.

We started to raise our cups when our stylists breezed through the door with a morning greeting, an apology for being late and a direct request to get into the costumes hanging in our dressing rooms. Obeying their instruction, we left our coffee on the counter beside our mirrors and headed to wardrobe up.

I finished changing in record time. The short-sleeved sweater I wore under a winter white pantsuit had diagonal red and white stripes. To round out the Christmassy look, I'd slipped into red pumps. My stylist pinned a glittery candy cane brooch to my lapel. Matching earrings dangled from my earlobes. I entered the common area to find Harrison ready and waiting in his swivel chair.

"Ah, you're a candy cane. My stylist told me we're *all* candy themed today in honor of the competition."

I almost giggled at his inflection, which I knew meant he'd voiced his displeasure at his wardrobe to his stylist. Harrison didn't like dressing in costume for the wedding-themed show. He was more comfortable in his suits or chef's attire. I examined his clothing. He was dressed in a brown designer suit. "Where's your candy?"

He turned toward me. Images of old-fashioned hard Christmas candy covered his necktie. A small boutonniere of plastic ribbon candy was attached to his lapel.

"Nice!"

He laughed. "I actually like it too. It's a costume with good taste."

"Hey, stop stealing my puns!" Skylar entered the area. A better sport about dressing in theme, he wore trousers and a long-sleeved shirt, both black, with a crazy Christmas jacket. The print on the green jacket looked delicious: images of chocolate Santas. "I'm going to get hungry wearing this today." He slipped into his chair.

Our stylists appeared and started working their make-up and hair magic. Soon after, Shannon entered the area tugging on the skirt of her dress with an annoyed expression.

She sat and huffed. "They ordered the wrong size. Wardrobe let out a seam and I'm still afraid to breathe. It's cute though."

Like the dress she wore last night, the seams looked ready to burst. The white dress had a fitted bodice and full skirt. Red and green gumdrops dotted the skirt fabric. Her green pumps matched her gumdrop pendant and earrings.

"Let's toast." Skylar reached for his mocha.

Before the rest of us could grab our beverage, shouting filtered through the door. A male and a very familiar female voice grew louder as the argument traveled up the stairs.

Kinzy shouted, "Leave me alone."

"No, you need to come to Montana and settle Harold's estate."

"Is that Kinzy and Leon?" Shannon drawled.

"I think so," I said.

"I'm not going to Montana and I'm not settling his estate." They had to be standing right outside of the door because it sounded like they were in the room with us.

"You have to. You're the executor." Leon used an authoritative tone.

"No way. Why would he do that? He didn't love me. He didn't want me. I haven't seen him in years. Years!" Kinzy shouted the last word.

"Should someone stop them?" Harrison asked. "Do they know we can hear them?"

"Umm . . . I'm not going to get between them." Skylar looked at his stylist. "Just keep working, this will blow over."

It didn't.

"Believe me I tried to dissuade him from naming you. Your grandfather didn't listen to advice."

"Take my name off of the will and give it all to someone else."

"It doesn't work that way. You need to come back to the ranch with me and bury your grandfather. After his ashes are interred, I'll file the required paperwork and we can settle this matter."

"I'm not going to Montana or anywhere else with you. If I never go back to that state, it'll be fine with me."

"He's your grandfather. You owe it to him to attend the funeral and settle his estate as soon as possible." The irritation in Leon's voice took an angry turn.

"I have a job. I know him and all his cronies, which includes you, thought I made a bad career choice. I didn't. I'm making a name for myself."

"Don't use the excuse you're too busy concentrating on your new director job to pay your respects. I have the power and means to kill your career. You need to do the right thing and get back to Montana to settle this estate or I swear, I will ruin you." The threat in Leon's tone struck fear into me. Kinzy, however, responded with anger, screaming obscenities while telling him where he could put the will and estate.

Before Leon could respond the door swung open and

Kinzy entered the room. "And leave me the hell alone," Kinzy hollered, then slammed the door so hard the coffee maker and mugs on the counter along the wall rattled.

I'd dropped my gaze when the door opened and now chanced a look her way via her reflection in the mirror. I expected to see red-faced upset or perhaps angry tears. Her expression surprised me. No signs of anger or sorrow.

Kinzy cleared her throat. "I'm here to escort you to the set." Her voice held its normal tone.

How could she go from sad news to arguing to normal? Even if she didn't like her grandfather, she had to feel something, indifference or regret. Factor in the argument with Leon and it wasn't a normal day for her, yet she was acting as if it were. Was she in denial? Shock?

Skylar and Harrison stood. Although they'd been camera ready, they'd remained seated during the fight outside our door. Shannon's stylist finished spritzing some flyaway hairs around her face, smoothing them into place. I noticed her cheeks looked fuller with her hair pulled into a braid and rolled into a bun on top of her head.

My stylist slid the straightening iron through the last section of my hair and fogged me with hairspray.

Shannon and I rose at the same time.

"Oh, my!" Kinzy looked Shannon up and down.

"What?" Shannon's tone was edged in confrontation.

Kinzy drew her lips into a perturbed line and kept quiet. Her gaze still scanned Shannon.

I knew why. Shannon's dress was tight. One deep breath might test the integrity of the dress's construction.

"What?" Shannon asked again. She stared at Kinzy with arms crossed over her chest, daring her to answer.

"Let's go." Kinzy didn't bite. Guess she'd argued enough this morning.

"Wait," Skylar said. "We need to make a toast with our peppermint mochas. They might be cold though." He looked disappointed. With all the commotion outside of the door, no one even touched their coffee.

"Mochas are good cold." Shannon grabbed her cup. "We'll take them with us."

Skylar glanced at Kinzy. "Sorry, Kinzy, I only bought four."

We held up our cups ready to toast when Kinzy replied, "I could drink Shannon's. By the looks of her wardrobe, she doesn't need the extra calories."

Harrison and Skylar beat a path to the door to get away from a possible cat fight. Kinzy followed on their heels. I stuck with Shannon. A soft sheen of moisture covered the sparkle in her blue eyes.

"You okay?"

She sniffed. "Kinzy's out of line saying that to me. They ordered the wrong size. Wardrobe did the best they could. She's so arrogant and bossy now Quintin's on board with the show." Shannon paused to catch her breath. "I'm going to complain to Brenden, then give Quintin a piece of my mind." She started out the door. I put a hand to her arm to stop her.

"I agree with you the comment was mean spirited and out of line, but we do need to remember she's grief stricken. Leon delivered sensitive news in a harsh manner. Maybe you should cut her a break this one time."

Shannon cocked a brow while considering my words. "All right. But if she makes one more insinuation about my weight I'm going to kill her." Shannon stormed out of the room.

I cringed at her word choice. I knew Shannon used the term figuratively. The sad truth was that on *The American Baking Battle* set, it'd become a literal fact. I'd hoped to get through the filming of this special without hearing the words "kill" or "murder." Or seeing another crime scene.

Shannon and Kinzy's confrontation worried me. Eric had offered Kinzy the director job on Shannon's and my new show, *City Meets Country*. We'd all been ecstatic when she'd accepted. Was it the reason for Kinzy's boldness about Shannon's weight gain? Would Shannon want to work with her after her comment?

I couldn't stand here all day wondering. I hurried down the stairs and joined Shannon by the commissary table.

"The set's so cute and festive! I made out the shadowy shape of a tree when we arrived and trudged upstairs this morning. I guess I didn't expect this." Shannon popped a donut hole in her mouth.

"It's great and so apropos for a baking show," I answered, glad Shannon's anger, or hurt, had dissipated.

The set designers had run with a gingerbread theme. Gingerbread house façades arched over the refrigerators in the corners. They'd covered the doors to look like slatted wood. The tree Shannon mentioned was made of lighted gingerbread boy and girl yard decorations. The designers somehow attached them together in a pyramid to create a tree shape. The front base of the kitchen counters had various shapes of gingerbread houses. All the kitchen utensils matched the red of the decorations' outline icing.

"Good morning, Courtney and Shannon."

I turned to see Pamela Mills approaching.

"Hi, Pamela. We were just getting some breakfast." I glanced at Shannon. She'd heaped her plate with carbs. "Want to join us?" I scooped a serving of veggie egg bake onto my plate.

"No, thanks. I've eaten. I wanted to let you know that I'm your security detail again." Pamela wore a long-sleeved red polo with the embroidered Nolan Security logo over her heart. She fit right into the Christmas theme of the show.

You'd never know it by looking at short, petite Pamela that she could provide security for anyone. I learned the hard way how effective she was at her job. "I'm glad." Last season I wasn't glad when Sheriff Perry insisted I have my own security person to keep me out of trouble. I'd felt insulted. I don't get into trouble; trouble finds me. Although when it did, Pamela shielded my body to protect me from an attempted stabbing, so I'm forever grateful to her. Even if she crushes on Eric Iverson, my producer and maybe boyfriend.

"Is Eric here?"

Boy, she wasted no time bringing him up. "Not yet. He'll arrive later this morning." While Eric and I tested the waters of a personal versus working relationship, we were keeping our couple status a secret. However, Pamela really liked Eric, and I liked Pamela, so to be fair, Eric and I needed to tell her about us. I made a mental note to discuss this with Eric.

"He actually got to spend Thanksgiving with his family," Shannon muttered behind us.

Is that why she was so moody? Change of holiday plans?

"Good for him. I celebrated Thanksgiving here."

"As a guest?" I asked.

"No, working. Nolan Security did spring for a nice Thanksgiving spread though. We had to get our base set up. Then we assisted Sheriff Perry."

I finished my breakfast. "What do you mean?" Had something already happened before any of us arrived?

"He's set up an onsite office just in case something happens. It's peak skiing season so the resort refused to cancel or turn away guest reservations. He's hoping his presence at the resort will deter any felonious behaviors."

In layman's terms, murder. I prayed Sheriff Perry was right. Two murders this year was enough for me. The first one threw me into a defensive mode since I was a person of interest. The second I jumped into to clear Skylar's name. Both times the murderer used kitchen utensils as their weapon of choice. I shuddered to think of the mistreatment of culinary utensils. Then again, who was I to judge? I used kitchen appliances to escape the murderers' clutches and aid Sheriff Perry in their capture. He would say I meddle. We both know I aid.

"Bring in the contestants." Brenden's voice carried over the setup noise of the crew.

Kinzy went to a side door and signaled for the bakers to enter, then went and stood beside Quintin and studied her tablet.

"Oh look! They're wearing your aprons." I pointed to the bakers filing onto the set.

Shannon's reaction surprised me. I'd expected excitement that her product line was featured on the show for all the world to see. That's how I'd feel if my knife set, which was still in development, was used on the show. Instead, she started to cry. Not small sniffles. Streams of tears ran down her cheeks. Had I missed something? Stepping closer to Shannon, I asked, "Are you okay?"

Sadness radiated from her eyes when she looked at me. "I don't think so."

CHAPTER THREE

"Kinzy! What's going on? The contestants aren't in the proper order."

Brenden's raised voice pulled my attention from Shannon to the main set. Brenden stood hands to hips.

Kinzy looked up from her tablet. Her gaze hit Brenden, then the contestants. She rose from her chair scowling. "Contestants, find the placard with your name. That is your kitchenette."

The contestants looked down and around. Mya held up the sheet of paper with her name on it. "I'm where I should be." The five other contestants followed her lead to show they'd found their names.

"I thought we'd discussed that I wanted them in a random order, not sorted by gender," Brenden said. He flicked a look at Quintin and braced, since Quintin constantly lectured him that wasting time cost money.

"I did place them randomly by their birth months." Kinzy tapped on her tablet and lifted it to show Brenden.

"Just fix your mistake so we can start filming."

"I didn't make a mistake." Kinzy walked closer to Brenden and shoved the tablet at him. "I used this contestant placement chart."

"Well, clearly," Brenden waved a hand, "they aren't in that order. A mistake has been made. Fix it."

Narrow-eyed, Kinzy said, "I will do my job, as I did the first time. You're wrong to say I made a mistake. Someone else did. They switched the placards." Kinzy employed the same belligerent tone she'd used with Leon.

Brenden drew a deep breath. Before he could answer, Victoria, who'd been sitting in Brenden's director chair, rose. Her heels clicked over the hardwood floor until she stood next to Kinzy. "How dare you speak to my son that way? You're his subordinate and need to do your job."

My eyes widened at Victoria's words.

Her icy stare didn't deter Kinzy, who had opened her mouth. Before she could rebut Victoria's remarks, Brenden pushed his body between them.

"Kinzy, please make the correction. Mother, come with me." Brenden walked Victoria to the edge of the set, close to our group standing by the commissary table. "This isn't your boardroom. You don't run the show here. No pun intended. Besides . . ." Brenden glanced over his shoulder. Satisfied Kinzy was out of earshot, he continued, "Her grandfather died. She's grieving. I'm sure Kinzy doesn't even realize she made the mistake."

"That's no reason to argue with you and use such a know-it-all tone."

"Mother, I'm happy to have you on set, but please refrain from butting in."

Displeasure etched every inch of Victoria's features. "All right. I'll watch from over there." She strode toward the cast chairs. Her unbuttoned cape-coat flapped with the breeze her brisk steps created.

Brenden returned to the set and I gave my full attention to Shannon. I noticed she'd dried her tears. "Sorry for the interruption. Tell me what's wrong."

Shannon waved a dismissive hand. "I wasn't prepared for the pride I'd feel seeing the contestants wearing my aprons."

I didn't buy it. Her expression while she cried was one of despair, not pride. "Are you sure?"

"Yes," Shannon drawled. "You'll know the feeling when they're using your knife set."

"I guess." If that day ever came, I hoped my expression and any tears would be ones of joy. "You remember Eric's planning on a dinner meeting tonight to discuss the kitchen design for our show."

"Hmm . . . I think there's something else we need to discuss and consider."

Although I suspected I knew the answer, I asked, "What's that?"

"Rescinding the job offer to Kinzy. After her actions this morning, I think she lacks professionalism."

I started to speak, and Shannon held up a halting hand. "I know, she's grieving or shocked or angry about other aspects in her life, but she can't take those things out on others."

"True. She's young. Maybe she doesn't realize she's doing it."

"That's why she does it, young and inexperienced. I think our offer to have her direct our show went to her head."

I didn't care for Shannon's pointed tone, yet I couldn't really argue with her. Kinzy had become cocky after her promotion to assistant director. Since our offer, it seemed to ramp up to another level. It was something the three of us needed to discuss and then meet with Kinzy. Directing our show was a good career opportunity for her. If Shannon expected her to act professionally, we needed to be held to the same standard. The only way to do that was an open dialog with Kinzy. And we'd have to consider her personal situation. Sometimes grieving people lash out. "Yes, it's something the three of us need to talk about or at the very least bring Eric up to speed on."

Brenden clapped three times. "Skylar and Courtney, take your places."

Skylar stood and laid his magazine in his set chair. Together, we walked to a gingerbread house façade. Our tape marks were placed where a door should be. Skylar, as always, stood so the camera captured his good side.

"Is everyone ready?" Brenden looked around the set.

"No."

The voice came from the contestant area.

"Is there a problem with your kitchenette?" Brenden walked toward Marley Weaver.

"No. I have a problem promoting a product line." Marley untied the apron he wore and slipped it off his head. He wadded it into a ball and tossed it toward the corner. "I'm here to bake, not to make Mrs. Collins richer. I'm ready now."

"No, you aren't." Kinzy stomped over to the corner, picked up the apron and walked over to Marley. "Put it on."

Marley clasped his hands behind his back and shook his head. "I don't need an apron to cook."

"Everyone's wearing one and you will too." She pushed the wrinkled fabric at him.

He grabbed it and rolled it into a tighter ball. "I'm not supporting product endorsement." He tossed the apron.

I didn't see where it landed.

"Look." Brenden stood in front of Marley, the counter between them. "It's part of the show."

"It's more than part of the show." A raised voice boomed through the quiet area. All heads turned toward Quintin. "It's in your contract. All of this was defined in the papers you signed. If you had a problem with it, that was the time to argue the point. Not now."

I tore my eyes from the scene on set to check on Shannon. I flicked my gaze over the entire area. I couldn't find her. Had Marley's protest upset her, and she'd run off the set? "Do you see Shannon?" I whispered to Skylar.

"She slipped out the main door when Brenden called us to our marks. Thank goodness, she isn't here to see this. Who screens the contestants anyway?"

"Good question." I breathed a sigh of relief Shannon wasn't witnessing this. After all, who wouldn't want to wear one of her cute aprons? The print on the one Marley tossed had Santa in a chef's hat in the midst of cookie baking. The front pockets looked like oven mitts.

"Are you sure it was in the contract? I don't remember reading it." Marley crossed his arms over his chest.

"It's in there," Kinzy snipped.

"Okay, I'll wear it. I don't like it though."

"Find him a new apron that isn't wrinkled." Quintin looked at Kinzy.

"I'll text the wardrobe people to bring one."

"Okay, everyone can relax for a few minutes." Brenden followed Quintin to a side area of the set.

I decided to use this time to speak with Kinzy. Maybe if she knew someone cared, her attitude might change. I walked over to where she waited by the contestant entrance. "I want to extend my sympathy to you and your family at the loss of your grandfather. If there's anything I can do to help you, please let me know."

Kinzy smiled. "Thanks." Her tone was civil and grateful. "It's unnecessary though. I haven't seen Harold in fifteen years. He was a stranger to me even when I lived with him. I do appreciate your gesture though."

The ring of Kinzy's cell phone interrupted us. Kinzy glanced at the screen and denied the call. "It's Leon. He won't leave me alone. He texted earlier that we needed to meet, and I said no. You'd think he'd have received the message loud and clear this morning." There was no longer civility in her tone.

Although I wondered why she was estranged from her grandfather, I decided to stick with the original conversation. "Well, if you need to talk or anything . . ."

The door popped open. A woman carrying an apron pinned to a hanger stepped into the room.

"Thanks." Kinzy grabbed the apron and started for the set. "Better get into place, Courtney," she called over her shoulder.

I walked over to the gingerbread house, feeling bad for Kinzy. Was she in denial or shock about her grandfather's death? Even estranged, shouldn't she have some feeling of loss even if it was regret over what might have been or a small hope that someday things might be different between them? It was only human to experience those emotions. Right?

I met Skylar in the doorway of the gingerbread cottage. We waited for our cue to kick off the competition with the first challenge of the day. Brenden counted down with his fingers and said, "Action."

Skylar smiled into the camera while I delivered the first line. "Candy is synonymous with Christmas time."

"Our wardrobe may have given away today's challenges." Skylar flapped his jacket and posed with hand on hip.

"That's right," I said. "We're testing your skills on making Christmas candy."

Skylar took over. "You'll compete in three challenges today. Candy from the past, present and future. We're starting with the past."

"You'll have three hours to complete this challenge. In the envelopes on your counters you'll find the recipes for Christmas candies from bygone days and . . ." I paused for suspense. "The preparations will mirror the time the candy was popular, which means." I looked at Skylar and we read the monitor together.

"Hand-beat fudge, hand-beat divinity and no use of a candy thermometer to make the anise candy."

Marley and Carol groaned just before Skylar and I said, "The baking begins now!"

Brystol looked around at the other contestants with a fear-filled expression. "I don't even know what anise is."

After Brenden cut Skylar and my filming, we joined Shannon and Harrison in our studio chairs.

"Bless her heart." Shannon jerked her head toward Brystol. "She doesn't stand a chance with these old-fashioned recipes."

"Maybe." I didn't like to underestimate young people. My guess was she and Dylan were on even ground with this challenge, but some of the others might be right there with them. It all depended on the cooks in a family. I was glad the show provided recipes, although basic, for this challenge. "I'm not sure I could prepare these candies with success."

Shannon laughed. "I guess if I'm honest, I couldn't either. I'm looking forward to sampling the treats."

I looked around for Kinzy. I didn't want her to overhear our conversation and make another weight retort. She stood by Quintin, so we were safe. "When I'm done interviewing contestants, I need to run to the *Cooking with the Farmer's Daughter* set at the resort. Want to come along? We could get a head start on the conversation about our show."

"Sorry," Shannon said with no apologetic tone in her voice. "I have an appointment. See you this afternoon." She stood and walked off toward the stairs.

"Courtney and Skylar, we're ready for you to do the interviews."

"Any particular order?" Skylar asked.

"Not this time," Brenden said.

After a brief discussion, we decided to go front to back on both sides, which would leave Brystol until last, giving her more time to concentrate on the challenge.

"Hi, Tim. What confection did you begin with?"

Tim stirred a pot. "The anise. It takes a while to harden. I'm assuming I must break it into pieces for the judges to taste. I wish they had anise liqueur instead of extract." He wrinkled his nose.

"Better flavor?" Skylar asked.

"My trademark." Tim dribbled red food coloring into the pot, then the extract.

We moved over to Mya. She stirred a deep pot too.

"Have you ever eaten hand-beaten fudge or divinity?" I asked, wanting to test my theory about age.

Mya nodded.

"Which of the three are you working on?" Skylar asked.

The licorice scent of the anise permeated the room, so it was hard to tell what anyone was working on, and all three candies had a syrup base.

"The divinity. My anise is cooling."

"Really?" Skylar looked around. "Already?"

"Yes. The cooling takes the longest. I put mine in candy molds."

"Good thinking! It will harden faster." I stretched my neck to look at the silicone molds. She'd used a square mold like the traditional candy.

"Thank you."

"I didn't get a chance to ask you about your cooking background last night."

She looked up and smiled. "I run a candy store. I'm a chocolatier."

Skylar laughed. "No wonder your anise is prepared and cooling already."

We moved on to Marley, who stood looking into a saucepan. When he saw the camera, he pulled the neckband of the apron over his head and let the protective chest fabric flop over the skirt. He stepped closer to the counter, so the apron was out of the camera shot.

I pursed my lips. Was it my place to say something? This wasn't really wearing the apron.

Marley spoke first. "Think this fudge will thicken up? I've beat it for a few minutes and my arm's tired." His question was directed at me as he lifted a wooden spoon. The brown, sugary mixture ran right off.

"Courtney can't answer your question. It'd be cheating." Skylar waggled his finger at Marley.

"Okay." Marley pulled an eight-by-eight pan close to him. From my vantage point I could see it wasn't sprayed or buttered. "I'm calling it done." He dumped the runny mixture into the pan.

I kept my expression neutral, knowing full well the fudge wouldn't set. It had no texture or shine. I wasn't certain he'd cooked the syrup long enough before beating.

"Next," Marley said, pushing the fudge aside and sliding a different recipe to him.

I motioned for Skylar and our cameraman to follow me. We walked to the front kitchenette in the next row.

Dylan had whipped his divinity into shape. He'd spooned the candy into an icing bag and piped out even, bite-sized bits on parchment paper. Although it looked great, divinity was usually dropped in spoonfuls for a rustic rather than a consistent shape.

"Are you going to add nuts to your candy?" I asked.

"No, because of allergies." Dylan finished filling the lined cookie sheet with perfectly formed dollops. "While they set up, I'll try the fudge." He stretched his neck to see what Brystol was doing, then whispered, "I don't know what anise is either so I'm leaving it for last." He left his kitchenette to visit the pantry.

Skylar and I approached Carol. Before either of us could comment or question, Carol shot us a deadpan look. Her wooden spoon tapped against the pan while she beat a deep brown mixture. "I don't have the muscle for this anymore. I used to help my mom make this every year. It's my favorite. I didn't even need the recipe." She stopped stirring and pointed to her temple. Then she lifted the spoon. The glossy candy stuck to the utensil with none falling back into her pan. "It's ready."

"What are you trying next?" I asked, watching her fold chopped walnuts into the fudge.

"The anise. My arm needs a break."

Brystol looked up from her work when we moved to her area. "Do people really eat this? It smells bad." She'd poured the anise candy onto a cookie sheet. The clear sugar glistened under the bright lights.

"Anise is usually red." Skylar inspected her pan.

"What?" She grabbed the recipe. Her eyes roved the paper. "I added the extract twice instead of food color. What do I do?" Panic etched her features.

"Move on. If there's time left, try again. We'll leave you alone." I flicked my gaze to the clock. An hour had passed. If she remade a batch of anise, I doubted it would harden in time.

I climbed into the covered cart that waited outside the door. Once I'd buckled up the driver took off. The day had turned out sunny, although low clouds lingered, hiding the peaks of the Pocono Mountains. With fewer contestants, it took less time for the interviews, which worked great for me. I needed to get back to the resort.

I appreciated the roof of the transport vehicle, which blocked the glare and allowed me to see my phone screen. I'd received a text during filming. I woke up my cell and smiled at what Caroline had written: "What a great way to kick off the toy drive!" over a screen shot of Quintin's very large pledge to our cause. I tapped out a quick text that I'd call and explain later, then wished her luck with all the media promotions today.

My ride dropped me at the main entrance and I hurried inside. The jacket to the pantsuit didn't provide much resistance to the cool outside air. Giving a slight shiver, I thought about heading to Castle Grounds for a latte. I walked through the lobby. Massive wreaths decorated with white lights and blue and silver ornaments hung on the walls and over the check-in desk. I stopped short. The coffee shop line snaked around the tables and almost out to the door. What an excellent indicator of the peak skiing season. I didn't have time to wait so I headed back through the lobby and down the hall to the conference room that housed our set. As I rounded the corner and pulled the key card from my jacket pocket, a door down the long corridor announced its closure. Involuntarily, I turned toward the sound.

I caught a gasp in my throat. I couldn't believe my eyes. What was Shannon doing coming out of a first-floor hotel room that wasn't her own, with her clothes and hair a mess?

Before she caught sight of me, I waved my key and hurried through the unlocked door. Had Shannon been lying down? If so, why wasn't she in her own suite? I swallowed hard. Or was something else going on?

CHAPTER FOUR

"Courtney?"

Eric's voice drew me away from staring at the suite door and my perplexity about Shannon. I turned and walked toward the kitchen counter, where Eric sat on a stool. "Hi." My greeting lacked luster.

"Everything okay?" Eric asked. His expression and voice both held concern. He stood and met me halfway.

"Yes." I brightened my tone. Whatever was worrying me about Shannon might be nothing, so I wasn't sharing my concern with him yet. "Did you have a good flight?"

He wrapped me in a clumsy hug. The spectacular kiss we'd shared changed our relationship. Not for the better. Our once easy comradery seemed filled with awkward conversations and innuendo. The official dates we'd been on fell flat and left us both on edge. No matter what we did, we couldn't find our "couple" groove, which was now bleeding over into our work rapport.

"I did." Eric broke the hug, took my hand and led me over to the stools.

I knew his holiday went according to plan. He'd accompanied his family on their early bird Black Friday madness, one of their family traditions and something my family never partook in since the toy drive kicked off on that day every year. My heart squeezed at the thought of Caroline handling the start of the fundraiser alone. I sure hoped the spa weekend Quintin promised made it up to her.

"Is something wrong with the knife set?" I took a seat.

Eric, dressed for a business meeting in a houndstooth sports jacket and black polo and trousers, centered his laptop between us and adjusted his stool so we were both visible on the screen, then dialed up a Skype meeting. "I don't think so. They want to talk to us before sending the prototype for you to test."

In no time a representative from the company making the knives connected. He had the prototypes in front of him. He lifted each individual knife to the screen so we could see the detail. "Are the brushed stainless-steel handles to your liking?"

"Yes." The company had pushed for a faux wood or black plastic handle. I thought the stainless-steel reflected a more professional kitchen look and quality product.

"Okay, we will overnight them to your office in Chicago."

"No," Eric said. "I'll email you the overnight address. We'll be working offsite for about a week. Courtney's anxious to try out the knives."

We said our goodbyes and signed off.

"Speaking of work," Eric said and closed his laptop, "what day do you want to film the holiday special segment? We need to decorate the set to reflect the season."

The cooking network that aired *Cooking with the Farmer's Daughter* had a special in the works for the holidays. This one spliced together most of the network stars preparing a favorite holiday food. My segment fell into the cookie category. Eric talked me into making a favorite of his, rosettes. I'd never even tasted them, let alone made them.

"The day after tomorrow? If filming goes according to Quintin's plan, we should be on the finale, so they'll have tougher challenges with longer times to prepare."

"It's a date."

I grimaced. "Let's not call it that."

"Courtney, stop!" Eric sighed. "I get it though. We do better when we don't think of our time together as dates. I think we're trying too hard and steering the dates in the wrong direction. We're nervous. We need to relax. After all, we know each other, so it should be easier than being on our best-impression behavior."

"I agree." It's nice to be past the good-impression stage. I liked that Eric had seen me without makeup and in exercise clothes, yet our dates fell flat or ended up with hurt feelings. We'd argued about the size of pizza to order at a restaurant we frequented when we used to buy a large and split it between two take-out boxes. The smack talk during what was usually a fun and friendly game of bowling started to hurt my feelings thinking Eric now thought less of me. Silly, I know. Then Eric wouldn't stop apologizing because he'd never want to hurt me. After that date, I'd been wondering about something. Now seemed like a good time to bring it up. "You don't think maybe we developed false feelings because we work so closely together, are planning another show and, well, we're thinking about our own mortality in light of the tragic murders?"

Anger or aggravation flickered through his eyes. I wasn't certain which. He exhaled, loud and dramatic. "My feelings are true."

"Are you sure? When was the last time you dated someone?" I posed my questions in a gentle tone.

"A while, I guess because I'm interested in you."

"I know. I'm interested in you too, yet . . ." I paused, searching for a good way to say this without causing hurt or starting an argument.

"Just say it like you used to." Eric used encouraging words in a discouraging tone.

Taking a deep breath, I said, "I guess I'm just saying being with each other day in and day out is a habit. Were we in a habit of seeing each other, or having someone to do things with, that maybe we didn't consider other people?"

Okay, in full disclosure, I was attracted to Drake. I like dark-haired, dark-eyed men and he wore both those traits well, but the more I talked to him, the more I knew his personality didn't match what I looked for in a relationship. Then there was Pamela and her not so subtle feelings for Eric. Another topic I needed to broach.

The door jamb released at the same time someone knocked. The door opened a sliver. "Can I come in or am I interrupting?"

Talk about on cue. "No," I said at the same time Eric answered "yes" while throwing me a look.

Pamela stopped a step into the room and looked confused. Finally, she said, "I just came by to say hello to Eric. I can come back." Her cheeks turned pink.

One of us needed to at least mention to Pamela that we were dating, maybe not well, but dating just the same.

Eric, gentleman that he was, exchanged pleasantries with Pamela before turning to me. "The resort's event co-ordinator sent up some of their extra decorations." He pointed to four large boxes sitting in the far corner.

I walked over and rummaged through them. Although the baking competition set was cute and appropriate, it was cartoonish. I wanted something different, something that reflected the theme of our show. I ruled out the first box, which held replicated Victorian ornaments in deep maroons and greens. Next, I found scenes that illustrated *The Night Before Christmas*. From the third box I pulled out a folk-art Father Christmas dressed in white with a long forest green coat and matching hat both trimmed in white fur. The four-foot figure held the reins of a caribou with a burlap bag harnessed to its back. The accents in the box were items from nature, pinecones and fir boughs with sprigs of holly interwoven. A perfect fit for a country-themed show. Plus, I thought Shannon had an apron dec-orated with forest animals that could complement these decorations. If the show had one for the contestants to wear, maybe they'd let me borrow it. "This one." I didn't bother looking in the last box.

Eric nodded.

"I need to get back to the set. Pamela, do you have ac-cess to a vehicle? And more importantly, is it covered?"

"Yes, and yes. Let's roll. See you later, Eric." Pamela headed for the door.

"Bye, Eric. I'll see you at dinner." I didn't peck a kiss

to his cheek or give him a hug. We had agreed to no public displays of affection while working.

"Courtney, we're going to continue our conversation."

"I know," I said and slipped out the door.

Pamela led the way through the resort so we could exit at a staff door. As we went through the lobby area, Victoria called out to us. "Are you going back to the workshop?"

"We are," I answered. I hadn't noticed she'd left the set.

"Could I catch a ride?" The wool cape Victoria wore in a concord-grape tone matched a stripe in her dark gray dress pants and her pumps. As she pulled on gray gloves, I wondered who had designed her ensemble.

"Yes." Pamela continued toward the staff door. Once we reached the vehicle, I deferred the shotgun seat to Victoria and slid into the rear seat. We secured our belts and Pamela took off.

"I'm so excited to see Brenden work I couldn't wait until after lunch. I'm so proud of him. He's making a name for himself with this show." She didn't have to tell us she was proud of her son; her face beamed with it.

"I wanted him to go into the family business, mergers and acquisitions."

"Like hostile takeovers?" Pamela glanced at Victoria.

"Sometimes. I wanted to groom him for the Chief Executive Officer position because someday I'd like to retire." Victoria held out her hand and admired her gloves. She sniffed. "He'd have no part of it. I suppose that's okay. He's so naïve and trusting."

"You say that like it's a bad thing." I'd never thought of Brenden as naïve. I'd say concerned and trusting.

"Those are bad traits in the business world, dear. They can derail a career." Victoria smiled over her shoulder. "I don't have to tell you about ruining careers though, do I?"

I didn't dignify her remark with an answer. She referred to my recent apology to my fans for the network misleading them to think my farm girl persona was real. Of course, Victoria's passive aggressive implication was that my fans were the simple and trusting people. Which wasn't true; my fans were trusting, not naïve, and most of them stuck with me after I came clean about my background. I received a few hate emails and some bad press in rag magazines, not enough for the network to fire me or stop the development of my knife line. Eight weeks after the announcement, the network told Eric I had a one percent drop in viewing. Much better than any of us anticipated.

Pamela stopped the vehicle, and my roving thoughts, with a jerk in front of the workshop turned set. In addition to running a coal mining business, Henry Cole had dabbled in inventions and had built this large workshop set about a mile from the castle with three outside connecting paths and a hidden tunnel from the inside. The tunnels! The resort staff and catering used the tunnel to avoid guests and to transport items. Security also used the tunnels. Drake had led me through them, which is how I knew they existed. Why weren't we using it to travel back and forth to the set to stay out of the cold elements? Was it because most people, including Brenden and Quintin, knew nothing about them? Wouldn't it be smarter and more secure? I'd ask Drake or Sheriff Perry the next time I saw them.

Victoria had exited the vehicle without a thank you

and was halfway to the door. I raised my voice a notch to point out the rudeness. "Thanks for the ride, Pamela."

It didn't seem to faze her. She neither turned around to thank Pamela nor held the door for me.

"You're welcome. I'm sure I'll see you later." Pamela sped off. She must have felt I was momentarily safe and didn't need my own personal security guard.

I hurried into the workshop, making a mental note to wear my outer jacket next time I made a trip to the resort, or better yet, to take the tunnel since I knew what door in the workshop opened into it. Of course, getting back out without a pass key was the hard part, as I knew from experience.

Shannon sat on the fringe of the set, now groomed to perfection. I pulled my chair close. "Don't forget about our dinner plans with Eric tonight. He wants to nail down the kitchen design for our show. I told him we agreed it shouldn't resemble either of our sets. I think he might have some sketches."

"Right." Shannon fanned her hand by her face. "It's warm in here. How do you stand that jacket on?"

Although it didn't ward off nature's chill, it was perfect for the inside temperature. "I'm comfortable."

"In a heavy jacket and pants?" Shannon pulled a face. "Are you coming down with something? My dress is sleeveless and I'm roasting."

I refrained from asking her if *she* was feverish. She didn't look flushed. "I feel fine. Do you have any ideas about the kitchen? I'd love stainless-steel appliances."

Shannon wrinkled her nose.

Okay. I'd try another angle. "Light marble counter tops with . . ."

"I'm so warm." Shannon cut me off and stood. "I can't take it anymore." She walked off without a goodbye or "we'll talk later" or "sorry I interrupted you." Hurt poked at my heart. Was she warm or trying to avoid me? Was she having second thoughts about our show? Did she feel I took Kinzy's side over hers this morning? Something was wrong. Maybe if I asked during dinner, she'd tell me.

"Time's up," Skylar and I said in duet.

The contestants looked panicked or fearful, none exuded confidence. As I'd predicted, Marley's fudge failed. By the looks of the tiered tray at the end of his counter for the display of his treats, none had turned out. It stood empty, surrounded by the pans of what he thought was his finished product.

Most of the other contestants managed to get their challenges on the display tray, although several didn't look very appetizing.

"Courtney, you'll accompany the judges today."

Nodding to Brenden, I fell in behind Harrison. Shannon had the lead. She stalked over to Marley. "Put that apron on right for filming." Her tone bore no argument.

So, she had noticed what he did. Had anyone else?

Marley narrowed his eyes and set his mouth. "This isn't right. . . ."

"Do it!" This time Shannon raised her voice loud enough that she caught everyone's attention.

"Is there a problem?" Quintin called.

Marley lifted the apron into place.

Shannon glanced over her shoulder. "Not anymore."

Harrison and I exchanged a look, then he stepped forward. "Why aren't your items on the serving tray?"

"Well." Marley tipped the fudge pan. The liquid pooled to a corner. "I did something wrong."

"On all of them?" Harrison perused the pans on the counter.

"Yeah. I think so. Maybe not the anise. It's still warm."

Marley had dumped the hard candy syrup into a deep bowl rather than a baking sheet. It appeared gelatinous when Harrison wiggled the bowl.

"We'll need spoons." Shannon drummed her fingers on the countertop.

A crew member brought three over. I smiled my thanks with no plans to sample any of his results.

Harrison and Shannon tasted the chocolate syrup. Shannon spoke first. "The flavor's right. However, you didn't cook the syrup enough. It's sugary."

"Yes, and because of that, you could've beat the mixture all day and it wouldn't get thick."

They both agreed the anise tasted right and would've cooled and turned out had he poured it into the pan size listed in the recipe. His divinity needed more beating. Like the anise, the taste was there.

Where most other contestants would've looked contrite, Marley smiled, taking the good points as a win. I shook my head as we moved on.

"This presentation is gorgeous!" Shannon marveled at the creative way Mya made her own tiered trays out of Christmas stemware and plates. Her anise came out in perfect squares. The divinity had formed a crust on the top yet tasted delicious.

"Your fudge is to die for." Shannon snatched a second piece of fudge and popped it in her mouth while Harrison gave Mya pointers on how to improve the divinity.

"Anything else?" Harrison asked Shannon.

"Just one more piece of fudge for the road." Shannon sunk her teeth into another sample.

She wasn't paying attention to the other contestants, but I was. Disbelief etched Brystol's features while anger settled onto Carol and Dylan's faces. Marley stared expressionless while Tim's dark brown eyes smoldered with an if-looks-could-kill glare aimed on Shannon.

CHAPTER FIVE

Shannon didn't notice. She'd closed her eyes while savoring the confection.

I watched Tim. He flicked his gaze to Quintin, set his jaw, then pinned his stare back on Shannon, whom Harrison had guided over to his station.

Tin-soldierlike, Tim stood by his arrangement. He'd used a cut-glass platter, placing his confections in gold and silver foil candy cups.

"A-plus on presentation," Harrison said. "Very elegant and party friendly."

Tim cleared his throat. With his threatening stare aimed at Shannon, he said, "I'd like you to cleanse your palate with water, so the taste of my creation isn't mixed with the last one."

Shannon flashed him a clueless look as she licked her lips.

"Splendid idea." Harrison motioned for bottles of water. He'd noticed Tim's disgruntlement too.

After they'd each had a few sips, they judged Tim's candy. He'd nailed the flavors on the fudge and divinity, but both were a little too soft. His anise was perfect. Because of the strong flavor, Harrison and Shannon's judging involved just a lick or two of the hard anise candies.

"Would you like to try another piece of my fudge?" Tim posed his question to Shannon.

My shoulder muscles tensed waiting for her response. I cast a look toward Quintin, who was involved with something on his phone. Brenden and Kinzy were watching the exchange.

"Time to move on," Kinzy called. Everyone had noticed Shannon's favoritism of Mya's fudge.

Tim narrow-eyed Kinzy for a few seconds, then said, "Thank you." He nodded toward Harrison and ignored Shannon.

Carol displayed her challenges in Christmas tins. "I used too much powdered sugar. The fudge is dry." She pointed out her mistake before either judge greeted her.

When Shannon lifted a piece, it crumbled. "The taste is there. Not the right mouthfeel."

Harrison picked at a fallen bit. "I agree."

"Hmm." Shannon lifted a piece of anise candy from the tin. She and Harrison exchanged looks before they tried the candy. Shannon flashed an apologetic look at Carol. "It's obvious your candy didn't reach the hard crack stage. I know you tried to save your anise by rolling it in sugar so it wasn't sticky and could be served, which worked. That's not the recipe though."

Carol nodded. "I tried."

"For home serving that's a good fix. For the baking

battle, it would have been better to leave the candy sticky since we must judge on the exact recipe. However, you succeeded on the divinity," Harrison said with a smile.

He moved to Dylan's kitchenette. Shannon, the cameraman and I trailed behind. I'd yet to sample any of the goodies. I was curious about Mya's fudge. Was it the taste, texture or both that appealed to Shannon?

Dylan earned a scolding from both judges. All his challenges came out too soft. His presentation did nothing to make his candy look attractive. He didn't use a Christmas or serving tray. He placed dollops of the candy in dark brown paper bonbon cups tucked into a mini-cupcake tin. I'm sure he thought the pan would give them form. Wrong! The candies stuck to the paper liners, making it difficult for Harrison and Shannon to taste.

To Dylan's credit, he held his head high when he admitted, "I spooned everything into the cups because I knew they wouldn't hold their form on a platter."

"We see that." Shannon spooned out a small sample of fudge. "It sugared."

"So did the divinity." Harrison set his spoon down. "I think you rushed your process for all of the challenges."

By the time we walked over to Brystol, a sheen of moisture covered her eyes. She threw her shoulders back and braced for the judges' comments. I wasn't sure why. Her presentation, Christmas-decorated bonbon wrappers filled with her challenges, were arranged on a long silver serving tray in the shape of a Christmas tree.

"Fun presentation!" Shannon clapped.

Harrison started with a piece of fudge. The once square edges had drooped, making it look melted on top. "Just a few more minutes of beating would've fixed this problem."

"It tastes great though. The consistency is good," Shannon added then picked up a piece of divinity. She tasted then nodded. "Nailed it."

"Yes, you did." Harrison had taken a small bite of the candy and instead of putting it down, he ate the rest.

A wide smile broke the worry on Brystol's face. "Really?"

"Really." Harrison smiled back. "Probably the best batch we've tasted today. However, although the texture's right on your anise, the color should be red . . ."

Shannon, who'd taken a lick of the candy, interrupted him with a cough. "Too strong. Way too much flavoring."

Brystol looked down. "I know. I put in more extract instead of food coloring. I didn't have time to make a new batch like Courtney and Skylar suggested."

"Remember to double-check your recipe. All in all, you did quite well though." His praise coaxed Brystol to raise her head and smile. "Thank you."

Harrison turned to the cameraman. "That's it."

Brenden moved to center stage. Victoria hovered close by, reminding me of a stage mother. "We'll break for lunch now. Kinzy, when you're done escorting the contestants to their exit, take the confections to the back filming area. We'll shoot the judges' discussion segment after we kick off the second challenge."

Shannon walked through the vacant kitchenettes, stopping beside Mya's. She took another piece of fudge and leaned against the counter eating it.

When all the contestants filed through their door, Kinzy returned to the set. "What are you doing?" She stopped in front of Shannon. "We need their challenges for filming."

"I know." Shannon drawled out the word. "I want you to stack up her fudge on her tray. I definitely want more."

Kinzy huffed. "You don't need more. You're outgrowing your costumes."

In an instant, Shannon's cheeks blazed red. Her hands fisted. "How dare you say that to me? This is the second time you've insinuated I'm fat when wardrobe ordered the wrong-sized clothing. Where's Quintin and Brenden?"

Neither man had been paying attention until they heard their names. A quick look at the scene playing out had them moving double time.

"What's going on?" Quintin asked.

"Your employee has insulted me twice today." Shannon pointed at Kinzy. "I can't even enjoy a piece of fudge."

"Wait a minute," Kinzy said, tone pointed. "You enjoyed several pieces of fudge during judging. You have clearly gained weight. You need to stop eating. In addition, it isn't fair to the other contestants that you're favoring Mya's fudge."

"Courtney, we're going to lunch," Skylar whispered in my ear. "Want to come?"

I shook my head. I wanted to be there for Shannon. I heard their retreating footsteps increase in speed when Shannon spat out, "That's not true. I only ate one full piece."

"Not true? We have playback, Shannon." Kinzy turned to Brenden. "Tim wasn't happy about it either."

"I don't have to stand here and listen to this." Shannon approached Brenden. She poked a finger at his chest. "Your talent should be treated better than this. Do your job and keep your employees in line."

She turned, strode past me and rushed out the door. Should I grab her coat and run after her? Her sleeveless dress was no match for the late fall temperatures. I wanted to support her, yet maybe she needed to walk off her anger. This was all so unlike Shannon. I considered her the poster child for Southern grace.

"What exactly did you say to her?" Brenden pinned Kinzy with a look. His tone held accusation and pulled me back to my surroundings.

"To stop eating the fudge. Can any of you honestly say you didn't notice she's put on weight? She's outgrowing her wardrobe. Her stylist suggested we order new outfits. Do you want to stop filming while we wait for additional clothing to be shipped to us?"

Brenden scratched his head. "I guess we could've had wardrobe place an overnight order."

"Do you know how much the costumes cost?" Quintin entered the conversation. "Kinzy's right. Shannon shouldn't be eating any of the contestants' challenge food, just sampling. It looks like favoritism. Gaining weight isn't an issue. Not notifying someone on the show about the change in her weight is, because of the costuming. Isn't there a clause in their contracts about what to do?" Quintin drew his cell phone from his jacket pocket, dialed a number and walked away.

Brenden threw a perturbed look at Quintin's retreating back, then directed it at Kinzy. "In the future, watch your wisecracks. You were unkind to Shannon and need to apologize."

"For doing my job? I don't think so. No one else stands there eating the challenge food. No one else has put on quite a few pounds. You should've spoken with her when she arrived. Get a backbone and do it now."

"Stop speaking to my son in that manner. I've told you before, he's your superior. Shut your smart mouth and do as he says." Victoria planted herself in front of Brenden.

Talk about a mama bear!

"Mother, I've got this." Brenden took a step. They were shoulder to shoulder.

"Really, you're going to fire this rude little . . ."

"Mother!" Brenden cut her off just in time. "I told you, Kinzy's grieving. This isn't her normal behavior. Please go back to the resort and get us a table at the steakhouse. I won't be more than fifteen minutes."

Victoria glared at Kinzy while answering Brenden. "Are you sure she's grieving, because I don't think so. I've been in the business world a long time and I know a ladder-climber when I see one."

"Mother." Brenden placed a hand on Victoria's arm. "This isn't your boardroom. It's my set."

Victoria stared at him for a few seconds, pursed her lips and stomped away. I knew Brenden was exhibiting the behavior Victoria referenced on the ride to the workshop. A hard-core businesswoman, she saw weakness in his gentle and compassionate ways.

"Brenden, I'm not grieving. Stop bringing my grandfather's death into every situation. None of this is about me. Shannon's out of line." Kinzy huffed out the words.

I shared his worry that Kinzy's anger was a result of her grief.

"I respect your opinion, but you aren't acting like a professional stating it in such a rude manner. You'll get everything to the back room and filming ready before you go to lunch. Understood?"

"That's not fair." Kinzy searched for Quintin and marched over to him. He pocketed his phone, listened to

Kinzy recant the situation, then said, "I think Brenden's idea is an excellent plan. You can take your full lunch once everything's ready."

Kinzy's demeanor changed from challenging to submissive, but her tone remained confrontational. "Fine," she said and stomped over to the kitchenettes.

Both men wore a satisfied smile. I shook my head. They obviously didn't know when a woman hissed the word "fine," it meant anything but.

"Action!"

Skylar and I stood front and center of the kitchenettes. The camera circled us in a sweeping shot and Skylar angled his head so his best side would be filmed while he said, "Bakers, your next challenge is Christmas candy of the present."

"You'll have two hours to replicate a candy bar of your choice." I turned toward the camera. "With a twist. Your candy bar must taste like a better version of what's found on store shelves."

None of the contestants appeared surprised, nervous or scared because they'd been practicing and fine tuning this recipe. The contestants were aware of at least one of the baking challenges in each episode in order to practice. Even if they perfected it at home, that didn't mean it would turn out during the competition.

Skylar picked up his cue. "The baking begins now."

"Cut. Great." Brenden shooed us back to the wings of the set with his hands. "Have either of you seen Shannon?"

"Not since she stormed out of here before lunch. Maybe Harrison saw her come in while we were filming." I surveyed the area and found him sitting in his chair scanning his phone.

Our trio walked over to him.

"Did you notice if Shannon came back?" Brenden asked in a whisper.

He shook his head and stood.

Brenden cranked his neck to spot Quintin. Secure in the fact Quintin was busy, Brenden grumbled, "Why are women always late?"

"Excuse me?" I heard the exasperation in his voice, yet I didn't like the generalization.

"Sorry, Courtney. My mother was late to lunch because she got tied up taking care of a business matter at her office. Now Shannon isn't here, and I want to get the judges' discussion session filmed so Skylar can do quick interviews with the contestants." Brenden started to pace. "Kinzy isn't here or I'd have her track Shannon down." He exhaled. "Would one of you mind calling her? She's a little on edge and . . ."

What Brenden didn't say said it all. He didn't like confrontation and knew if he called, it was a possibility. "I'll contact her." I fished my phone from my jacket pocket and thumbed out a text. As I hit send, the heavy wooden entry door blew open. Shannon ran into the room disheveled and breathless.

"Are you okay?" I asked.

"Yes." She tugged on her dress and walked over to our group.

I knew the skeptical looks on the others' faces matched my own. Wrinkles covered the front of the skirt of her dress. Her hair was flat and matted in the back. Her mascara flaked under her eyes. Had she taken a nap and just woken up?

"What?" Shannon asked.

Did she not know she looked a mess?

"You need to get to wardrobe and makeup. Pronto." Brenden looked her up and down. "Tell them they have ten minutes to get you camera ready. Your dress will be hidden under the table so leave the wrinkles for now. We need to start filming your discussion segment. Meet us in the back corner." Brenden turned away from Shannon. "The rest of you to the back room." Brenden waved over a cameraman.

Shannon didn't argue. She hurried over to the stairs.

I took the lead, with Brenden falling in behind me. The room was on the opposite end of the large workshop building. It was small with thick walls, so the sound didn't carry to the main set. Skylar and I took on many roles while filming the openings in this area. The first season we were hippies. It was a blast.

With Shannon on the premises and getting ready, Brenden cheered up. "We moved the baker's rack and bistro table inside. The set designer made a nice backdrop of a frosted window with curtains. There's a Christmas tree decorated with antique metal cookie cutters."

"Can't wait to see it. Where will Skylar and I shoot the openings for the episodes? Or aren't we doing that for the Christmas special?"

"You are. We're still negotiating with the resort about using the fireplace area. It's a scheduling problem more than a space problem. They don't want us filming during the coffee shop's peak hours. You know some of their guests are very important people on vacation who don't want to worry about being caught on camera. Not that they would be."

"I'm just glad the judges don't have to bundle up and film outdoors. Although the snow-covered Pocono Mountains would make a pretty backdrop," Harrison said.

"You're right. Maybe if there's a bright sunny day, we can shoot one of the openings outside." Brenden sounded like an idea was forming.

"Thanks, Harrison. Courtney and I didn't really want to bundle up to film either," Skylar said in mock aggravation.

Harrison laughed. "Sorry, pal."

"You don't sound sorry," Skylar and I said in perfect timing before our laughter joined his.

My merriment died the moment I opened the door to the set area. I stopped short. A gasp stuck in my throat. Instinctively, I stepped backward. Brenden, who couldn't see around me, kept walking and bumped into my back. His momentum caused me to stumble-step forward and release my breath.

"Courtney! Are you all right?" He grabbed at my arm to steady me, thinking I'd gasped because I feared falling.

That wasn't it at all. I kept backing up bumping into Brenden. I wanted out.

"Oh, no!"

Brenden had looked around me to see what was wrong. He grabbed my arm and backed us out of the room, closing the door. I wished shutting the image of what was in the room out of my mind was that easy.

Kinzy lay draped over a wicker bistro chair. Her right cheek rested on the cut-glass serving tray Tim had used. Her tongue hung out of blue lips, while her open vacant eyes stared toward the door. Some of the baker's confections were stuck to her face and hair. Mya's display tray lay smashed on the floor. Fudge, divinity and anise littered the floor around the table and chair. An apron rested over her back, attached to her by the tightly twisted neckband around her throat.

"What's happened?" I heard the alarm in Harrison's voice.

"It's Kinzy," I managed to choke out. "She's been strangled with an apron from Shannon's line."

Chapter Six

I knew the drill. I fingered my phone from my pocket. Hands shaking, I tapped out a number and waited through three rings.

"Hello, Courtney."

"Pamela? I thought I called Drake." My voice cracked. "I guess I made a mistake."

She read between the lines on my tone or my error. "Tell me what's wrong."

I stumbled and stammered and sniffled. This was the third time I'd made this kind of call. I thought I could relay the facts. I couldn't. Finally, I blurted, "Kinzy Hummel's been murdered."

"Hold tight." Pamela ended the call.

"They won't make us look, will they?" Skylar stopped pacing. His eyes searched my face. Fear etched his own.

"No, I don't think so." I patted his arm. Squeamish, Skylar hated the sight and smell of blood. I almost assured him there wasn't any blood. I didn't because I felt certain the first thing Sheriff Perry would do was clear the area.

"Why does this keep happening?" Brenden slid down the wall. Sobs shook his shoulders.

Wide-eyed, Harrison looked at me. "I'll take care of Skylar. You comfort Brenden."

After I nodded, he led Skylar to the opposite corner of the room. When Harrison moved fast and grabbed the first receptacle he saw, a janitorial bucket, I knew Skylar had recalled the bloody scene when his stalker was stabbed in his room, making him the main person of interest.

Certain Harrison had Skylar under control, I forced my wobbly legs to walk over to Brenden. Since my costuming was white, I didn't sit on the floor beside him. I placed my hand on his shoulder and squeezed.

He reached up and clasped my hand. "Oh, Courtney. She was so young. Had so much life ahead of her. Who would do this to her?" He looked up at me. "Why?"

A question I couldn't answer, though it caused my brain to spin through recent scenarios, creating a list of suspects and reasons why. I'd witnessed a lot of hostility between Kinzy and several people in a few short hours. All things I'd have to report to Sheriff Perry.

"Courtney!" Pamela called. "Where are you?"

In my shock, and her haste, had I told her where we were? Had I even said we were in the workshop?

Pulling my hand free of Brenden's with a promise I'd be right back, I hurried to a more open area of the back of the building.

"We're back here."

More than one set of footsteps beat a hurried rhythm on the wood flooring. They all came into view at the same time. When Sheriff Perry tried to push around Pamela, she held her ground and her lead. She reached me first and grabbed my shoulders. "Are you okay?"

"I am. Shook up, but okay."

"Where's the body?" Sheriff Perry had stopped. His gaze roved the area. Was he already looking for evidence?

"She's in the back room the show has set up for filming."

"This way." Drake pushed through our group and walked with determined steps to the corner.

When we arrived in the short hallway, Brenden still sat on the floor, head between his knees, sobbing. Skylar too had taken a seat on the floor. Harrison squatted beside him.

"She's behind this door."

Sheriff Perry and Drake opened the door and took in the crime scene. Pamela stayed by my side. Right by my side, our shoulders touched. Last season, I'd have stepped away. Not now. Not after she risked her life to save me. The slight touch brought me comfort.

"I'll call it in." Sheriff Perry backed out of the doorway.

"What's going on?"

Both Pamela and I jerked, startled by Quintin's voice. He frowned at Pamela. "Your hollering caused quite a commotion. For one thing, a microphone picked it up and now it's on the film. A few of the contestants stopped working, concerned for their safety given the show's track record. Explain yourself."

Unfazed by his gruff chiding, Pamela said, "There's a situation."

"Yes." Sheriff Perry turned. "Once again, your show has brought a murderer to my county."

"What? Who?" Quintin's gaze bounced around the room, landing on everyone involved in the show. His eyes widened and stopped on the door. Horror transformed his features. His breaths came shallow and rapid. "Is the body in the room? Is i . . . is it," his voice trembled, ". . . someone with the show?" He'd realized who would've been in the room. "Who?" His tone and eyes pleaded with Sheriff Perry.

I didn't think Sheriff Perry knew Kinzy's name, so I stepped away from Pamela and placed my hand on his arm. Quintin looked down at me. "It's Kinzy," I whispered.

"No." He shook his head in disbelief. "No!" He pulled his arm free and started for the door.

Drake stepped in front of him. "It's a crime scene. You can't go in."

"You're all mistaken. It can't be Kinzy. I want to see for myself." Quintin pushed into Drake, who teetered off balance.

Sheriff Perry pulled up beside Drake to make a human shield in front of the door. "You can't go in."

"Quintin."

He turned toward me.

"It's her. I saw." I kept my voice soft and my eyes locked to his.

He dropped to his knees, closed his eyes and hung his head. "Oh, Kinzy, Kinzy, Kinzy. Why did I make you stay behind?"

Taken aback by his reaction, I thought he'd ask how she died. I thought he'd keep it together in a calm, professional manner. Shock, like grief, does strange things to people.

Silent sobs shook his body. Brenden crawled over to him and wrapped him in a side hug. "Who would do this to our sweet Kinzy?" Together both men grieved for their Girl Friday.

After several minutes, Quintin sniffled. "Someone needs to go stop the competition and postpone filming." He looked up. "Courtney or Harrison?"

"I'll go." Drake stepped forward.

"Me too." Harrison left Skylar's side.

My surprise increased. Quintin wasn't one for shutting down production due to the cost involved. I guessed this time it hit home because he knew the murder victim.

"Courtney, you go too," Sheriff Perry said. "Pamela, take these two back to my onsite office."

"I don't want to leave Courtney. What if she's the next target?"

I swallowed hard at her question. It was a viable possibility since it'd happened twice before.

"She'll be with Drake. He'll keep her safe. I'll wait here for the rest of the team. Drake, when the set's cleared, escort Mr. Canfield to the office. Courtney, you report back here to me."

I didn't appreciate the perturbed look Sheriff Perry pinned on me. He thought I was trouble or attracted trouble, since I somehow always seemed to stumble upon the dead body. "I had nothing to do with this." I inflected challenge in my tone.

Sheriff Perry's expression hardened. "Just come back here when you're finished."

* * *

Drake managed to deliver the news and oversee the exit of the contestants and crew in about fifteen minutes. Shannon came down the stairs just as he assured them their questions would be answered later, possibly this afternoon. He called in his security detail to handle the transport of the contestants and secure the area.

"What's going on?" Shannon hurried over to me.

"We have a situation," Drake said. "You need to come with me."

"I'm not going anywhere until someone tells me what's happened."

I cringed. Now was not the time for grumpy Shannon to make an appearance.

Harrison stepped over and took Shannon by the arm. "It appears Kinzy was murdered."

"What? How?" Shannon looked at me.

"She was strangled." I paused wondering how she'd react to the next bit of news. I hated to tell her, but it was better coming from me than someone else. "With an apron from your line."

Panic masked her features. She opened her mouth and Harrison took her arm. "It's shocking. Just process, don't speak." He cast a glance at me. He, like me, had been a person of interest in a murder before. Given her current state, it was best Shannon kept any comments to herself.

Drake escorted Harrison and Shannon through the door. I walked to the back room. Why did Sheriff Perry want to see me?

Sheriff Perry had let his men in through a back door rather than the main entrance we used. I stopped at the outer hallway. The deputy guarding the door nodded to me, opened the door a crack and said, "She's here, Sheriff."

While I waited, I pulled my phone from my pocket and tapped out a quick text to Eric to let him know what had happened. Sheriff Perry came out of the room as I hit send.

Expression grim, voice gruff, he said, "Let's go."

"What? Are you arresting me?"

He quirked a brow. "You must have a guilty conscience."

"I do not."

Sheriff Perry walked away from me. I guess he wasn't in the mood for sparring. Without turning around, he waved a hand in the air for me to follow. He stopped in the hallway that housed the bathrooms and the janitor's closet, which was really an entry to the secret tunnel system in the resort. I'd found that out last season when we filmed, and I'd inadvertently locked myself in the tunnel and tried to find a way out.

He leaned against a wall and scrubbed a hand over his chin. "I'm beginning to believe you're cursed."

"Yeah." I sagged against the opposite wall. "Me too. I'm not in the mood for a lecture about attracting trouble."

"That's not why I kept you. Of course, I'll need to get an official statement from you, but you seem to notice things. From the moment we came on the scene, your expression told me that your *amateur* sleuthing wheels were turning."

I didn't like his condescending enunciation. I pursed my lips.

"You're not a professional. See, I notice body language too. What do you think you know about Kinzy?" He pushed the bill of his ball cap back to expose more of his face.

"She was the assistant director for the baking battle, and she was going to be . . ." I stopped. In all the shock and chaos of finding Kinzy, it hadn't occurred to me until now that Shannon, Eric and I had lost the director for our new show. Moisture sheened my eyes.

"Courtney?"

I sniffled and blinked to regain my composure. "Kinzy was going to direct Shannon's and my new show. It was going to be her big directorial break."

Sheriff Perry nodded. "Was there anyone else in contention for that? Someone who was angry they weren't offered the job?"

"No. We never interviewed. We offered her the job and she accepted. However, no announcement had been made because the contract hasn't been drawn up and signed yet."

"Did she mention anything about her grandfather's death?"

"Sort of. I expressed my condolences and she told me they'd been estranged for several years. She and Leon Chapski had a terrible argument this morning outside of our dressing room. He wanted her to attend the funeral and settle the estate. When she refused, he threatened to ruin her career." I rubbed my temple. There was something else said. What was it?

"What can you tell me about the murder weapon?"

"The apron?" I swallowed hard. I hated to implicate my friend, yet the tag was visible, so I was sure this was a test to see if I'd tell the truth about the apron. "It's from Shannon's new line of products. You already knew that."

"I did. You're hiding something. Spill it. You know I'll find out anyway."

"Kinzy and Shannon argued two times this morning."

"About?"

"Shannon's weight gain."

Sheriff Perry pushed off the wall. His eyes searched the ceiling.

I knew what he was looking for. "There aren't any security cameras."

He shook his head. "Not inside, no. Wait here while I get someone to drive you to the resort."

I slipped my phone from my pocket. I'd felt a text come through during our conversation. I tapped the screen to bring it to life. Eric had answered my text about Kinzy with shock and grief, then ended the message with a stern warning to stay out of the murder investigation.

How could I? Kinzy was a coworker and I feared Shannon would be considered a person of interest. Why wouldn't she? She'd argued with Kinzy and was angry enough that she said she'd kill her if she made another crack about her weight. Then Kinzy made a second remark. My heart dropped. When Shannon reported to the set late after lunch, I thought it looked like she'd been napping. Maybe not. A struggle with someone fighting for their life would rumple your clothing, mess up your hair and smear your makeup. Her hair and makeup had been fixed. Her wardrobe hadn't. I felt certain Sheriff Perry would notice.

I didn't believe Shannon murdered Kinzy. She'd stuck

by me with unwavering faith and I planned to return the favor.

Who else might want Kinzy dead? Maybe Leon? After their vicious argument this morning, then Kinzy ignoring his text, had Leon come to our set and confronted her? Had they argued again, and it escalated to murder?

"Are you ready, Miss Archer?" A young deputy pulled me from my pondering.

"I am." Not only for the ride to the resort to make my formal statement, but to start some sleuthing on the murder of Kinzy Hummel.

CHAPTER SEVEN

The cast had been called to a catered dinner in the party room of Fit for a King steakhouse. I chose black leggings and a burgundy pullover sweater to wear to dinner. My black boots skimmed my knees and provided comfort with a low wide heel. I opted for no jewelry other than diamond studs. I wanted to dress respectfully considering the circumstances.

Once the deputies took our statements, they released us. I'd considered joining Eric on my makeshift set for the rest of the afternoon, then opted to go to my room. After a therapeutic FaceTime with Caroline, I decided to do a little research on Kinzy's grandfather. It was time well spent. I found a plethora of information on the man. Harold Hummel ran a successful law firm in northern Montana along with one of the largest ranches in the state. He served the state as a representative for twenty years starting in the early 1980s and supported an oil pipeline. He'd held board positions on several charities and was active in his community and church. He seemed well respected. Everything I found indicated he was a good person.

So why were he and Kinzy estranged? Perhaps in private he was a different person? Kinzy's parents had lost their lives in a car accident. Had his grief overtaken him when he was out of the limelight? Was Kinzy a reminder of what he'd lost rather than what he'd had left? Was it a clash of personality between him and Kinzy, or a matter of money? From the information I gathered online, I'd say he was a millionaire several times over.

Which brought me to the question of whether there were other beneficiaries to his vast estate. Did they kill Kinzy to increase their inheritance? Was it possible they were at the resort? Leon was a partner in Harold's firm. Did he stand to gain something from Harold's estate?

I made a mental note to question Leon Chapski before I shrugged off my thoughts as I entered the steakhouse and was directed to the party room.

I scanned the area. Sheriff Perry, Drake, Pamela and Victoria were in attendance.

Pamela approached me. "You should've called me. I'd have escorted you down." The concern on her face was genuine.

"I know." I patted her arm. "I felt safe."

"But there's a murderer loose."

I nodded. No argument there.

I followed Pamela to the table and took a seat beside her. The mood was somber. Victoria sat beside Brenden, while Skylar and Harrison flanked Quintin. Drake and Sheriff Perry stood by the wall conversing. Everyone, other than those there on official business, had chosen dark-colored attire.

"We're waiting for Shannon," Pamela leaned over and whispered.

I wasn't surprised. Something was troubling Shannon. Her weight and personality showed it. I needed to get her alone for a private conversation. Since she'd been on edge before the murder, the change in her couldn't be attributed to shock. She was unhappy, but why? Was she having marital problems? That thought bothered me. A lot. She wasn't staying on set and chatting with the rest of us. She was leaving for appointments. Was "appointment" code for rendezvousing with another man? After all, I'd seen her coming out of a strange hotel suite.

As far as I knew *Southern Comfort Foods* was as popular as ever. She had two endorsements, a cookware set and now the aprons. I grimaced as the crime scene flashed into my mind. The inside fabric of the apron lay across Kinzy's back with the tagless brand stamp visible, as if the killer intentionally draped it that way to make a statement.

Or to pin the murder on Shannon. It was possible. Marley had argued with Kinzy over wearing the apron. Had he somehow stayed behind or come back to the set and strangled her, then pulled out the tag to make a point since he vehemently disagreed with product endorsement? Tim was also disgruntled over Shannon eating Mya's fudge. Kinzy had shut his argument down. Had he sought revenge?

"Sorry," Shannon drawled as she entered the room.

She walked across the floor, all eyes on her. I shook my head at her attire. She was wearing the same tight cocktail dress and stiletto shoes she wore to the meet and mingle, they were black, but they weren't appropriate. She slid onto the chair next to Pamela and smiled. Did she think this was a party? "How is everyone tonight?" she asked, her voice bright and happy.

"Miserable." Brenden sniffled. "I just don't understand." He turned sad eyes toward Sheriff Perry. "Who would do something like this to Kinzy?"

Drake and Sheriff Perry joined our group at the table. Victoria scooted her chair closer to Brenden to give Sheriff Perry more room.

Brenden hung his head. "What are we going to do without her?"

Although it was slight, I caught Victoria roll her eyes. Did Brenden's grief seem like a sign of weakness to her?

"It'll be okay," she soothed, reaching over and squeezing his hand.

Brenden looked up and gave her a weak smile. The expression she wore was nothing but sympathetic to her son. Her eye roll might have been aimed at making room for Sheriff Perry or the fact we were called to a dinner that no one wanted to attend. Or I'd completely misread her response due to the trauma of the day.

With a nod of his head, Drake cued a security guard, who opened a door to allow several waitstaff in. They delivered several casseroles, pitchers of water and carafes of coffee. Drake and Skylar started passing the food and once everyone made their choices, Sheriff Perry stood.

"I want everyone to know we're securing the area. Unfortunately, the resort isn't as cooperative this time. It's peak skiing season for them so it will make our job tougher. I can't roadblock the entry to the resort. All vehicles entering or leaving are subject to a thorough search. No one affiliated with the show or the victim can leave; this means eliminated contestants and one very unhappy Montana attorney. Drake and I are teaming together to have twenty-four-hour security at the resort. Thank you for your cooperation this afternoon and in the future." Sheriff Perry pinned me with a stay-out-of-the-investigation stare. I pretended not to notice.

He sat down. Silent minutes passed while a few of us ate and others pushed the food around on their plates with their forks.

Quintin stood. "I called this dinner meeting because we have a problem. I don't know what to do." His eyes flooded with tears. He sniffled and used a napkin to swipe the water from his cheeks. "The judging area's now a crime scene."

"And it will be for quite some time," Sheriff Perry added.

"Do we clear the kitchen and film the judging there? Do we not air the judging segment?" Quintin's eyes searched Brenden's face for an answer.

"I don't know." Brenden turned to his mother.

Victoria, doting mother that she was, picked up her cue. "Filming must go on or the special won't be ready to air in time, right?"

Both men nodded.

"Then it's settled. I'm not Kinzy or a director, but I will help out on the set so you can concentrate on directing the show." She gave Brenden a hug. "I can hustle the contestants in and out. I'll find a room for the judging or some type of solution and move the furniture."

"Sorry, no."

Victoria blinked and gave Sheriff Perry a look. "Excuse me?" Victoria didn't like to be told no.

"All of the furniture and decorations, including the spilled candy, are part of the crime scene and considered evidence. You don't just need a room. You need everything."

"I see." Victoria stared off into space, pondering.

"Maybe I should contact the network, cancel the contract."

I knew the shock registered on my coworkers' faces matched my own. Kinzy's death, or maybe the third murder during the filming of the show, had taken a toll on Quintin. He couldn't be thinking straight. He'd worked hard to get this special aired this year.

Victoria stood. "Let's not make any rash decisions tonight. If you let me help you out, I *will* resolve this issue and any others that pop up."

"You might want to contact the events coordinator at the resort." I looked at Victoria. "They lent Eric some decorations for my set. There were several boxes to choose from. Maybe they have extra furniture too." I turned to Quintin. "Probably not exactly like we had . . ."

"I don't think we have a choice," Brenden interrupted. "We can't reorder the furniture. It would take too long to deliver."

"Thank you, Courtney, for the constructive suggestion. I will speak to the events person tomorrow. Perhaps, we can use the grand ballroom. It's already decorated, and the Christmas tree would be a good backdrop."

"Oh, Mother. You think of everything." Brenden looked at Quintin. "Thoughts?"

"You're hired." Quintin pushed his chair away from

the table and stood. He hadn't touched his food. "Sheriff Perry, I'm confident you'll catch the murderer. Good night."

Quintin had addressed the sheriff while looking at me.

I knew why. He was depending on me to solve Kinzy's murder.

The next morning, the cast—except Shannon, who hadn't showed up for work yet—stood beside Brenden and Quintin in front of the kitchenettes. Sheriff Perry lingered in the wings in case he was needed to calm the group. After the contestants filed into their places, led by Victoria in a stunning designer suit, Quintin, voice shaking, announced that Kinzy had passed away.

"What's the yellow tape over there?" Marley pointed a finger. From his kitchenette, he had a clear shot of where the yellow crime tape started.

"What?" Dylan jogged over to Marley's area. "That's crime scene tape."

Eyes round with fear, Brystol asked, "Are we safe?"

"Yes." Quintin looked at Brystol first, then scanned the other contestants. "We have security and the sheriff has deputies onsite."

"What exactly happened?" Carol asked.

"Well," Quintin choked on a sob, "Kinzy was . . ." He hung his head.

Victoria, who'd stood on the wings of the set, strode front and center. "It's believed that Kinzy Hummel, the assistant director of the show, was murdered."

"In the workshop?" Mya's voice rose on the last word.

"Yes, but the workshop's very large, and the crime

didn't occur anywhere near our set. At no time were you in danger," Victoria reassured, although her statement might not be true.

"Then they know who did it?" Tim flashed a skeptical look at Victoria. "They've made an arrest?"

"I didn't say that."

The contestants looked at each other and began to murmur.

"Everyone, please quiet down and listen." Victoria walked down the center aisle between the kitchenettes. "We're safe. Nolan Security and the sheriff's staff made a thorough search of the building. They'll continue to process the crime scene while we continue to film a baking competition. They'll use a different entrance. We won't even know they're back there."

"But . . ."

"No buts." Victoria walked up and down the aisle, making eye contact with each contestant. "The building's swarming with law enforcement and security. We couldn't be safer. What happened to Kinzy's tragic and we need to honor her memory by finishing this baking competition. She loved this show. She loved her job."

I noticed Quintin and Brenden nodding their agreement.

"We owe it to Kinzy to make this the best *American Baking Battle*. Are you with me? Do you want to honor Kinzy?"

The contestants murmured acquiesce.

"We can do better than that. There's a lot at stake here. A hefty prize and a chance to honor Kinzy. I'll ask again. Are you with me in continuing to film this baking competition?"

I caught myself before I said a resounding yes along with the bakers. Victoria was a compelling speaker. Something I'm sure she honed convincing CEOs selling their company was the right thing to do so she could acquire their assets.

A blast of cool air and natural sunlight cut through the room. I turned toward the door to see Shannon run through. She stopped a minute for her eyes to adjust and started for makeup and wardrobe.

Sheriff Perry moved out of the shadowy wings and closer to the stairs, eyes fixed on Shannon's every move. Had he received a tip? Did he find evidence the killer was really after Shannon? I swallowed hard. Or had he found evidence that tied Shannon to the murder?

When Shannon noticed everyone staring at her, she looked around, frowned and joined the group.

Victoria pursed her lips, probably because this deflated her rallied spirit.

"We're starting fresh today." Brenden stepped forward. "You'll get to redo your first challenge."

"Why?" Tim asked.

"Well, it didn't get judged."

"Sure it did. When the judges sampled," Tim countered.

Brenden looked to Quintin. Victoria jumped in. "What you said is true, Tim. They did sample and could judge. However, the show's set to film the judging segment and well, the candy's part of the crime scene. So we're offering you all a second chance to improve your creations. Don't you want a second chance? Don't you want to try to make it difficult for the judges to decide?"

"I do." Marley raised his hand.

Which brought out laughter and smiles, easing some of the tension.

Brenden continued, "We won't refilm the kickoff; we'll just get you started on baking. Again, you'll have two hours to complete the three items. If you please take your places, I will give a countdown. Courtney and Skylar will get you started."

We waited for everyone to apron up, including Marley. Once the contestants faced us, Brenden got a thumbs up from the lighting and camera crews and counted us down.

"The baking begins now." Since it wasn't being filmed, it didn't have to be perfect, which was good because both of our voices lacked a happy lilt.

I turned and noticed Sheriff Perry leaning against a wall, homing in on Shannon.

He wasn't the only one. Victoria held Shannon in her gaze. She walked over to her. "You're late. Get up to wardrobe and makeup." Her commanding tone earned her an ugly stare from Shannon. Victoria didn't back down. "Go."

"I'm afraid that's not going to happen." This time Sheriff Perry answered. "She's coming with me."

"No, I'm not." Shannon started for the stairs. "I gave my statement yesterday."

I could tell Sheriff Perry didn't appreciate her snotty tone.

"This isn't about your statement."

He'd found something or knew something. "Shannon, I'll go with you. We have two hours before we need to be back."

"You're not coming along," Sheriff Perry snipped out.

"I'm not going either." Shannon got one foot on a step when Sheriff Perry caught her arm.

"You *are* coming with me." He took long strides and Shannon had trouble keeping up.

As they got to the door, Shannon demanded, "What more do you want from me? I've told you all I know."

"I don't think you have, Mrs. Collins." Sheriff Perry opened the door and pulled Shannon through it. Before the heavy door closed, I heard him ask, "Why were you exiting through the back door adjacent to where Kinzy was murdered at her approximate time of death?"

CHAPTER EIGHT

I sprinted for the door, never giving a thought that my pantsuit provided little protection from the nearly freezing air. I made it outside before they made it into their transport vehicle.

"Shannon, you don't have to answer that question!"

They both turned toward me. Shannon looked dazed. Sheriff Perry didn't hide his aggravation. "Go back inside, Courtney."

I ignored Sheriff Perry's orders and continued my path to them, clamping my hands to my arms trying to shield from the cold. How did Shannon stand it in her sleeveless dress? The least Sheriff Perry could do was find her a coat.

"You told me there were no security cameras in the area of the workshop where the murder occurred," I challenged Sheriff Perry.

"And there aren't. However, there're security cameras outside of the back door we've been using to process the crime scene. They caught Mrs. Collins fleeing from the building at the approximate time of Kinzy's death."

Shannon came out of her stupor. "What? No . . . I . . . air . . . needed . . . hot . . . remember . . ." Her eyes searched mine.

I vigorously shook my head, but Shannon didn't pick up on my message. She kept stammering, looking and sounding guilty.

"I think what Shannon's trying to say is . . ."

"To get your nose out of my investigation and go back to work?" Sheriff Perry gave his pants a hitch. "Get in the vehicle Mrs. Collins. Courtney," he pointed, "get in the workshop."

This time Shannon didn't resist or argue. She climbed into the backseat of the vehicle and Sheriff Perry pushed in beside her. "Go!" he ordered the driver like he feared I'd jump into the passenger seat.

I stood watching them get further and further toward the horizon using the main path to the resort. I hoped Shannon heeded my warning and at least stopped talking long enough to gather her thoughts and make sense when she did. Thoroughly chilled, I hurried back into the building.

Skylar and Harrison waved me over to the commissary table.

"Obviously, you didn't stop him from taking Shannon." Harrison topped off his plate with fresh fruit. "You get some breakfast and meet Skylar and me upstairs. I'll make us coffee. You can tell us all about it."

Frustrated with the situation this morning, I loaded my plate with carbs, blueberry muffins and hash brown casserole. I sighed. I didn't need to outgrow my wardrobe too. I fitted a scoop of scrambled eggs and turkey sausage onto my plate and stepped up to the makeup room.

"I wish we still had our table." I set my food on the counter ledge in front of the makeup mirror.

"I bet Victoria could get it back for us," Skylar said between bites.

"Yes." Harrison handed me a freshly brewed cup of coffee from our private brewer. "She's a powerhouse."

"I think I'll mention it." I sipped my coffee. The aromatic scent of roasted hazelnuts hit my senses. "We have flavored coffee now?" It wasn't quite as effective as a latte, but more than a reasonable facsimile.

"We do." Harrison brought his cup over and took a seat between Skylar and me. "What'd you find out?"

"Not much. Although, Sheriff Perry did say the outside security cameras caught Shannon leaving the building at the approximate time of death."

"Should he have told you that?"

I looked at Skylar. "I don't know. Now you ask, probably not. Do you think he wants me to try to figure out how the murderer came and went?"

Both men responded with an emphatic "no."

I frowned, broke a muffin in half and munched on the top. How did the murderer get in and out? Assigned security stood at the main door. I guessed I was the only one who knew the workshop entry or exit to the tunnels except for Nolan Security personnel. "They must have used the contestant entry." Unless it was security or resort personnel who committed the crime. It'd happened before.

"It's a possibility." Harrison sipped his coffee. "But you need to stay safe and let Sheriff Perry figure that out."

"I agree."

Harrison and Skylar were starting to sound like Eric and Sheriff Perry. I'd almost come to harm twice when I'd ask too many questions, making the murderers nervous. They'd thought if they eliminated me, their secret was safe. It was true I'd narrowly escaped both times I found myself in a murderer's clutches. I was more seasoned now in my investigating skills and doubted I'd put myself in the same situation. I planned to disclose any information I gathered to Sheriff Perry right away and insist he listen to my theories. Besides, I had to make some inquiries. I'd read between the lines last night. Quintin was counting on me to find Kinzy's killer.

"I'm concerned about Shannon. She's not her cordial self," Harrison continued.

"She's lost her Southern hospitality, that's for sure." Skylar sipped his coffee. "And she has gained weight, Kinzy wasn't wrong."

Nodding, Harrison said, "I've never seen her enjoy so many sweets either. Maybe she's stress eating?"

Skylar and Harrison both showed concern in their tone, so I knew they weren't fat shaming.

"Has she confided anything to you?" Harrison swiveled his chair toward me. "Is everything okay with her family, her show?"

"She hasn't told me anything." I shook my head. "I've wondered the same thing."

"Maybe she's on a new medication or something? Look what Ambien did to my system."

Skylar referred to getting drugged with the sleep aid and experiencing the severest of the drug's side effects. "I hadn't thought of that. I want to talk to her in private. Every time I invite her to go somewhere with me, she puts me off. She says she has appointments. I'd hoped to talk to her about it during a dinner meeting last night, which was postponed due to the cast gathering." I kept the part about seeing her leave the hotel suite to myself.

"Appointments? Like at the resort spa or something?" Skylar asked.

I gave him a deadpan look. "The resort has a spa?"

Harrison roared with laughter. "Courtney, you need to come to the resort when you aren't doing double duty for the network. You're missing a lot of the amenities here."

I couldn't argue. Last season I learned there was a bowling alley in the basement.

"But back to Shannon and Kinzy." Skylar sobered. "They were at odds. Shannon was really angry about Kinzy's cracks concerning her weight."

"And Kinzy was angry Brenden dressed her down," I added. "You don't think Shannon went to the back to confront Kinzy, do you?"

"It's a possibility." Harrison looked sad.

"I refuse to suspect Shannon. She stood by me with unwavering faith when Mick was killed. She supported you too, Skylar." I didn't add Harrison. Although he'd been a person of interest at the same time I'd been, he'd been standoffish and arrogant to the rest of us. He didn't form a bond with his coworkers until Mick's murder was solved.

"I know. You said Kinzy had been strangled with an apron from Shannon's line. What I can't figure out is how the apron got there. Neither Kinzy nor Shannon wore one that day." Skylar stood and gathered the breakfast garbage. "I'm heading back down to do the interviews."

"I'll go with you." Harrison followed Skylar.

With the close of the door I was left alone with my

thoughts. Skylar made a valid point. If Shannon—and that was a big if for me because Shannon never wavered in her belief in my innocence and I planned to return the favor—had confronted Kinzy, she wouldn't have taken an apron. Kinzy had no reason to wear one either. The contestants' candy was transported via a cart. The show liked the judging segment to be professional and dignified. An apron wouldn't be part of the décor.

I shut my eyes and conjured up my memory of the crime scene. The apron band was around Kinzy's neck with the body of the apron lying over her back inside out showing the designer branding stamped on the fabric. Whoever strangled her had twisted and twisted the band until it cut off her air supply. Even looking at the wrong side of the cloth, I remembered it was printed. Santas wearing toques blanches. My eyes popped open.

The apron that strangled Kinzy matched the one Marley had refused to wear.

Was it the same apron? I wracked my memory. What happened to the apron Marley discarded? The first time he threw it, Kinzy picked it up. The second time he cast it off, my memory was fuzzy. Did he toss it harder and further? Where did it land? I had no idea because I'd focused on the altercation taking place. I didn't pay attention to the apron because it didn't seem important at the time.

The contestants' wardrobe person brought a fresh apron, which meant extras weren't kept on the set. Who'd picked up the apron when everyone else's attention was on Marley? Could Kinzy have picked it up and put it on the cart when she'd transported the challenges? Or maybe I thought he'd tossed it further and he just threw it down by his feet. I concentrated harder but failed to bring a clear detail to mind. Marley was adamant he wouldn't endorse a product. Did Quintin and Kinzy's insistence make him angry enough to kill?

Or did this have to do with Kinzy's personal life? Kinzy had told me Leon wanted to come back to the set and speak with her. Our set wasn't on lockdown so security wouldn't have stopped him from entering. When she didn't answer, had he entered the workshop and hidden somewhere until he could get Kinzy alone to talk to her? While most eyes were on Kinzy, Marley and Quintin, had Leon snatched the apron from the floor? Did he hide somewhere until he could get Kinzy alone to talk to her, which escalated to an argument and ended with her death? Or had he plotted to murder her? I'd heard him threaten her and by the position of the body I'd say Kinzy knew and trusted her murderer because she'd turned her back on them. Or had she dismissed Leon yet again, inciting his fury?

I pulled my phone out and accessed my internet search program, intending to dig around on both Marley and Leon. A rap on the door followed by the turn of the knob drew my attention away.

Victoria poked her head through the cracked opening. "We'll be ready for you to count down in five minutes."

What? I checked my phone. I'd lost track of time. Two hours had passed. I stood. "I'll come now."

"Good. That way we'll be ready to go. We're running behind and that will cost the show money." Victoria smiled.

All business, just like Quintin. In silence, we stepped down to the set. When we reached the bottom, she faced me and straightened the pin on my lapel before walking off and whispering to Brenden.

Brenden approached me and waved Skylar over. "We're

going to reshoot the countdown. I think Harrison and Shannon will have a tougher decision on who won this round because today Marley acts like he knows what he's doing."

Skylar and I walked to the gingerbread house, put our toes to the tape that marked our spots for camera angles and waited for our signal.

"Five minutes," I called.

Carol glanced up while plating, missed her serving tray and dropped a piece of divinity on the floor.

I felt bad for her. The clock was ticking, and she needed to plate all three items.

"Three minutes, bakers," Skylar said.

Mya tapped her candy molds of anise onto a cookie sheet and transported them to her trays. She dumped them out, then arranged them. Her other treats were ascetic perfection.

Movement in the wings of the set caught my peripheral vision. Relief washed through me. Shannon had returned. She must have answered Sheriff Perry's questions to his satisfaction.

Brenden held up one finger. Together, we said, "One minute."

Marley glanced at us, then his pan. He sighed and set the pan beside his tiered tray just like yesterday, although today there was divinity and anise candy on two of the tiers, so it was his fudge that failed.

"Time's up," I said.

Everyone backed away from the end of their counters. The cleanup crew hurried in to straighten the area for the judging shot.

"Courtney, you'll go with Harrison and Shannon again. In case we want to use both yesterday and today's judging in editing." Brenden turned his attention to Quintin, who sat with his head hung low.

While I waited, I read a text from Eric inquiring if Shannon and I could do lunch since our dinner plans were cancelled last night.

I walked over to where Harrison and Shannon stood and addressed Shannon. "Eric's wondering if you'd like to have lunch today to discuss our show."

Shannon stared at me, expression blank like she had no idea what I was talking about.

"Are you okay?" I touched her arm.

"Yes." She flipped a dismissive hand through the air, one of her endearing habits. "It slipped my mind we'd missed our dinner meeting last night. I'm sorry. I can't make lunch. I have another appointment."

"Let's get started," Brenden called before I had a chance to inquire about her appointment or meeting with Sheriff Perry.

I hung back, whipped out my phone and replied to Eric that he was stuck with just me over lunch. I joined Harrison and Shannon at Marley's kitchenette where I'd been correct. His fudge was a runny disaster, but he'd fared better with his anise, pouring it into a thin layer on a cookie sheet.

Most of the contestants made improvements to their candy and earned praise from the judges for listening to their critiques yesterday. Mya had beat her fudge to perfection. Brystol's anise was the right color and flavor strength. The confections Tim presented mirrored yesterday. Harrison took the lead on Mya and Tim and managed to move Shannon along so she couldn't oversample Mya's fudge. I tried a few of the treats and found them very good. Harrison and Shannon agreed they had a tough decision for the first round of candy.

"Cut," Brenden hollered. "We'll take a twenty-minute break while Kinzy gets the candy moved."

A hush fell on the set. Brenden hadn't even realized his slip of the tongue until Marley piped up, "Hey man, she's dead."

"Hi, Eric." I entered the *Cooking with the Farmer's Daughter* set. "We need to talk."

"I agree. About our conversation yesterday, I'm not for dating others."

Eric's statement was matter of fact with no hint of anger or jealousy. Crossing the room, I noted, and appreciated after yesterday on the set, his nonconfrontational demeanor. "We do need to continue that discussion. It's not what I meant though." I slipped onto the stool beside him. "Kinzy's death bothers me."

He reached for my hand and squeezed. "It doesn't get easier to see someone murdered, does it?"

Kindness shone in his eyes. I leaned into his soft navy cashmere sweater that he wore with jeans. He slipped his arm around my shoulders and I relaxed into the comfort of his embrace. Seeing him made me feel better about the entire situation. "It's worse when you really know and care about the victim." I sniffled a little. "Brenden just made a faux pas. He mentioned Kinzy like she was alive and working. One of the contestants blurted out that she was dead. Brenden and Quintin both began to sob. Brenden kept looking at everyone and saying, 'I'm sorry' over and over."

"It probably hasn't quite sunk in for Brenden yet."

"I know. Thank goodness, Victoria decided to visit Brenden. She took charge of the situation. She sent both men upstairs to the makeup room, opened the commissary table to the contestants and phoned the resort. After a few minutes, she announced that security would transport the challenges to the resort's kitchen until she could meet with the event planner at noon. She's going to have them start the second challenge without Skylar or me telling them to begin. I'm not needed on set for about an hour and a half, so I came here to unwind and talk to you." I glanced up into his familiar blue eyes.

Eric gave me a sympathetic smile. "I'm glad you're here. Poor Brenden. It must be very hard for him. He depended on Kinzy."

"I know. His reaction doesn't surprise me; however, Quintin's does. He's really broken up for only working with Kinzy a few weeks."

"He is?"

I was glad Eric shared my surprise. "Brenden's slip of the tongue sent both men into uncontrollable sobs. Last night Quintin excused himself from the dinner he'd called and catered." I stopped there. I wasn't mentioning I felt Quintin had directed me to find Kinzy's killer.

"Maybe his gruff confidence is a cover for a soft heart?"

Thinking about his donation to the toy drive and offer to spring for a spa weekend for me and Caroline, I said, "I think you're right."

"I mean no disrespect to Kinzy, but her murder leaves us without a director for *City Meets Country*. I'd really hoped Shannon could make lunch so we could discuss it."

I sighed. "Me too. I've tried to talk to her about the show twice and she leaves the conversation."

Eric looked at me, expression blank.

I sat straight and faced him. "Literally, she walks off. I'm worried about her, especially since Kinzy was murdered with an apron from her line."

"You think she's a person of interest because of her apron?"

"Yes and no. I don't think the apron ties her to the murder as much as other events do. She and Kinzy had argued. Security cameras show Shannon leaving out the back door of the workshop at the approximate time of Kinzy's death. Sheriff Perry came and escorted her back to his office for further questioning this morning."

"Well, when you were a person of interest you were free to live your life within the confines of the resort. So even if Sheriff Perry considers her a person of interest, we should still be able to have our meetings. I really hope she can come tonight. We need to make decisions." Eric reached for his phone. "I'm going to text Rafe about finding a new director. We've been working closely on the show. Maybe he'll want to join us via Skype. I'll know in a minute or two. He's a prompt responder."

Shannon depended on her husband, Rafe, like I did Eric to take care of business matters.

Once he sent the text, Eric turned to me. His expectant expression told me he wanted to continue our relationship conversation, but I needed to talk about Shannon, and Kinzy's murder. So I dived right in. "I'm worried about Shannon."

"Because of the murder?"

"Only a little bit because of the murder. She acts sad

and not about Kinzy's death. It's something else. She has gained noticeable weight. Women sometimes do that when they're unhappy about something."

"What would Shannon be unhappy about? She has a great career and husband." Eric checked his phone. The corners of his mouth drew into a slight frown.

"Rafe didn't answer?"

He shook his head.

I took a deep breath and delved into my suspicions. "I'm wondering if she's having marital problems."

"What would make you say that?"

"She hasn't talked about Rafe once since we arrived. Really, she hasn't talked about much at all. She isn't excited about the new show or her product line. As soon as her shot's over, she leaves the set. When she comes back, late I might add, she's a disheveled mess."

Eric pulled a face. "What are you saying?"

"Yesterday when I came into this suite, I saw Shannon leaving a room down the hall."

"So?"

"It fit the walk of shame scenario, messy hair, clothes and makeup. Then after lunch when she came back to the set, late again, it was worse. She'd looked like she'd slept in her clothing."

Or wrestled with a person struggling for their life. I pushed the thought to the back of my mind.

"Are you going where I think you're going with this conversation?"

My shoulders sagged. "I'm afraid she's having an affair." *That's better than committing murder, right?*

Eric considered my words for a moment. "I don't think Shannon would do that."

"I know, but what other reason would she have to be in a hotel room that isn't hers?"

"I'm sure there's a better explanation than marital affair." Eric gave me a pointed look.

Now I said it out loud, it sounded ludicrous. Shannon was a loyal person. She'd never cheat. "You're right. I just need to talk to her. Get her to share what's bothering her."

"*We* need to talk to her. We need to start taping by the end of January. We must decide on the design of the set kitchen. With the upcoming holidays it might be hard to find, and interview, potential directors." Eric checked his phone again. I could tell Rafe hadn't answered.

"Brenden might have helped us out, but given his emotional state, I think he's going to want to take a break when we wrap the Christmas special."

"Probably." Eric stared at his screen like that would make the message appear.

"I did some checking on Kinzy's grandfather."

His head snapped up. "Courtney."

"Hear me out. He was wealthy. With Kinzy gone, I wonder who stands to benefit from his estate. Is there a way to find that out?" I paused, but not long enough to give Eric a chance to respond. "Leon Chapski is a partner in his firm. Do you think the firm's named in the will? Could Leon stand to inherit it all? Then there's Marley. He didn't want to wear the apron. He and Kinzy had words about it."

"What?" Eric's brows peaked with his interest.

I nodded. "He refused to wear the apron because he didn't want to endorse a product line. Kinzy argued with him. He took off the apron and threw it. She brought it back and he did it again." I wished I'd seen where it landed the second time. "Quintin intervened, saying it was in his contract, so he agreed. The wardrobe person for the contestants had to bring a fresh apron to the set. During filming he dropped the front of the apron, so it hung over the skirt and out of the camera's view."

Eric opened his mouth and I continued. I wanted to get all the information out before I received a lecture about staying out of the investigation and staying safe. "Shannon insisted he wear it correctly for the judges' filming segment. Although he didn't like it, he righted the apron. This morning when I was thinking about things, I figured out that the apron used to strangle Kinzy was Marley's original apron."

A storm of emotion rumbled across Eric's features. I braced, waiting for his normal warning, which didn't happen. Instead he asked a simple question I didn't want to answer.

"Did you tell Sheriff Perry all of this?"

CHAPTER NINE

I was saved by the bell (okay, phone chime), so I didn't have to answer Eric's question. Of course, I hadn't told Sheriff Perry. In my defense, I'd just figured it out.

I read my text. "It's a call back to the set from Victoria." I held up my phone for Eric to see. "I need to go. I'll be back for lunch."

Eric stood and walked me to the door. He pulled me into his arms. His concern-filled gaze rested on mine. "Talk to Sheriff Perry. I think the information about the apron and the contestant is important."

"I will. I promise." Although Eric always encouraged me to talk to Sheriff Perry, this was the first time he expressed that my suspicions could provide a clue to Kinzy's death. I'd promised Eric and myself not to withhold information from Sheriff Perry, so I needed to contact him the first chance I had.

Pulling me closer, Eric's eyes dropped to my lips. I leaned in. I wanted the goodbye kiss as much as he did. He dipped his head. The alluring scent of his woodsy aftershave greeted me as I stepped closer, circling his neck with my arms. His grip tightened around my waist. Our lips brushed, then the door handle clicked. I caught my breath and pushed away from Eric just as Pamela entered the room.

"Hi. Victoria sent me to fetch you back to the set." Pamela looked back and forth between us. "Sorry, did I interrupt again?"

Did my expression show the panic I felt at being caught in Eric's arms? I glanced at Eric. He'd set his jaw, with lips in a thin line. He was perturbed. Was it at the interruption? Or my reaction?

Eric spoke first. "Not really. See you later, Courtney. Bye."

Hurt edged his tone. I cringed internally. My reaction bothered him. Why had I pushed him away? Why did I worry if someone saw us kiss?

He walked toward the counter and his laptop while I exited the room with Pamela.

"Eric doesn't seem like himself," Pamela said when we were situated in the covered transportation. "I guess the murders are affecting everyone."

Guilt cut through me over my rude behavior with Eric and the fact that we needed to tell Pamela we were dating. Should I tell her now? I opened my mouth, then couldn't. What if we'd decide to test my theory? I didn't want to mess anything up for him. That was my reasoning, albeit weak, for sealing my lips and not saying a word. The few minutes it took to get to the workshop were quiet. I thanked Pamela for the ride, and we said our goodbyes.

I watched my own personal security person drive away. She didn't seem to be sticking to me like glue. Had they found conclusive evidence in the murder, so Drake and Sheriff Perry felt I'd be safe? Would they tell us if they had? As Pamela rounded a bend on the path, I realized I'd missed my chance to inquire on the status of the investigation.

Victoria waited inside the door. She perused my appearance. "You need a few touchups to your makeup. I have the makeup artists waiting for you over by your chairs." She smiled. "It saves time, which is money."

My face must have shown the question in my mind. Victoria was even more money conscious than Quintin. I joined Harrison in our set chairs. A few minutes later, Victoria instructed Skylar to join us. It didn't take long to get us camera ready. With no sign of Quintin or Brendan on the set, Victoria directed us in what to do, which was call time on the second challenge, recreating a popular candy bar. She decided to film us standing front and center of the kitchenettes. Skylar and I followed her cues to count down from five minutes, then together we said, "Time's up, bakers."

Shannon hurried through the door, went to her set chair and dropped into it. She fanned her hand in front of her face. How could she be warm coming from outside sans a jacket? The movement caught Victoria's eye. She looked at Shannon, then the clock, and frowned. Shannon was twenty minutes late.

"Great. Cut." Victoria told a stylist to get Shannon touched up, then walked into the kitchen area to oversee the cleanup of the kitchenettes in preparation for the judging. When everything met her satisfaction, she approached us. "Courtney and Skylar, you'll both accompany the judges." She turned to Shannon. "The judges will take small samples of the challenge and no more. I abhor favoritism."

Shannon's cheeks blazed red and her eyes narrowed.

"Now, get to work." Victoria dismissed us before Shannon could say anything.

I pushed between Shannon and Harrison. "You okay?"

"Yes," Shannon snapped.

I noticed the gleam of moisture forming in her eyes. "Are you sure?"

She blinked rapidly, then nodded. "Let's get started. I need to get to lunch."

Stepping back behind the judges, I exchanged a look with Skylar as we followed Harrison to Brystol's area. Harrison studied her offering. It was a layered bar. The bottom was chocolate and peanuts, the center a light pink filling, topped with the chocolate and peanut mixture. She'd cut them into small circles with a cookie cutter. "What's this?"

"My version of a regional candy bar sold in the area where I grew up. I loved this candy bar as a child. The original candy bar is a round dome with the cherry center covered by the chocolate and peanuts. I think the cherry filling is too pretty to cover so I improvised. I'm calling my challenge cherry chocolate delight." She chewed the corner of her lips while watching all of us try a bite.

"It's very good," Harrison said.

"Actually, better than the candy bar." Shannon reached for another, thought better of it and pulled her hand back.

"I agree." Harrison faced the camera. "In full disclosure, so our viewers know, if the contestants chose to replicate a regional candy, the competition had some shipped in so we could taste it. I agree letting the cherry marshmallow filling show makes for a nice presentation."

"Especially at Christmas." Shannon smiled while eyeing the treats.

Brystol beamed at their praise. We moved on to Dylan.

"It's messy." Shannon held up a brown paper bonbon cup. I assumed Dylan had tried to replicate a peanut butter cup.

When she tilted it to look it over, I saw hard globs of chocolate on top of the filling that to my surprise wasn't peanut butter.

"You overheated your chocolate." Harrison took a bite. "Your version of a marshmallow cup is a unique choice."

"Standout, really, had it turned out." Shannon set her sample back on the tray. "The bottom chocolate and marshmallow cream are the perfect consistency and tasty. However, the stiff chocolate on top isn't appealing and didn't seal the filling inside your cup."

"Let me guess," Harrison said. "You melted all your chocolate and set it aside while adding the filling."

Crestfallen, Dylan nodded.

"Next time melt it in small batches." Harrison set his fork on the counter.

Shannon moved to Mya's station. "We don't have to guess what these are!"

Harrison smiled. "They're perfect."

We all took a turtle from the crystal serving tray.

"These are divine," I said without thinking. "Oops, sorry judges."

"I concur. The flavor's out of this world. Sea salt in the caramel, right?" Harrison asked.

"Yes." Mya smiled.

"The caramel's so soft and creamy, the placement of the pecans so precise, and the size is uniform. Do you sell these in your store?" Shannon asked.

"I do."

A loud harrumph sounded in the room. I turned to see Tim frown.

"I agree, Tim. Not fair. She's a candy maker," Marley said like we weren't filming.

"Cut." Victoria's heels clicked across the floor. "Contestants don't comment during judging."

I glanced at Mya. Her smile had faded.

"But . . ."

"No." Victoria cut off Marley. "Your vita sheet said you specialize in cookies. Maybe Mya doesn't. Your time to shine will come." She turned to Tim. "Yours too." She walked over to our group. "Ms. Brooklyn, I know you're a chocolatier and not a television star, but when I say action, please say what you said before and show all the exuberance you feel. That's what we want to capture." Victoria looked at the turtles then back at Mya. "And quite frankly, I'd say you're deserving of every accolade the judges gave you. Your candy looks delicious." Victoria marched back to her chair and hollered, "Action."

"I do." Mya sounded happy and enthusiastic.

I grinned. I wanted to say to Victoria, "I see what you did there. You knew they hurt her feelings and you built her back up." Victoria jumped up a few rungs on my ladder of admiration. More women needed to be like her and build each other up.

We moved on to Tim and learned why he'd scoffed. His attempt at a Snickers bar had failed miserably. Shannon had lifted her bite to her lips when Harrison started to scold him about the overuse of alcohol. Chiming in, Shannon laid her sample back on the tray. I wished I'd done the same. The liquor gave the nougat too much moisture. It was sticky and the alcohol left a bad after-taste. The expression on Tim's face made it clear he disagreed.

Shannon gave him no time to respond. She walked over to Carol's area. Carol, like Mya, did well with her version of a bite-sized peppermint patty and admitted they sold it in their candy shop.

Marley had attempted a salted nut roll. Although they weren't better than the original, they tasted good even though they didn't look appetizing. The caramel ran off the nougat, taking the peanuts with it and creating a sticky pool at the base of the candy bar. He'd also used dry roasted peanuts to make them healthier; however, as Shannon pointed out, the success of the original candy was that it appealed to the sweet and salty snacker. Harrison suggested he learn to be patient until his syrups, in this case caramel, cook and thicken.

When they finished critiquing Marley, Harrison stepped back to address the group. "I want you to know that uniformity and neatness count on these challenges. Any chef will tell you people eat with their eyes before their mouths. When serving guests, each person should get a visual and palate-pleasing treat. Please remember this going forward."

"Cut. Thank you judges. Nice speech, Harrison. I'm sure it won't land on the editing floor. Contestants, please file to the exit door. A security person will take you back to the resort for lunch."

I'd hung back by Marley, hoping to make small talk and find out about the discarded apron. Maybe I could turn the conversation to where he thought he'd cast it off. Or even see if he knew what happened to it. The more information I gave Sheriff Perry, the better.

"Crew, take your lunch. Cast, find your coats, you're coming with me," Victoria said. "I'll go get Brenden and Quintin." She clicked off toward the stairs.

"What about our lunch?" Shannon asked.

Victoria stopped and turned.

"I have a . . ."

"Where we're going affects you. You can eat your lunch when we return while Skylar and Courtney kick off the third challenge."

"But I have an appointment."

Victoria didn't seem affected by Shannon's excuse or argumentative tone. She continued toward the stairs. On the first step up, she looked at Shannon. "You work for the show and will do as I tell you." Victoria briskly walked up the stairs.

Shannon stood with her mouth open wide.

"Finally, someone put her in her place." In a rough manner, Marley freed himself of the apron he'd worn and wadded it up in a ball.

I held my breath. Would he throw it the same way he threw the murder weapon? At least then I'd have an idea of where it might have landed. I exhaled and frowned when he dropped it on the countertop and dashed my hopes.

"Maybe now they'll make her be a fair judge," he muttered, stalking off and taking my chance to ask about the discarded apron with him.

*   *   *

"What do you think?" Victoria turned to Brenden.

Stoic, he walked around the area. Quintin, eyes red-rimmed, strolled to the focal point of the room, a square stained-glass window that took up most of one wall. Wide strips of rough-cut pine framed and accentuated the glasswork, a snowcapped mountain range. The varied pink hues of a spectacular sunrise surrounded the mountain-top. The artist used shades of green to light and shadow the valley below. I was certain the Pocono Mountains were the artist's inspiration.

"Was this a chapel at one time?" Quintin faced the front of the room.

An arched entry led to a small alcove. I walked over to check it out. The space was large enough to hold a chair and possibly a pulpit. Now it held a large modern sculpture of a sun and a moon.

"Yes. The event planner said it was changed to a meditation room several years ago." Victoria turned a circle. "There it is." She walked over to a corner. "They had a wicker table and chairs and wrought-iron baker's rack in storage."

"Wrong color." Quintin moved to the table and traced his fingers over the brown woven wicker.

"We can cover that up," I said. I turned to Victoria. "Do you think they'd lend us linens?"

"I like where you're going." Victoria smiled and pointed at me. "Crisp white linen tablecloths and chair slipcovers with red bows like in the ballroom."

I nodded.

She tapped a note into her tablet.

"We'd have to move chairs." Brenden looked at Quintin. "The window's a great backdrop." He'd perked up. "We can angle the baker's rack like this," he moved his hands in an area by the window, "and it will be in most of the shots." He stepped back to envision the camera shots and angles. "We'd need something to balance the other side for wide shots."

"A Christmas tree?"

Brenden looked at Victoria. "Not lighted. That'd be too much distraction from the window, although trees would work well with the nature theme." He stared at the area and tapped his chin with his index finger while in thought. "The narrow artificial kind with burlap bag bases. They come in varying sizes. We can make a small forest."

"I like it. Since these segments are usually shot outdoors, it will give it an authentic look and give our audience what they've come to expect." Quintin turned to the rest of us. "What do you think?"

Shannon plopped down in a chair. "You didn't need me for this." She spat out the words while crossing her arms over her chest.

Victoria quirked a brow and set her jaw.

Everyone was on edge with the murder, and I could tell Victoria didn't appreciate Shannon's surly attitude while trying to find alternative areas for filming. "I think it's perfect." I jumped in trying to deflect more angry words since we'd all seen Victoria in Mama Bear mode protecting her son.

I really needed to have a heart-to-heart with Shannon especially after Marley's comment. Hopefully that would happen tonight after dinner.

"Will the resort have the types of trees Brenden wants?" Skylar asked.

"I'm sure a big box store in town has some. We aren't

locked down, so our set designer can go in and out." Harrison looked around the room. "Outstanding job, Victoria."

"Yes, Mother. You did a great job."

"And in such a little amount of time." My tone held the marvel I felt at Victoria's accomplishments.

"Thank you, everyone, but this is what mothers do to help their child succeed." She wrapped an arm around Brenden and squeezed. Brenden pecked a kiss on her cheek and Victoria's face beamed with love.

A sudden longing to see my parents stabbed at my heart. Moisture sprang to my eyes. I hadn't seen them in almost a year. Although we had a video chat once a month, I hadn't realized how desperate I was to see them. Blinking away the tears, I quickly typed a text message asking them about their Christmas plans, telling them I missed and loved them. Would Dad's schedule with Doctors Without Borders allow them to return home for Christmas?

"The event coordinator said they'll close the meditation room to the public for the remaining time we're here. She'll have the facilities staff arrange it under our direction." She glanced at her tablet. "I'll ask about the linens and the trees. I'll tell her how we want it set up. I'll also mention there may be some tweaking in our floor plan so she can have a facility person assigned to us." She looked at Quintin. "Anything else?"

"No. Quite frankly, you have everything under control. The show's in capable hands. So capable, I won't be returning to the set after lunch." Quintin nodded a good-bye and left the room.

Shocked, I watched the door close. Quintin had been hands-on during the shooting on the second season of filming. Was he this broken up over Kinzy's murder? Was he worried the show would get a bad reputation or possible cancellation? Was he working with the network on damage control?

"Am I free to go to lunch now?" Shannon's question drew my attention back to the room. She stood, fists on hips.

"No," Brenden said. He seemed to have snapped out of his grieving. "We need to get back to the set. Your lunch is on the commissary table."

Victoria started to herd us from the room.

"Speaking of lunch on set," I said, "the first season we had a nice round table where we could eat our lunch in our makeup area. It was removed for our last filming. Is there any way we can get it back?"

"It's very unappetizing eating in the chairs where our hair and makeup is done," Harrison added.

"I didn't know it was gone." Brenden looked at Victoria.

"I'm on it," she said with a bright smile while we filed through the door. As she fell in behind me. I heard her mutter, "I suppose another harebrained idea of hers."

I pulled a face and kept walking. Victoria obviously found the event planner unprofessional. Would it be her job to prepare the area for the show? Had she thought it was unnecessary since they added a coffee bar? Maybe someone from facilities moved it unbeknownst to the event planner. Either way, I knew a table would grace our room once again.

"Brenden, are you ready to take over for the day? If so, I'll stay here so I can meet with the event planner and hopefully we'll have the room set up for filming later."

"Yes. Thank you, Mother." Brenden kissed her cheek before ushering us to the covered cart.

Shannon slipped onto the bench seat furthest to the back of the vehicle. Brenden, Skylar and Harrison climbed into the cart and sat right behind the driver. With an empty row between us, I thought now might be a good time for Shannon and me to talk.

"Mind if I sit with you?"

"Of course not." Shannon, who wore no coat, scooched over when she didn't need to.

"Aren't you cold?" I'd pulled a brown wool cape over the white pantsuit.

She pulled a face, then looked down at the sleeveless dress. "No, I'm not cold."

I wasn't being deterred by her snappy tone this time. "How can you not be?"

She heaved a sigh. "I'm just not. Okay?"

"Shannon," I slid closer to her and kept my voice low. "Is something wrong?"

She lifted her eyes to meet mine. Again, I saw a sheen of moisture. "Nothing is wrong." She reached over and squeezed my hand. "Bless your heart for caring, though."

I knew "bless your heart" had two meanings for Southern women, and by her tone she meant it in the derogatory way. She wanted me to butt out.

I didn't. "You'd feel better if you talked about your problem."

"Well," Shannon said, wrinkling her nose, "the only problem I have right now is hunger. Unless you have food in your pocket, you can't help me."

This was more than Shannon being hangry. "Shannon." I leveled her with a don't-mess-with-me look.

"I'm fine." Her sad expression belied her words.

I knew I wasn't getting anywhere so I changed the subject. "Want to talk about our new show over lunch? We can be prepared for our dinner meeting with Eric." I put more room between us.

She shrugged in a noncommittal way. Was she having second thoughts about our show? Was that why it seemed she was avoiding conversations with me? My mood soured at the thought. I was excited and happy. I wanted her to be too. "We need to talk about our set and director. Without either we don't have a show."

"Well," she finally looked at me like she could see me, "I think we dodged a bullet with Kinzy's death. Having her as our director wasn't going to work."

Stunned by her statement, it took me a minute to recover. "You voted for offering her the job too."

"Yeah, well, we were excited. We made that decision too soon. She didn't have enough experience."

That I couldn't argue. She'd only been assistant director one season on *The American Baking Battle*.

"We need someone who knows how to treat us. Not a snippy young thing like Kinzy turned out to be."

Were Shannon's feelings still stinging over Kinzy's comment about her weight?

"Don't you agree, she was less than professional?"

"I don't agree. Kinzy handled a lot of things in a professional manner."

"She didn't. Trust me, I know." Shannon flopped her hand.

"How?"

"I just do." Shannon drawled out the last word.

We arrived at the workshop and Shannon jumped from the vehicle. I watched her walk to the door. What did she know about Kinzy? Did it have anything to do with these appointments Shannon had been going to?

Like me, she'd wanted to give Kinzy her big break in directing a show. Women supporting women like Victoria had for Mya. What had changed? Had Shannon met or had conversations with Kinzy in the past few weeks? Or was she referring to the times Kinzy noted Shannon's weight gain? Something was bothering Shannon. Was she deflecting those feelings on Kinzy?

"Courtney, are you coming?" Skylar stood with his hand out to assist me with my exit from the vehicle.

I accepted his chivalry and followed our small crowd into the workshop.

"Harrison and Shannon, go ahead and get your lunch. Courtney and Skylar, I'm sending word for the contestants to be brought back to the set. We'll film the opening of the third challenge, then you can break for lunch. All right?"

We agreed. It didn't take long for the bakers to arrive and file into their respective kitchenettes. With our toes to our tape, our stylists touched up our makeup and hair. Brenden conferred with the cameramen and turned. "Ready?"

We nodded and he began a finger countdown.

"Well, bakers. You've survived the past and present portion of the candy challenge and it was sweet." Skylar smiled wide at the camera. A few contestants laughed.

"Now, it's time for you to create a future favorite Christmas candy!" I read the monitor. "And just for fun, you'll get a special ingredient to incorporate in this challenge."

"Christmas is the season of giving," Skylar continued. "In front of each of you is a gift."

"In it you'll find what we think will be a popular food

trend in the future and needs to be incorporated into your candy." I flashed the camera a Cheshire cat smile.

Fear etched every inch of Dylan and Marley's faces. The remaining contestants stared skeptically at the box in front of them.

"Without further ado"—Skylar waved his hand in the air—"please open your gifts."

Most lifted the wrapped box off the item at the same time.

"Great!" Mya covered her mouth and looked wide-eyed at the camera.

I knew she was worried she'd said something she shouldn't, so I adlibbed, "It's okay to be excited over a gift." She'd received the perfect item for a chocolatier, ancho chiles.

Brenden indicated to keep rolling, so Skylar said, "Brystol, what did you get?"

"I don't know." She held up a round spikey fruit.

"Dragon fruit." By her expression, my explanation didn't help.

Marley held up his item. "Wasabi?"

Dylan said, "I got chickpea butter," before he made a gag face.

Carol laughed. "I'll trade you. I have matcha."

"Neon sugar." Tim crossed his arms over his chest.

"Well, bakers, your gifts will put your skills to the test. You have two hours to complete this challenge," I said. They'd had enough time to get over their shock at the surprise ingredient.

Skylar and I smiled into the camera. "The baking begins now."

"Great, cut. Go get some lunch," Brenden said.

Skylar and I walked to the table. "Hope there's something good left," Skylar said.

"I'm sure there is. The resort's catering takes good care of us." I was right. We found plenty of the main course left. We filled our plates with chicken stir-fry and egg rolls.

Movement in the shadows of the room caught my eye.

"Sadly, it's my turn to accompany the judges. I don't think I'd want to sample some of the items." Skylar laughed. "I can't wait to get upstairs to tell Harrison and Shannon about this challenge. Their palates may never be the same."

I gave him a weak smile. He'd have to wait to tease Shannon. With his back to the contestant door, he hadn't seen her sneak out of the workshop like I had.

CHAPTER TEN

After lunch, Skylar and I, along with a camera and lighting crew, were whisked away to the resort. Since Shannon was nowhere to be found, Harrison agreed to interview the contestants while they prepared their challenges so we could film the opening for this segment of our show. I was bummed because I'd hoped to speak with Marley again. I wanted to have good information to share with Sheriff Perry about the murder weapon.

Victoria met us at the door to the coffee shop. "We're filming in front of the fireplace. You'll have to hurry and set up. We have an hour before the shuttle returns from the slopes with cold, thirsty skiers."

I marveled at this take-charge woman.

"Skylar and Courtney, please sit on the hearth in front of the fire so we can block the camera angles."

Castle Grounds wasn't closed for business. The tables closest to where we were filming were marked reserved. A few resort guests occupied tables across the room reading or talking quietly. My eyes homed in on a patron carrying a laptop bag who had just entered the area. Leon Chapski. He walked to the "Order here" sign.

My spirits rose. I wasn't getting a chance to talk to Marley, but this was the perfect opportunity to inquire about Kinzy's grandfather and the will. I hoped the lighting crew hurried so I could make my move.

I kept my gaze on Leon. He'd ordered plain coffee. To my relief he walked to a table, sat down and pulled out his laptop. If I couldn't speak to him before we started the filming, I might have a chance afterward.

"You can take five." Victoria called to Skylar and me. She turned to the props man and started pointing.

I didn't stick around to see what they'd come up with for us to use. I walked to the table where Leon sat in front of a long-arched window.

"Hello, Mr. Chapski." I held my hand out. "I'm Courtney Archer."

He stood before he took my hand. "It's a pleasure to actually meet you."

Leon wore a black suit. The Western-cut yoke of the jacket seemed a direct contrast to the white tie with a black silhouette of a city skyline over a starched white shirt. His dark hair, hidden the first night I'd seen him by a cowboy hat, lay in waves across the crown of his head. The distrust in his brown eyes eclipsed his cordial greeting.

With time against me, I cut to the chase. "I'm sorry for your loss."

He arched a brow and sat down without offering me a chair. "My loss?"

"Wasn't Harold Hummel your partner?"

"Ah! Yes, he was. Thank you."

He acted like he'd forgotten Harold died. I studied him a minute. "Did you think I was talking about Kinzy?"

His shoulders stiffened. "You wouldn't be the first to extend sympathy to me over her death." He snorted a laugh.

Was he mocking Kinzy's murder? I checked my ire in lieu of finding out more information. "So you didn't know her well?"

"I didn't say that." Leon wore a blank expression. Probably his practiced trial face.

"How's the rest of the family taking the loss of Harold and Kinzy?" Leon didn't know that I knew there was no other family. Maybe he'd tell me about close friends or something to give me a clue as to who else was listed in the will.

"Coy doesn't work for you." Leon took a sip of his coffee, never once breaking eye contact. "I never mentioned I was Harold's partner. What do you really want?"

I cut a glance to the filming area. I didn't have much more time. "Who is next in line to receive Harold's vast estate after Kinzy?"

"Why would you ask that?"

"Because they might have wanted Kinzy out of the way to claim it for themselves."

"So you think Kinzy stood to inherit a fortune?"

From what I found on the internet, yes. I managed not to voice my thought. Leon already suspected I'd researched him. He didn't need to know to what extent. "Are you interrogating me?" I crossed my arms and waited.

The distrust in Leon's eyes intensified. "Isn't that what you're doing to me?"

Of course I was. Another quick glance at the fireplace told me I was running out of time. I switched tactics, ending the game of cat and mouse. "You do know that the entire cast heard you and Kinzy arguing yesterday morning."

He broke his stare and gazed out the window toward the snowcapped Poconos. I had the upper hand. He'd had no idea what and who was behind the door Kinzy had gone through.

"Well," Leon said, looking back at me. "That explains why I'm stuck at the resort. Sheriff Perry won't let me leave. One of you made me out to be the bad guy."

The threatening edge in his tone didn't deter me. "I'm sure we all told the truth."

"Did you?" Leon bounced his knee and rapped his fingers on the table.

Did his body language scream nervous or guilty? Was he trying to figure out his next move now that he knew someone had heard that argument? Had Sheriff Perry questioned him, and had he not been honest in his answers? I didn't answer his question, mostly because I couldn't think of how to counter with a question of my own. My silence worked in my favor.

"Thanks to you and whoever heard the argument, I'm losing money every hour I'm here."

My brows pinched.

"Attorneys make our living via billable hours," he said just before his lips curled into a sinister smile. "Although I can settle Harold's estate from here, and by the end of the year to boot, with Kinzy out of the picture. All I need is a copy of Kinzy's death certificate," he enunciated her name, so it was clear who he was talking about.

Anger burned through me at his disrespect to Kinzy and her memory. This time I couldn't hold back my wrath. "You know she was murdered? She died in a violent manner. Her life was worth more than her grandfather's estate, which by the sounds of it she didn't care about, but it's obvious to me that you do."

Leon pinned me with a blank stare and a smirk. "Thanks for the chat."

He closed his laptop and gathered his things, leaving me with burning anger and the knowledge he was cold-hearted. Was it his occupation? Had his line of work desensitized him? Or was he a killer who thought he'd covered all his tracks and now found out people had heard him threaten Kinzy? As a partner in the firm, was he next in line to inherit Harold's estate? How could I find that out? Was it public record?

"Courtney, we're ready to film," Victoria called across the room.

Still dazed from my conversation with Leon, I walked over to the fireplace.

"Let's run through the script."

Skylar and I sat at an angle on the edge of the wide hearth, a couple of feet from the glass shielding the gas flame. With my jacket on, it was toasty. Our props were Christmas mugs showing a character from *A Christmas Carol*. Skylar's mug had Scrooge in his nightcap, mine

Tiny Tim leaning on a crutch. I knew they'd been chosen because of the past, present and future theme of the episode.

The monitor sprang to life. I began. "It's Christmas season on . . ."

Victoria's vigorous shaking of her head alerted me I'd read the script wrong.

I wasn't surprised I'd messed up. My anger at Leon's blatant disrespect of Kinzy still burned. I took a deep breath, hoping to clear my mind, and tried again. It didn't work. Tongue tied, I couldn't spit out the word *Christmas*.

Victoria frowned. Leon's insolence toward Kinzy and the obvious fact that money meant more to him than a person's life bothered me. I knew I had to push my thoughts about Leon out of my mind and focus on my job. I tried to not think about my previous conversation. It didn't work. I read Skylar's line as well as my own.

"Courtney." Victoria walked into the shot. "We only have thirty minutes to film this opening. Please concentrate." Victoria gave me a sympathetic look. "It's a difficult time for all of us. We must strive to make this special really good to honor Kinzy's memory."

Victoria stepped out of the camera frame and said, "Action!"

"It's Christmas on the set of *The American Baking Battle*." I smiled into the camera, then looked at Skylar.

"I'm so excited for the past, present and future candy challenge. Do you think our contestants stand a ghost of a chance pleasing the judges?" Skylar took a fake sip of coffee, making sure that Ebenezer faced front and center to the camera.

I shrugged. "They may receive a merry greeting." My turn to pretend to drink.

"Or get a bah humbug." Skylar mocked contemplation. "There's one thing I know for certain about this show."

"What's that?" I asked in an innocent tone.

"Our contestants are glowing with good intentions."

We both gave an amused look to the camera and lifted our cups in a toast to make sure viewers saw the characters on the mugs and got the wordplay using lines from the book in the opening.

"Cut. We'll go with that." Victoria glanced at her fitness band. I knew I'd blown my lines enough we'd run short on time. The cameraman, prop person and light person started tearing down the shooting area.

My mind drifted back to my conversation with Leon. I wondered if Sheriff Perry was in his onsite office. Maybe I should talk to him while I was in the building. Everything Leon had said niggled at me. Our conversation left me suspicious of why he wanted the estate settled so quickly. I didn't like the coldness he displayed for Kinzy, but if he was Harold's friend and partner, he probably knew why they were estranged. Perhaps, out of loyalty to Harold, he despised Kinzy.

Was there anyone else who'd know the background on their estrangement? There were no other living relatives listed in Harold's obituary. Were there other partners in the firm? I could suggest Sheriff Perry or someone in his office call and speak with them.

Between Marley and the discarded apron and my question-and-answer session with Leon, I decided a quick trip to Sheriff Perry's office was in order. He might scoff at my theories, but at least I could clear my mind.

My phone vibrated in my jacket pocket. Excitement curled through me. Had one of my parents returned my text? Anxious to connect with them, I pulled out my phone and unlocked the screen. Disappointment squeezed my heart when their names didn't fill the screen. The text was from Eric. He wanted to see me if I had some downtime.

I cleared a brief visit to my set with Victoria and walked toward the suite housing my set. I reached the door and hesitated. I looked down the corridor. Was Shannon in the room down the hallway? Is that where she went every time she sneaked out of the workshop? What kind of appointment takes place in a hotel room? I pursed my lips at the first thought that popped into my head. She'd always seemed so happily married. It couldn't be another man. Could it? I thought about walking the length of the hallway. What would that prove? I knew which door she'd exited from, but I had no plans to knock anyway. With a sigh, I entered my set.

"That was fast!" Eric greeted me with a smile.

"We just finished filming the opening for the segment in front of the fireplace. What's up?"

"This." Eric slid an overnight delivery box across the countertop.

"My knives!" I hurried across the room.

"I thought you'd want to do the honor of opening the box as soon as you possibly could."

He knew me so well. "You are correct, sir." The product delivery improved my mood. I tore into the box and carefully removed the cutlery from the packaging. I laid them out in a row on the counter, shivering a little when I took out the eight-inch butcher knife. That was the type of knife used to kill Skylar's stalker just a few short weeks ago. I wondered if I'd ever look at a butcher knife the same again.

"What do you think?" Eric stood beside me, inspecting the prototypes.

"I like the look of all stainless steel. I know the company wanted different handles, but this looks more professional." I lifted each one. "The weight feels good. I don't have time to try them out now but promise I will later tonight."

"Great. We have a lot to cover for the new show. Shannon's joining us?"

I supposed I should tell Eric about her lack of enthusiasm for our show. Instead, I sighed and said, "That, Eric, is a question I can't answer."

I stood beside the coffee shop exit looking out the window. The fir tree branches danced in the wind. The flats I wore insured I could walk the path to the workshop without discomfort, yet the sway of the trees and ripples of bent grass discouraged me. In addition to the chill of the brisk air, I did have my camera-ready hair to think about. I should've asked Victoria to send the shuttle back for me.

"Shouldn't you be working?"

Deep in thought, I hadn't heard Sheriff Perry approach me. Still looking out the window, I moved my eyes from nature's beauty to his ghostlike reflection in the glass. "I am working. We filmed in front of the fireplace."

He kept his feet planted and turned his torso to look across the room, which now looked normal.

"We've been finished for a few minutes. I went to chat with Eric."

I turned to face him. When he smiled, I realized I'd offered information he didn't inquire about or really need to know. "Does that happen a lot to law enforcement? People oversharing?"

"Only the ones with a guilty conscience."

I pinned him with a look. "I'm not guilty of anything."

"But you have something on your mind?"

"Yes. I need to get back to set and don't want to walk in the wind." I patted my hair.

Sheriff Perry nodded, yet his expression told me he didn't buy it. "You're coming with me."

"What! Why? I didn't do anything."

Amusement twinkled in his eyes. "Yet," he said. "I thought I'd give you a ride to the workshop, but if you'd rather walk—"

"I accept your offer," I interrupted. This was the perfect opportunity to talk to him about Kinzy's murder. I followed him through the lobby and out a side door to where several police cruisers and catering trucks were parked. He unlocked the vehicle and I climbed into the passenger seat while he slid behind the wheel. He exited the parking lot and turned the opposite direction from the workshop.

"Where are you taking me?"

"Where do you need to go?"

This was like talking to Leon. I harrumphed.

He heaved a sigh. "We're going to the workshop. Sit back and enjoy the ride."

I leaned back into the seat.

"Do you know what's troubling Shannon?" Sheriff Perry never took his eyes from the road.

Ah! He needed to talk to me too. "I don't. I do know she didn't kill Kinzy."

He chuckled. "You're always so sure of yourself. What makes you think that?"

"Well, she stuck by me when you thought I murdered Mick." Mick's real name was Bernard Stone. An investigative reporter, he'd entered the first baking competition under an assumed name, trying to get an exposé on an incident in Harrison's past. Sadly, he was clobbered to death with my iron fry pan of cherry cobbler, making me a person of interest.

"Any other reason?"

"Why would she do it?"

"I don't know. She was seen leaving the scene of the crime area. The next time I saw her, her appearance was in disarray."

I knew he'd noticed her rumpled clothing.

He continued, "I'd think once the cast was in their hair and wardrobe for the day, they'd try their hardest to stay polished for filming."

I didn't answer. I watched unfamiliar landscape creep past the windows. The cruiser was living up to its name, practically idling along the road.

"Is that a true statement? The right way for a non-celebrity to think?" Sheriff Perry probed.

I hated to admit it, but I did. "Yes. We try to only require touchups."

"Is she having any personal problems that you know of?"

"What do you mean?"

"Sounds like you're avoiding my question. Does she have relationship, financial, employment problems? You and I both know she doesn't look or act like the same woman who left the resort a few short weeks ago."

I frowned. I had been trying unsuccessfully to find an explanation for this myself. He cast a glance my way, so I finally answered, "I know."

"You all told me that she argued with Kinzy."

"But that doesn't mean she killed her."

"True, but the murder weapon came from her apron line, and we have footage of her sneaking out a back door."

"Was she sneaking or just walking out?" I turned in my seat as far as the safety belt allowed, although I didn't really need it because the car moved just a notch above a standstill.

He glanced at me for a brief second before returning his eyes to the road. "She peeked out the door, then looked behind her before she exited."

My heart sank. That mirrored her movement today when I watched her sneak out the contestant door.

"I think you need to talk to your friend."

I thought so too, but I wasn't telling him that. "I think you need to consider two other people as suspects."

"Who would that be?" Sheriff Perry guided the car around a bend and the back of the resort came into view.

It surprised me to see a large cement parking area with a loading dock bay. I'd never thought about deliveries in and out of the resort. Yet there would be many, including our production equipment and supplies.

"Do you think that whoever murdered Kinzy used this back exit to enter and leave? There's a lot of tree cover." Tall pine trees lined both sides of the road, a landscaping technique to hide the business side of the resort from guests. I hadn't checked out all the amenities in the building, but I knew that from any angle on the paths or the grounds these trees would hide delivery or garbage trucks.

"I wouldn't be much of a law enforcement officer if the thought hadn't crossed my mind."

I heard the sarcasm in his statement.

"This is the way they take the contestants in and out." He pointed to an exit door on the opposite side of the loading bay before he pulled into a parking space close to a door just around the corner. He pushed the gear shift into park, then gave me an expectant look. "Who are your suspects?"

"Leon Chapski and Marley Weaver."

"Why?"

"Leon and Kinzy argued the morning of her murder."

"So I've been told by every one of you. He's on my radar."

"I know. I spoke with him earlier and he's unhappy that he can't leave the premises."

Sheriff Perry pursed his lips. I braced for a lecture on staying out of his investigation. Instead, he asked, "What do you know about Marley Weaver?"

What? Did Sheriff Perry need my assistance? "I wanted to talk to you about him too. Personally, I don't know much about him, but the day Kinzy was murdered, he argued with her and Shannon about wearing one of Shannon's aprons on the air. As a matter of fact, he took it off, wadded it up and threw it. Twice. The first time, Kinzy retrieved it. The second time, I don't know where it went but . . ." I needed a moment. I took a shaky breath. "The next time I saw the apron it was wrapped around Kinzy's neck."

"Why didn't you tell me that in your statement?" Sheriff Perry's question was matter of fact.

"I didn't think about it then. When it came back to me and I ran it past Eric, he told me to tell you. This is the first chance I've had. Do you think it means anything?"

Sheriff Perry pointed. "That door will take you to a back hallway. Follow it and it will lead you past the restrooms and onto your set."

"You didn't answer my question." I pulled on the door release.

"And I don't plan to."

Miffed, I exited the vehicle. Before I closed the door, Sheriff Perry said, "Courtney."

I bent down and looked at him, waiting for him to answer the question I'd posed.

"Stay out of my investigation."

Not what I'd expected to hear. His response stung and his satisfied grin made it worse.

I slammed the car door, stomped across the parking lot and entered the building. A Nolan Security Guard nodded as I strode past him.

The nerve! Sheriff Perry had played me. He needed me to verify a piece of information, and I obviously had. But what was it? I replayed our conversation. He'd asked about Shannon and Marley. I'd offered up the information about Leon and all he'd said was Leon was on his radar. Did that mean he was watching him and considered

Leon a person of interest? Did he find something personal in Shannon's life that made him think she was under enough pressure to commit murder?

Then there was Marley. Had they found something that pointed to him as the murderer? Or was Sheriff Perry placating me about my theories to throw me off the track of the real information he was trying to confirm or expand upon? He had ended our conversation abruptly after I'd told him about Marley throwing the apron. Was my theory about the apron backed up by hard evidence? Had Marley Weaver killed Kinzy with the apron he didn't want to wear then used the contestant access to flee the scene?

CHAPTER ELEVEN

With my mind on the murder, I wandered through the corridor, not really noticing anything until I passed the restrooms and janitor closet doors. With their backs to me, Harrison and Skylar sat in the wings of the set. I approached them, intending to sit down beside Skylar.

"Courtney!" Harrison shouted my name. "There you are!"

Harrison stood so fast and forcibly that his chair clamored to the floor and startled me. I jumped back.

"Thank goodness you're here." Skylar rose too.

My eyes widened. "What's wrong?" My gazed bounced between the two men. "Has someone else been murdered?" I realized that couldn't be the case as soon as the question came out of my mouth, because I had been with Sheriff Perry and he wasn't called to a crime scene.

"No. It's Shannon," Harrison said.

Skylar gripped my shoulders. "She had a meltdown. Something *is* wrong."

"Really wrong." Harrison emphasized the last word. "She was crying and babbling. You have to talk to her."

"I will." I looked at Skylar, then Harrison. "But I need to know what happened."

Skylar released his hold. "Right." He took a deep breath. "I'll let Harrison start."

"I was almost finished with the interviews when she appeared out of nowhere." He scratched his head. "She marched up behind me like she was going to join the interview segment. Of course, I was in the middle of interviewing Tim with only Marley left." Harrison stopped.

I waited for Skylar to pick up the story. Neither man did. "And?"

"That's when it happened," Harrison continued. "Brenden yelled cut because she just barged into the scene. Tim made a snide remark about his interview getting messed up and what an unfair judge she was because she liked Mya's fudge."

I grimaced. Tim hadn't hidden his displeasure at the time. I should've known he'd store up a comment for ammunition later. Marley had called her an unfair judge too. Did all the contestants share that opinion? "I guess we should've expected this after the fudge incident."

"Actually," Harrison said, "the meltdown happened when Brenden asked Shannon to move out of the camera frame."

"She lost it," Skylar interrupted. "I came back from the resort in time to see her hysterics. What we could understand didn't make any sense." His expression turned sad. "I'm worried."

"Me too," Harrison added. "You need to get to the bottom of this."

I'd put off talking to Shannon for too long. "Where is she?"

"Upstairs," Harrison said.

I looked around the set. "Is Victoria with her?"

"No. Victoria stayed behind in the resort. Brenden took her up there."

Brenden was back on the set, so he'd left an upset Shannon alone. I turned to go.

"You'd better hurry," Skylar said. "We call time in fifteen minutes."

I took the stairs two at a time and threw open the door. Shannon sat in a swivel chair, elbows resting on her knees, head in hands, crying.

"Shannon." I said her name softly while I closed the gap between us. I placed my hand on her shoulder and she raised her head. "What's troubling you?"

Sadness mixed with fear clouded the sparkle in her eyes. She swiped at her tears with her thumbs, smearing her mascara. Finding a tissue, I handed it over while she sniffled. "Nothing is wrong."

I scowled. "Shannon, something *is* wrong."

She stared in the mirror and attempted to mop off the mascara. Calmer, she sat back in the chair.

I leaned against the makeup counter. "Tell me what's troubling you. I might be able to help."

She dropped her gaze. "It's nothing. Really, it's not."

I knew she was lying. She acted heartbroken. "We're friends, you can tell me anything." Although I didn't think so, I asked, "Does this have anything to do with the murder?"

There was the off chance that she was feeling remorse

that there were hard feelings between her and Kinzy at the time of Kinzy's murder.

Shannon snapped her head up. Her expression was blank, and then an emotion crossed her face. "Yes. That's it."

Again, I suspected it wasn't, but maybe if we had this conversation she'd eventually tell me the truth.

"Do you need to talk to someone? Quite frankly, I think the network should have provided onsite grief counselors since the first season."

"No!" Shannon shot up out of her chair. "I can accept death. It's part of life. Am I shocked that Kinzy was murdered? Yes. Do I like that she was murdered with an apron from my line? No. I'm probably going to have to pull that product line. At a very lucrative time of the year, I might add. What I'm tired of is these murders happening every time we film. And now, I'm the suspect." She started to pace behind the chairs. "It's so offensive. No, degrading. The questions that Sheriff Perry asked me." She threw up her hands in exasperation. "You just can't believe it."

I could. I'd lived through them too.

"He kept probing about that apron. He asked me the same question, reworded, several times. Like I'd give a different answer. I didn't bring the aprons with me. The company that makes them shipped them to the show. The contestants' wardrobe person oversaw them, not me. Is anyone questioning the wardrobe people?"

I didn't answer. I just listened. In one way it was good she was venting, in another way, I was even more concerned. She'd changed moods on a dime. She'd been sad and crying when I entered the room; now the fires of her anger had control.

"Did he do that to you?" She'd stopped in front of me. I nodded.

"I won't go with him again. I won't be accused of something I didn't do. I won't sit through the humiliation another time." She leaned towards me and I leaned back. "I don't have to stay here and take this abuse. That's all that's happened since I set foot in the door to film this special. I will not be mistreated." She stomped toward the door.

"Where are you going?"

"To find Quintin and give him a piece of my mind." The door closed with a bang.

I blinked then blinked again. What had just happened? I came in to console my friend and try to find out what was really bothering her. She'd turned the tables on me and worked herself into a rage. I wasn't certain who she was angry with. Sheriff Perry? Kinzy? The wardrobe personnel? Quintin? Or was her anger a smokescreen to keep everyone on edge and at arm's length so they didn't find out her true secret. What was she hiding behind her anger? I thought of the hotel suite and appointments during all hours of the day. Was she having marital problems? Was she having an affair?

I hated to think along that line. Why wouldn't she confide in me? Nothing could be that bad, short of murder that is. Whatever she was trying to hide, whatever secret she had that she thought was too horrible to share, the wall she was putting around it was making her look guilty of Kinzy's murder. How could I convince her of that?

An incoming text message jingled and broke into my imaginings. I knew I was needed on set. I walked down the steps, noting that Shannon sat in a chair while her stylist worked his magic. My stylist stepped over to me, powder-puffed the shine from my face, then smoothed and spritzed my hair.

"To the gingerbread house." Brenden pointed like Skylar and I didn't remember where it was.

Toes to tape, Skylar angled to feature his good side. I stepped in beside him and we began the countdown.

"How does time go so fast?" Carol asked, voice raised. She scurried around the area looking for a serving tray of some sort.

Dylan and Brystol both glanced at the clock, losing valuable plating time.

Tim threw his hands in the air, stepped back from his creation and leaned against the stove.

"One minute," Skylar warned.

I watched Marley fill a cut-glass candy dish in a beautiful shade of green with hard candies. Had he finally hit his stride?

Brenden pointed to me. I hit my cue. "Time's up, bakers."

Mya fanned herself with a tea towel. She'd worked right down to the last second arranging molded chocolates on a Christmas-themed tray.

"Great." Brenden clapped his hands. The gesture warmed my heart and made him seem more like himself. "Skylar, your turn to accompany the judges."

My spirits sank. I wanted to see what Marley made and taste one of Mya's chocolates. However, I knew I'd be able to do both of those things later when we filmed the judge's segment.

After a short break so the crew could get the kitchenettes spiffed up for judging, Harrison, Shannon and Skylar entered the set. I knew I wasn't needed and could relax in my studio chair, but I stood beside Brenden just inches from the action. I wanted to be close in the event Shannon had another meltdown.

Marley's jaw dropped when the judges walked to the back corner to start with Mya. "Hey, I thought you'd start with me." He scratched his head. "I thought my candy turned out great this time."

"Thank goodness the camera isn't rolling yet," Brenden whispered. "How many times have I told him that he can't talk during the judging? What a space case."

I smiled while Brenden once again explained how the judges rotated the order and that the contestants had to remain quiet while the judging was filmed.

"Okay." Marley nodded. "But I wanted them to see I used candy molds and everything."

"They will," Brenden assured him before he held a finger to his lips to indicate it was time for Marley to be quiet. "Action."

Harrison, Shannon and Skylar looked excited to try Mya's candy. I kept my eyes peeled on them while I spoke to Brenden. "Victoria's doing a fantastic job."

"She is." There was a smile in Brenden's voice. "It helps that she's a control freak."

I looked at him and saw mirth on his features. "Really?"

"Oh, yes! In the boardroom and at home, but sometimes I must admit it pays off. I really don't know what we would've done without her. I think Quintin and I would've shut down the show. She basically saved all of our jobs."

"I guess I hadn't thought that far ahead. She told Pamela and me that she runs a company."

"The family business. Her father made her work from the ground up to learn the mergers and acquisitions business. He didn't give her any breaks." Brenden paused at looked at me. "That's back when it was a man's world. She broke some glass ceilings."

Now I knew why she'd rushed in to build up Mya. She'd worn the same shoes, only in a boardroom. "Good for her."

"Yes. She wanted me to follow her into the family business. I couldn't do it. I'm not the cutthroat type. I'm tickled she finally seems happy about my career choice and interested in it." Brenden grinned. "It's nothing short of a Christmas miracle."

"This is the hardest part of our job," I whispered to Skylar.

"I agree. Harrison and Shannon made the decision, they should have to be the bearers of the bad news." Skylar chuckled. "We should be used to it by now."

Brenden started his five-finger countdown. At his fist, Skylar said, "Contestants, you've made it tough on the judges, not only for choosing who stays, but also who goes. Candy is a staple during Christmas. The judges were disappointed that many of you just couldn't hit the mark on creating treats to satisfy the most discriminating sweet tooth or look appealing on display."

I followed with, "The baker of the day came close to nailing every challenge, and sadly was the only one. Bakers, the judges want to see you succeed. Please try harder in the next round." I hated scolding everyone, but Shannon and Harrison both thought at least three of the contestants should be leaving the kitchenettes.

"The baker of the day is Mya." Skylar smiled wide.

I'd drawn the short straw, so I had to send the first contestant home. "We had runny fudge." I looked at Marley. He wasn't going home, but I wanted him to be aware he was walking a thin line. "Overheated chocolate and a duplication on a recipe. The chickpea butter cups weren't original or tasty. Dylan, you're the contestant leaving the kitchen today."

He'd hung his head when I mentioned the overheated chocolate. Brystol, Mya and Carol moved into his space and whispered what I guessed were words of support because he raised his head and nodded.

Tim and Marley joined them. Marley patted his back. "Tough break, kid." Neither man congratulated Mya.

"Cut! You're all free to go for the day." Brenden motioned to the crew member now assigned to escort the contestants. He turned to us. "You aren't done for the day. Mother says the meditation room's set up and ready for filming. There's a vehicle waiting to take you back to the main resort. A crew member will get the challenges over to the room via another mode of transportation."

With outerwear on—even Shannon—we all piled into the cart. This time Harrison and Skylar took the bench seat farthest to the rear while Shannon and I sat on the seat right behind the driver.

"Are you coming to dinner with Eric and me tonight?" I needed to text Eric that our filming day would run later than I'd anticipated.

"Of course!" Shannon pinned me with a look. "We have to discuss our new show."

I turned my head so Shannon didn't see the expression of disbelief that I knew had morphed onto my features. Her mood had swung back to her normal self. I whipped out my phone and thumbed a text telling Eric we'd be later than planned and that Shannon was joining us so he should expect mood swings.

He answered with a thumbs-up sign.

In the time it took me to text Eric, we arrived at the resort. The cart dropped us off at the main entry. I realized that was easier for the drivers, yet several guests stopped and stared at us. A few greeted us, which was wonderful because we all loved our fans, yet we needed to get to the judging set, and it had been a long day.

When asked for a picture, Skylar smoothed it over and told his fan he was happy to pose, but we were still working. He promised to be in the lobby area around eight if they'd like to come back then.

"We may need to mention this to Brenden." Harrison glanced back over his shoulder at the small gathering of people watching us retreat down the hallway.

I thought of the secret tunnel as a possible alternative and wondered if it had an outlet close by. I didn't see any staff-only entries.

"There you are!" Victoria greeted us with open arms, then spun around like we were admiring her clothing. "What do you think?"

I knew she was talking about the set. "It's beautiful." Because there was so much green in the stained-glass window and trees, she'd gone with Christmas red linens. The tablecloth hung over the edge of the table enough that, in any shot, it wouldn't show the furniture as brown wicker versus the normal white. The red slipcovers on the chairs were tied on with an elegant bow in the back.

The set designers had dusted the small forest of trees with artificial snow and used sprigs of evergreen to give the baker's rack a festive flare. Dishes decorated with Christmas trees set the table.

"Stunning," Harrison said.

Victoria beamed. "Let's get started. I placed name cards on the chair seats. Once you're in a comfortable position, we'll do a light check, then we can get started."

It was more than a light check. Once the camera angles and lighting were okay, the trays of the finished challenges were situated around us and on the baker's rack. Victoria chose the best offering from each of the contestants.

"It's a shame we can't put all of Mya's on the table." She shook her head and moved Marley's pan of fudge to a lower back corner of the baker's rack out of the main camera shot. His tray of green candy graced the table.

Shannon rearranged the offerings on the table, sliding Mya's fudge tray closer to her.

Victoria turned around in time to see the switch. "Move that back." Her snippy tone brought a frown to Shannon's lips.

"No." Shannon stood and fisted her hands to her hips.

Victoria reached across Harrison and lifted the plate. "I want it front and center. She deserves it. You should want it prominent in the shot too since you like it so much." Victoria put Dylan's divinity in its original placement.

"I guess you're right." Shannon sat back down. "Off the record, I think Mya's clearly the winner."

"I don't know." Harrison looked at Shannon. "She's a chocolatier, so this was her forte. We don't know how she'll fare with the cookies and cakes."

Victoria looked up from primping the challenges.

"That's better than the script. Why don't you start the judging conversation out with that, only don't mention Mya's name? Just say one of the contestants."

Harrison and Shannon agreed. I thought of my conversation with Brenden. Victoria had particular tendencies that could be described as controlling. I couldn't help but wonder how Brenden was going to feel about her going off script.

Brenden came in on the start of the third take of the judging segment. If he noticed the script change, he didn't say a word. He either liked it or perhaps didn't even know what had been scripted for the judges to say. After all, without Kinzy, he was pulling more directorial duties than before. On the fifth take, Brenden called it good.

"Let's go eat," Shannon said, while nibbling on a piece of fudge.

"Don't you want to change your clothes?"

"No. I'm too hungry." Shannon grabbed another piece of fudge.

Victoria saw her take it. She frowned and came over to herd us out of the room.

I texted Eric about the dinner reservations at Fit for a King, the onsite steakhouse. "Eric said," I held up my phone to show the text screen, "the reservation is ten minutes from now so we shouldn't have a problem. He'll meet us there."

Shannon and I walked through the corridor into the main lobby. True to his word, Skylar posed with fans for pictures and autographs. I had no idea where Harrison had disappeared to. Probably his room. It'd been a long day.

The hostess seated Shannon and me in the back booth close to the kitchen and far from the door.

"What can I get you?" our waitress asked.

"I'd like a sparkling water and the appetizer sampler," Shannon said.

"A glass of burgundy."

Eric approached the table as the waitress turned to go. He smiled. "I'll have the same." He slid into the booth beside me.

"Wait a minute," I called to the waitress. "Shannon, you like burgundy. Should we just order a bottle to share with dinner?"

She wrinkled her nose. "I'm too hungry. If I drink wine now, I'll be tipsy."

"Two glasses for now," Eric said.

We filled Eric in on the judging area in the resort and the long day of filming until our beverages arrived along with three small plates.

Shannon pushed the plates behind the condiments on her side of the table.

I guess she didn't plan to share. Were the fried fatty foods her dinner? If so, perhaps this was the reason for her weight gain. She'd stopped eating healthy.

"Shannon, I texted Rafe the other day and haven't heard back. That's so unlike him. Is everything okay?" Eric asked.

Shannon had taken a sip of her sparkling water and started to choke. She grabbed her napkin, coughed and cleared her throat. "I think so. . . . I don't know." Her eyes widened. "Maybe he's busy. . . . I don't know. . . . How would I know? I'm here."

Whoa. Shannon and Rafe had Skyped almost nightly the last two times we filmed the show. They even had Skype dinner dates. How would she not know?

The waitress chose the right time to deliver the appetizer tray. Shannon eyed the food, so she didn't see Eric and me exchange a look. My stomach twisted. Had I been correct in assuming she was having marital problems?

We gave the waitress our orders and Shannon dug into her appetizers, making no motion to pass around the plate. Did she really need deep fried cheese and veggies in addition to a steak dinner?

Brave man that he is, Eric reached over and snagged a cheese ball. "The first thing we need to discuss," he began, "is our director."

Shannon gave Eric a perturbed look but said nothing about the stolen appetizer. "Can't the network just assign someone? I mean, they must have lots of directors. They have lots of shows." Shannon watched Eric pop the cheese ball in his mouth and slid the appetizer plate closer to her. "And we're filming off season. I can't believe one of those directors wouldn't want to pick up a show."

"We want the director to have the same vision we do for the show," Eric said.

"Right. We can't have someone assigned who wants us to make fancy tablescapes instead of focusing on our cooking." I'd seen that happen, when a chef or home cook did more table designing, including centerpiece arrangements, than cooking on their shows.

Shannon seemed to weigh what I said, then shrugged. "Okay. I guess we advertise and interview then?"

"Should we start with the directors of our respective shows?" I asked.

"Mine's good, but she's busy." Shannon's voice cracked. She looked up from the food, her eyes moist. "Maternity leave."

Here we go. Was she afraid that the director for *Cooking with the Farmer's Daughter* would treat her like Kinzy and Victoria? He was a family man, so I knew he wouldn't. "You'd love mine if he's free."

"I'll check," Eric said.

Shannon blinked, then smiled, and I knew I'd reassured her.

"Okay, now about the kitchen design. Since it's a country meets city, do we want to try to combine the looks?"

"Just a sec." Shannon pulled her phone from her purse and swiped the screen. A wide smile spread across her face. "I've got to go." She threw her napkin on the table and slid out of the booth.

"But your food," I said.

Shannon didn't hear me. She'd speed-walked away.

CHAPTER TWELVE

"Wow!" Eric closed the suite door behind us. "I can't believe she just up and left."

"I hate to think it's marital problems, but she seems to skirt any conversations that involve Rafe," I said.

We walked over to the counter in my set. I slipped off my jacket. Since it belonged to the baking competition wardrobe department, I didn't want to soil it during my knife testing.

"She acted like she didn't know Rafe's whereabouts. You don't think he's done something?" I swallowed hard. "Or left her? I think she's sad and using anger to push everyone away."

Eric's long and loud sigh echoed through the room. "Something's bothering her. It might not be what you think." He pinned me with a pointed look. "Maybe he's having surgery that he doesn't want publicized."

"Don't you think she'd be with him?"

Eric contemplated my question, then said, "The filming for this show came up fast."

"True. She made a comment about missing the holiday. Maybe they had a vacation or something planned." I thought a moment. "That doesn't explain the text messages. This isn't the first time she's received a text and left without an explanation. She's also arriving late to the set."

Eric sat on a stool while I found an apron to cover the rest of the wardrobe.

"Courtney, I agree Shannon isn't acting like herself, but stop making assumptions. It could be a million things."

"True. I wish she'd talk about whatever it is. She had a meltdown on set. When I spoke with her, she lied to me. I could tell by the look on her face. The worst thing is Sheriff Perry's aware of her change of behavior and sneaking around. Her actions make her look guilty in Kinzy's murder. I want to do something to help her with her problem."

"I know and I agree that she's troubled." Eric pulled out his phone, swiped the screen and scrolled. "I still don't have an answer from Rafe. I'll send another text just in case something failed. You know technology. It's about all we can do to help right now."

Eric was right. I couldn't force Shannon to be honest or confide in me.

I opened the box of knives and began taking them from their sheaths, excited to try them out. Looking around the set, I grabbed an apple and began carving. The handle fit well in my palm and gave me good control. In no time, I'd carved a poinsettia into the skin of the fruit. I held it up for Eric to see.

"Nice."

"Thanks. What do we have to chop?"

"There's a small beef roast and veggies in the refrigerator. I thought we could make a beef stew for lunch or dinner some night in the Instant Pot." Eric got up and retrieved the items.

"Or veggie beef soup?"

"Soup sounds good."

I set to work chopping, paring and cubing. The razor-sharp blades gave me speed and precision while cutting. Each knife had a good weight balance. Eric put the items into storage containers and refrigerated them while I washed the knives with a soapy sponge, rinsing them under hot water.

"They have my seal of approval." Excitement coursed through me. One more step, production, and I'd have my own product to endorse with two, soon to be three, cooking programs to advertise them.

"I'll email the company in the morning."

"Will they know a timeline of availability?"

"I don't know. I'll ask."

I cleaned up the counter and removed my apron. "Thank you, Eric, for making all of my dreams come true." I walked over to him and wrapped him in a hug.

He smiled and tugged me closer. "We made our dreams come true." He looked down at me, eyes shining with love.

My heart pattered with the anticipation of the dip of his head to kiss me. He didn't. Instead he released the embrace and took my hand. "We make a good team, Courtney, not just in business."

Disappointment cut through me on the near-kiss miss. Now I know how he felt when I'd pushed him away. "I know. We need to figure this out."

His fingers entwined with mine, Eric led me to the stools by the counter. "The only way to do that is to talk through the awkwardness that happens on our dates. I know you think we've developed false feelings. I disagree."

I'd never heard Eric use such a firm tone. "It was only a suggestion."

"It was a suggestion to date other people. Do you want to date someone else?" Eric released my hand. "It seems like that subject only comes up when we're here."

He was referring to Drake. I couldn't deny my attraction to Drake, yet a conversation last season led me to believe he and I had vastly different relationship ideas. "It has nothing to do with Drake." I paused. "Or Pamela."

"We need to tell her that we're dating," Eric said.

"I know, and the sooner the better." I didn't say it out of jealousy. I said it because I like Pamela and didn't want to see her hurt.

"At least we agree on that," Eric said.

"We agree on much more." I knew where Eric stood on politics, religion, family, business. "Maybe the problem is we don't have anything new to discover about each other?"

"Well"—Eric waggled his brows—"that's not entirely true."

A blush crept up my neck and devoured my cheeks. "Eric!"

His smile turned sly. "You're pretty when you blush. And I think we've found our problem."

"Flirty banter?"

He nodded. "And the romantic expectation or element of the dates. Courtney, you think they haven't worked because we're so comfortable with one another like an old married couple?"

I started to laugh.

He scowled.

I held up halting hands. "I thought of my parents, who can finish each other's sentences. They know what the other likes as a side with their steak or fish."

Looking thoughtful, Eric said, "Can they order their better half's deli sandwich exactly how they like it?"

I nodded. "That's us, Eric. We're trying to get that new person, new relationship feeling, and we can't because we know each other too well."

"At least we know the problem. How do we fix it?"

"This is what we need." I slid from my stool and wrapped my arms around his neck.

"Intimacy? So, like, public display of affection?" Eric drew me closer.

I wanted Eric to kiss me, but did I want him to do it in public? Subconsciously, I leaned back.

When Eric registered the movement, the emotion in his eyes faded.

"I'm sorry. I don't know why I did that. I want you to kiss me. I've wanted you to kiss me twice tonight, but . . ."

"Not so someone else sees?"

"No. Yes. I don't know. I guess I want to keep our relationship between us until we have it figured out. I don't want other opinions, suggestions or comments to taint it any more than it already is."

I earned a glare for my inept explanation. Which I deserved. I hadn't made the point I'd intended.

"Let's call it a night. I'll walk you to your room." Eric picked up my jacket and headed for the door.

"You don't have to."

He opened the door to allow me to go first. "In case you've forgotten, which I doubt, there's a killer on the loose."

The walk down the hallway and the elevator ride were filled with tense silence. Why was I surprised? This is how all our dates ended. When we reached my door, I pulled my key card from my purse.

"Eric, I'm sorry I ruined . . ."

I didn't get to finish. In a brisk move, Eric captured my words midsentence. His lips took control of mine. The kiss started soft and gentle then he deepened it. I leaned into him. My breath became shallow as his kiss softened again, then ended.

"Good night." He released my shoulders and walked off, leaving me breathless and wanton.

My breaths came in huffs as I watched him retreat to the elevator bank. With shaky hands, I unlocked my suite and stepped inside. Eric found what had been missing. The element of surprise, of not knowing what lay in store at the end of the evening. I dropped onto the sofa, reliving the last few moments. Giddy excitement coursed through me. Eric had me stirred up. I almost squealed with delight. I'd never sleep. My fingers searched my pocket for my phone. I couldn't wait to tell Shannon.

My thumbs hovered over the screen. Would she be excited for me? Two days ago, on my way here, I'd have thought so. Now, maybe not. I placed my phone on the cushion beside me. I wished she'd share her problem with me. She was so sad. No, not sad, heartbroken. Sure, she'd been sneaking in and out of the workshop and made the unfortunate choice to escape through the back door in the area where Kinzy had been murdered. But I knew Shannon's attitude had nothing to do with Kinzy's murder, which I didn't believe for one minute she committed, because Kinzy had experienced her moodiness.

Kinzy. Tears sheened my eyes. She was so young, with her entire life ahead of her. I believed her youth, and our job offer, made her cocky, which is why she had no problem telling Shannon about her weight. It had nothing to do with being a professional and everything to do with the over confidence of youth. I'd been so busy throughout the day, I'd pushed her murder from my mind. Quintin wanted me to figure out who killed her. I couldn't let him down.

If I couldn't talk to Shannon about Eric or the murder, I needed to focus on researching my persons of interest in Kinzy's case. I changed into comfy fleece jammies, grabbed my tablet and got busy. First, I entered Harold's name into a search engine. Many entries popped up for him, cases that were now public record. Had he put someone in prison who had a vendetta against him? I perused a few of the cases. They rang true with what the law firm website listed for him: family law, wills and adoptions.

Adoptions? Perhaps Kinzy had been adopted? It bothered some people enough to break ties. How would I find that out? Adoption records were sealed. I tried Harold and then Kinzy's name paired with "adoption." Nothing. I went back to Harold and continued to scroll through pages. I found a popular site that listed quite a bit of personal information. He must have grown up on the ranch;

it was the only address listed under his name. He had good credit, no bankruptcies or arrests. Kinzy was the only relative listed. I plugged in her name. Multiple addresses popped up. Like her grandfather, she had good credit, no legal issues and no other relatives.

I rubbed my eyes. Unless Kinzy had posted on social media, I doubted I'd find the reason she and Harold were estranged. With no other relatives listed for either, whoever was next in line to inherit Harold's vast estate wasn't related.

Leon Chapski entered my mind. I typed in his name. His record, like everyone else's. came back sparkling. I exited the background site and entered Leon's name in the search engine. Many public record court cases came up. Unlike Harold, Leon handled a variety of cases. Most were environmental issues. I tried Leon's name with Kinzy's.

Two entries caught my eye. One was an article about an environmentally friendly home being built on Harold's land. The person who would live there was Leon Chapski. The other entry was an archive of a church newsletter that talked about Kinzy's baptism and godparents. The woman's name listed meant nothing to me, but the godfather was none other than Leon Chapski.

I sent a text to Eric and Shannon before I started my morning routine, asking them to meet me in the coffee shop for a holiday beverage, my treat. Between the researching and my daydreaming about Eric's kiss, I lacked sleep and didn't care. I was filled with energy, hope and information. As I was finally drifting off to sleep the night before, I realized I should've looked up Marley too, but I would do that in my downtime today on set.

I also needed to bring the godfather issue to Sheriff Perry's attention the next time I saw him.

Dressed in jeans, boots and a heavy Chicago Bears sweatshirt, I would be more comfortable on the ride to the set. I ran a comb through my hair to remove my bed-head look and headed out to the coffee shop. When the elevator doors opened, I treaded lightly in my boots, so I didn't disturb the early morning quietness in the main floor hallway. At this hour, I walked the corridor alone. When I heard a suite door close hard behind me, I glanced over my shoulder.

Shannon!

She stared at the door, a frown on her face. She wore yoga pants and a matching tunic that stretched the seams to the limits and showed the outline of her cell phone in the front pocket. She carried her shoes in her hand. Her blond locks were matted and sticking up in a poof on her crown like she'd just rolled out of bed.

I didn't want her to see me or think I was spying on her, although a face-to-face meeting now would make it hard for her to lie about her whereabouts. Besides, she was probably headed to the coffee shop to meet Eric and me. I'd have a chance to question her then. I quick-stepped to the next adjoining corridor and rounded the corner, intending to backtrack so I arrived at Castle Grounds right after her.

My intention was good. My timing was bad. Preoccupied, I didn't pay any attention to where I was going and ran into a well-defined chest. Strong hands caught my shoulders on my bounce back, keeping me vertical.

"Good morning, Courtney. There're easier ways for me to sweep you off your feet."

My eyes met Drake's.

A thrill slipped through me, weakening my knees. My mind screamed "stop that," but my body didn't listen. Every nerve ending tingled.

"You look pretty in the morning with sleep still in your eyes." He held me just inches from his sturdy chest.

His spicy aftershave appealed to my senses, making me want to close the already too small space between us. "Um . . . thank you." I had to fight the effect this man had on my libido. The green long-sleeved Nolan Security polo he wore with jeans complemented his dark hair and eyes.

"What are you doing in this hallway? And so early?"

"I . . . I'm . . . going to get coffee." It was the truth and if Shannon overheard, all the better. I decided not to explain why I was in this hallway since it led to more guest rooms. With my back to the cross hallway, I wondered if Shannon had walked past yet. I shrugged out of his hold.

"I thought your producer brought you coffee every morning?"

I didn't like his emphasis on the word "producer," but it didn't surprise me. He and Eric had never exchanged a civil word. "I'm meeting him there."

"Oh." Drake snarled out the word while dismay covered his features. Had he planned on asking me to coffee? The hope that sprang in my heart annoyed me.

He leaned a shoulder on the wall. "So, shall we try to do dinner? I'm busy assisting Sheriff Perry with security around the murder site, but I think I can squeeze you in."

His charming smile replaced the dour expression and was a stark contrast to the unattractive dinner invitation.

Squeeze me in? My heartrate returned to normal and my nerve endings calmed down. "I think I'll have to pas—"

"The audacity!" Shannon's voiced boomed through the silent halls.

"What?" A familiar male voice, though not as loud, responded to Shannon. "Just because you expect us to hawk your wares doesn't mean we want to. Men wearing a frilly Christmas apron is silly and stupid."

"Enough!"

Drake and I rounded the corner to see Shannon raise her fists. Sometime between leaving the suite and the confrontation with Marley, she'd slipped on her sneakers. Hair askew and clothes wrinkled, she looked like she'd already been in a fight. Marley stood his ground in front of her with his palms up, ready to thwart her punches.

"What's going on?" Drake used a low yet firm tone as we hurried to the elevator area.

"He"—Shannon lifted her fists higher—"insulted me and my apron line. He's trying to bully me. It won't work." Shannon didn't lower her tone.

A couple of room doors cracked open. I'm sure the inhabitants surveyed the scene. Just what she'd need, civilians spreading stories about this confrontation. The rumors were sure to reach Sheriff Perry's ears.

I hurried over to her and pushed on her arms until she relaxed them by her side. "People are watching," I whispered.

"I don't care." She looked at me, then shook a finger at Marley. "He needs to keep his mouth shut."

"Hey, freedom of speech, lady. I don't like endorsing products so 'the man,' or woman in this case, gets rich. I don't think you're a fair judge. I don't think I like you." Marley appeared to be wide awake and dressed for his day in a blue tie-dyed T-shirt and faded jeans. This couldn't be a chance meeting. There was no reason for him to be in this hallway.

"Okay, buddy." Drake stepped in between them.

I thought I heard him sniff the air around Marley. Did he think that he was a drunk or high guest?

"He's Marley Weaver, a contestant on the show." I'd wrapped Shannon in a side hug, mostly to keep her planted in one spot. Her entire body had tensed at Marley's words.

"A contestant?" Drake looked from me to Marley. "Is that true?"

"Yes. I'm a part-time baker at a grocery store and trying to open my own cookie business." Marley scrunched his nose to push his wire-rimmed glasses into place.

"Okay." Drake sounded confused by Marley's lack of awareness of his location. Drake dipped his head and looked into his eyes. "What are you doing in this area of the resort? It's off limits to the contestants."

"No, it's not." Marley looked around like it was the first time he'd seen his surroundings.

"Yes, it is." Although not in unison, the three of us had the same answer.

"How'd you get here?" Drake asked.

"I don't have to answer that. I know my rights."

I was sure he did. It seemed to me that Marley held fast to the era of his youth, which probably included sit-ins or demonstrations.

"Answer or not, you're going back." Drake beckoned Marley in a follow-me fashion with his fingers, then took a step.

"I have every right to be here."

"No you don't. You're a contestant and aren't allowed in this area of the resort. If you were a guest, it'd be no problem."

Marley shook his head.

"See. See how he is?" Shannon flicked her gaze to Drake then back to Marley. "How'd you ever get on the show?"

I cringed.

"How did you get on the show? You're a lousy judge. You play favorites."

"I don't!" Shannon was incensed and it took all my strength to hold her in place.

"Enough." Drake looked around. "Both of you. People are trying to sleep. You're going back to your area, buddy." Drake took a hold of Marley's arm. "Can you take care of her?"

I nodded.

Marley didn't move when Drake started to walk, so he stumbled a few steps. "Take it easy, man. Let go of me. I'll go peaceful."

Drake released his arm. Side by side they walked down the corridor. Halfway to the main lobby, Marley turned and hollered, "Mrs. Collins."

My heart sank. By now they'd awoken people in the rooms along this hallway. Calling her by name identified her to listening ears or watching eyes. I was sure that was his intention. Marley was smarter than he let on. Was this scene over wearing an apron, or what he viewed as unfair judging of his baking? Fortunately, this time, Shannon didn't answer, although anger made her tremble.

Marley continued in the same volume, "Mrs. Collins, you still haven't answered my question. How in good faith do you think the contestants want to plug aprons that were used as a murder weapon?"

CHAPTER THIRTEEN

The trembles in Shannon's muscles grew stronger. I tightened my grip. Drake turned Marley around and, with hands on his shoulders, marched him forward.

I pulled Shannon to the cross corridor where Drake and I had bumped into each other in the event there were prying eyes and ears in this hallway. All she—or any of us, really—needed was for a cell phone video to hit social media.

"Are you okay?" I whispered my question.

"No!"

I put a finger to my lips.

Shannon read the signal and lowered her voice. "What's wrong with everyone? Why's this happening to me? I just don't need this stress."

I thought there'd be tears. None came even though fury had bloomed on every inch of her features.

"I'm talking to Brenden and Quintin. Marley needs to be removed from the competition. I don't expect contestants to like me, but I won't put up with being called an unfair judge. I'm professional and impartial."

I didn't point out the obvious—the multiple samples of Mya's fudge. Did Shannon not realize how that looked to the other contestants? She'd made a comment about stress. Was she stress eating and not even realizing it? "Wait until you've calmed down so you can speak rationally—"

"I'm rational." Shannon snapped out the words.

This time I decided to point out the obvious and brace for the consequences. "Shannon, you're not. You haven't been since you arrived for filming."

Her blue eyes narrowed and bored into mine.

"How can you, my friend, say that?" She had the audacity to look affronted.

Did she really think she'd been victimized with no just cause? "Because it's true. You shift between angry, snide and sad."

Her eyes narrowed further.

"Tell me what's wrong." I gently squeezed her hands, hoping that'd be the encouragement she needed.

Resignation washed the anger from her face. She opened her eyes, although her lips stayed pursed. Had I finally gotten through to her? She heaved a sigh, long and loud.

"I guess I have been on edge."

Now we were getting somewhere.

"The rushed scheduling of the show created chaos." She took a few steps backward, bit the corner of her lip and looked down the hallway toward the suite she'd exited. "And now, I'll probably have to pull my apron line off the market."

She'd been in a bad mood since I arrived, so whatever was troubling her had something to do with the rushed filming and the chaos she'd referenced. The prospect of having to pull her product line just deepened it. I found it odd that she looked down the hallway. Was she checking on the suite? Or if people had come out of their rooms? I'd deliberated about which item I wanted to question, then remembered she had no idea I'd seen her exit the suite two times.

Shannon stopped checking the hallway and picked up her conversation. "You of all people know how much work goes into landing an endorsement product, developing it and getting it ready to market. We had to push to get them released before Christmas."

"There isn't a truer statement. I don't know what I'd do without Eric to take care of that side of the business. What does Rafe think about the apron being a murder weapon and pulling the line?" After all, he was her business manager. I knew his opinions carried a lot of weight in her career.

Surprise covered Shannon's features, giving her a deer-in-the-headlights look.

Had she been lying about her concerns about the apron? Or was it something to do with Rafe? When Eric questioned her last night, she'd acted like she hadn't spoken to him in months. Was my theory about marital problems true? I waited for her to respond and raised my brows to encourage her to do so.

"Well . . . it's like this . . . um . . . I. . . . I don't . . ." She cleared her throat. "I . . . um . . . we . . . um, haven't discussed . . ."

"Why are you two standing here?"

Startled, my body jerked. I'd been so focused on watching Shannon stammer through what I thought was a lie, I hadn't seen Eric walk past, then return.

He looked from me to Shannon and back to me. I saw the slight widening of his eyes as he figured out something was going on. Of course, Shannon's appearance alone was cause for concern for anyone who knew her. Shannon was always well coiffed.

"Why don't we continue our conversation at Castle Grounds?" I took a step.

"Good idea." Eric smiled at Shannon. "It's not every day that Courtney offers to buy."

Shannon pulled a face. "What?"

In her anger had she forgotten where she'd been heading?

"Eric's talking about my text to buy a round of holiday coffee before we report to the set."

"What text?" Shannon sunk a hand into the front pocket of her tunic and pulled out her phone. She frowned when she looked at the screen, then stuffed the phone back into her pocket. "I can't go. I need to get to my room. I haven't been there since—" Shannon stopped and waved her hand through the air. "Maybe I can catch up with you later." With a forced smile, Shannon turned and walked away from Eric and me.

"What was that all about?"

I filled Eric in on the short walk to the coffee shop, including that I had originally thought, and was mistaken, that Shannon was sneaking out the first-floor suite to meet us for coffee.

"I still haven't heard from Rafe." Eric's expression showed the same concern I'd been feeling.

We ordered two gingerbread lattes and took a seat.

"Well, whatever Shannon's preoccupied with, it might affect her livelihood. If Marley raises a stink about her not being a fair judge, she could lose her contract with *The American Baking Battle*. In addition, she's not at all interested in discussing our new show." I thought for a moment. "Do you think that if she and Rafe parted, she no longer wants to work with him professionally?"

I swallowed hard after my question. I hadn't considered that scenario concerning Eric and my relationship either. Had Eric? If our dating failed, would we still have a successful business partnership? Or was that question on one or both of our subconscious minds, turning our dates into disasters?

My name was called. Eric started to stand.

"My treat, remember." I left him at the table to consider my question and really hoped he'd have a counter to my whole separated theory. I really didn't want Shannon and Rafe to be splitting up.

I handed off his coffee, took a seat and waited for his response. When he didn't answer, I said, "Well?"

His eyes focused on his cup. "I don't know. It would be hard, but some people manage to do it."

He glanced at me for a second, long enough for me to know that his thoughts had gone to the same place mine had. Did we really want to wreck the professional relationship we'd created?

"Do you think Marley will complain to the right people about Shannon being an unfair judge?" Eric unskillfully changed the subject.

"I don't know. But really, she's fair, or he wouldn't still be on the show, right? Not just because she'd want to be rid of him, but because, in my opinion, he failed at all the competitions. Harrison and Shannon had a tough choice between him and Dylan. Sadly, Marley's saving grace was Kinzy's murder and the do-over of the challenge. He did listen to the judges and showed improvement."

"Do you think he'll make it through the double elimination today?"

"Maybe, cookies are his forte." I sipped my latte and noticed Sheriff Perry had entered the area. As he paid for his order, he looked around the coffee shop and seemed to zero in on me.

He walked over to the table. "Do you mind?" He started to pull out a chair.

"Our pleasure." I flashed him a sweet smile.

"Good morning," Eric said.

"'Morning." He sat and pushed the bill of his cap back. He wore a long-sleeved uniform shirt with blue jeans. "Thanks." He looked up and smiled at the barista who delivered his coffee.

"Guess it pays to wear a badge."

He shrugged. "Some people have respect for it." His expression challenged me, yet I saw a glimmer of humor cross through his eyes.

I smiled wider. "What brings you to the coffee shop and our table this morning?"

"I couldn't stomach the coffee my deputies make in our onsite office another day. I sat down to see if you're managing to stay out of trouble." He lifted his cup and must have decided the liquid was too hot to drink so he set it back on the table. "Or maybe you're not and I just don't know about it." Sheriff Perry looked at Eric, then back at me. "Anything you need to confess?"

I took that as my cue to discuss who might have murdered Kinzy and share the information about Leon being her godfather, which connected him to the family in an aspect other than a partner in the law firm.

"I have researched a couple of people who should be on the person-of-interest list."

"Courtney!" Eric admonished me.

Sheriff Perry lifted his cup and took a sip, then said, "I'll humor you. And they are?"

"Well, no one new. The same two people we talked about before, Leon and Marley."

He nodded. "Marley's the one who didn't want to wear the apron?"

"Right. Have you talked to him?"

"No."

"Run a background check on him?"

"No."

His quick one-word answers started to raise my ire. Hadn't he taken me seriously at all yesterday? I tamped it down and said, with what I thought was a nonchalant tone, "You should. He was in the main part of the resort this morning arguing with Shannon." I knew I was giving him a Cheshire cat smile because I felt that was information he didn't know.

Sheriff Perry pinned his gaze to me, and I saw a twinkle in his eye. "That's what Drake said."

Drat! I should've known Drake had filled him in.

"Anything else?"

"Not on Marley." I didn't add that I'd forgotten to research him. "But I did find something out about Leon."

My turn to take a sip of coffee to build suspense. Although I think it backfired because Sheriff Perry also sipped his beverage in a lackadaisical way.

"Did you know that Leon was Kinzy's godfather?"

Sheriff Perry's eyes shot to mine.

"You didn't?"

He set his jaw and shook his head.

"I found it in a church newsletter archive on the internet. Buried under most of his environmental cases." I wanted him to know it was from a creditable source.

"Did you know that Leon lives on Harold's ranch?"

"That I knew. Anything else?"

"Yes, I'm thinking that with Leon being Kinzy's godfather, living on ranch property and being a partner in the law firm, that he may be next in line to inherit Harold Hummel's vast estate."

Sheriff Perry wore a thoughtful expression as he took a sip of his coffee. "What makes you think his estate is vast?

"Well." I leaned closer. "The article in the paper about Leon's eco-friendly home stated the number of acres of land owned by Harold. I guess I don't know the actual value of land in Montana, but two hundred thirty acres seems vast to me. That's bigger than Coal Castle Resort's property."

Sheriff Perry nodded at my reasoning.

"Then there's the law firm."

"I don't know," Sheriff Perry said. "It's a partnership. Harold may have held the highest percentage, but it's probably drawn up so if a partner dies, they get to buy out the shares equally. Usually not as much as you'd think." He sipped his coffee.

"Still, I think the value of the ranch was enough to kill for and isn't it possible Leon felt he'd lose his home if Kinzy took ownership? You really need to find out who was listed in the will besides Kinzy," I said.

Sheriff Perry stood and slid the chair under the table. "I suppose I do. Anything else?"

I gave him a satisfied grin. "No."

"You can wipe the smug look from your face. Although you gave me something to think about, you left out an important suspect."

I leveled him with a look. "Who would that be?"

He picked up his coffee. "Kinzy's onsite boyfriend." Without saying goodbye, he walked off.

With my mouth agape, I looked at Eric. "Who's Kinzy's boyfriend?"

Eric and I walked the main path to the workshop since it was an unprecedented calm sixty degrees this morning. Dressed in black corduroys, black turtleneck and a red V-necked pullover sweater, his clothes shielded him from the temperature like mine did.

With our coffees in hand, we fell into step. "Who do . . ."

"We aren't talking about murder suspects," Eric said, cutting me off. "You need to stay out of the investigation and stay safe."

"I've only done internet research and spoken to Leon once."

"That was one too many times. If he's the murderer, he knows you suspect him."

"But . . ."

"No buts. I'm not talking about this anymore." He cast a side glance my way. "I'm actually ticked off that Sheriff Perry dangled the carrot of Kinzy's boyfriend in front of you."

"He wasn't dangling. He was rubbing my nose in it."

"Either way, he knows you well enough that the information will pique your curiosity and you'll poke around, putting yourself in danger."

I drew in a deep breath of fresh mountain air. I didn't tell Eric that I thought Sheriff Perry might have hit a wall in the investigation and needed a civilian perspective, which is why I thought he dropped that bomb.

We walked in companionable silence. I tried to enjoy my surroundings. The velvety green lawn had turned dormant brown. Although snow covered the mountain elevations, only a dusting covered the valley. Commercial-sized Christmas baubles, alternating in red and green, lined the resort driveway and created a festive welcome. The tinsel inlaid in their frames glimmered and shimmered in the morning sunshine and slight breeze. Huge wreaths were hung between the castle windows on the second floor and all the trees surrounding the building sparkled with multicolored lights.

My mind wandered back to Sheriff Perry's words. Did Kinzy date someone affiliated with the show? She seldom conversed with anyone but Brenden, Quintin and the cast. Was he behind the scenes? Could he be in wardrobe? Perhaps the apron that strangled the life from her wasn't the one Marley tossed, but a fresh one? I shuddered a little, recalling the murder that took place during the filming of our wedding show. Crimes of passion were a real thing. We all lived through it a few short weeks ago when a bride was stabbed and left as the gory topper to her wedding cake.

I really needed to speak with Marley to see if he knew where he'd tossed the apron or if he saw someone pick it up. Depending on the shooting schedule for the day, maybe I could do some research and have a few prepared questions for him in addition to inquiring on the cast-aside apron. I should also ask him how he got into the main resort area. Another thought hit me. Had he and Shannon met by chance or had Marley been following or watching her? If he was the murderer, had Shannon been his next target?

"Was Caroline disappointed?"

"I'm sorry, what?" I'd been so deep in thought I'd totally missed what Eric had said.

He huffed. "Stop wondering about the boyfriend and Kinzy's murder. I asked if Caroline was disappointed."

"I think so. She said she wasn't and that she understood I had to go to work. Still, organizing the toy drive is a huge obligation to take on by herself."

"It's only for about a week, then you'll be back to help. You both work on this every year. It's a well-oiled machine."

"I know, but getting it kicked off is a big deal. Notifying media outlets, doing interviews for local television and radio stations. Caroline likes me to do those because of my celebrity. In addition, there're the other fundraising efforts and dealing with volunteers. I need to text Caroline. I meant to but with all that's happening . . ." I sighed. "At least we didn't schedule my cooking demonstrations for the kickoff."

"Right. Selling raffle tickets for people to win you as their personal chef for a night should bring in a lot of money at the end of the drive."

"I sure hope so. Most years we need a big push to reach or exceed our monetary goals at the end. Hospitalized children deserve the best Christmas ever. They worry about if Santa will find them, and then many times the parents are strapped for money because of the illness or accident."

"Your dad was the visionary behind the drive, right?"

My heart twisted. I really missed my parents. I'd hoped spending time with Caroline over the Thanksgiving holiday would fill up my familial need. "He was. I miss my parents," I blurted out.

Eric found my hand and squeezed.

"I texted them asking if they'd be home for Christmas. It'd be so nice to finish up the toy drive with Mom and Dad there."

"It's a very worthwhile thing he does."

"I know. I feel selfish when I miss them and ask when they'll be home. They gave me a good life and taught me so much about giving back yet . . ."

"It's okay to want to see your parents. I know the work with the toy drive goes right up until the twenty-second of December, but if your parents can't come home, you're welcome to join my family."

I stopped and looked at Eric. Spending a holiday with his family would be a big step in our relationship. I knew most of his family from their visits to Chicago so it wouldn't be uncomfortable, but it would take our relationship to the next level. I smiled. I felt okay with that. "Thank you. I may take you up on the offer."

Eric gave me a hug. "I'm not letting you spend another Christmas alone, especially under the circumstances that's happened during the filming of *The American Baking Battle*. I'm beginning to think doing this show wasn't our wisest decision."

We broke our embrace and started to walk. "That's not entirely true. It has been good for our careers. We have another show scheduled, I got an endorsement product and came clean on the farmer's daughter persona. Only the first murder was a direct result of the show. The last one had nothing to do with filming the show and everything to do with an obsession."

"True."

"And we don't know about Kinzy's murder yet."

"Maybe it was a crime of passion."

Eric's response surprised me. "I considered that too, but now I don't think so. If her boyfriend's onsite and was the jealous type, we'd have seen him. Don't jealous men keep close tabs on their girlfriends?" I cast a side glance at Eric. He shrugged.

We'd reached the entrance to the workshop-turned-set. Eric faced me. "Don't get involved in this murder. No more research. Sheriff Perry's capable of figuring out who killed Kinzy Hummel without your help or interference."

I just looked at Eric and didn't say a word.

"Courtney? Promise?"

"See you later." I turned on my heel and hurried toward the heavy wooden door. I heard him holler my name again. He wanted my promise to stay out of the investigation. I hated not turning around, but how could I make a promise I couldn't keep?

CHAPTER FOURTEEN

When I stepped it up to wardrobe, Harrison's voice boomed through the door and into the hallway. Cringing, I turned the knob and pasted a smile on my face. "Good morning."

Skylar looked at me and smiled. "Hi, Courtney."

Harrison, however, turned a sour look my way. "I'm not happy."

I didn't bother saying I knew that before I opened the door. We'd all dealt with an unhappy Harrison when we taped the first show. I'd even seen him enraged before the stress he was under was relieved when he'd told the truth. Once the murderer was apprehended, he'd turned into a pretty fun guy and encouraging chef. I knew the same would hold true for Shannon. If she'd confess her troubles, she'd feel better and be back to her bubbly and positive personality.

I broke my gaze with Harrison and looked at Skylar. "Dare I ask why?"

Skylar's blue eyes twinkled with merriment. "You'll know soon enough." He pointed to my wardrobe room. Furrowing my brow, I studied both men. Their stylists had caped them for their hair and makeup, but I assumed— which I knew could be a dangerous thing to do—it had something to do with our wardrobe. Since Skylar looked pleased and Harrison disgruntled, it must mean we had a thematic costume for the show today. Harrison didn't like wearing "silly costumes" (his words, not mine), so I knew something horrendous waited behind door number one.

I entered my dressing room and broke out laughing. I'm sure the outfits for today surpassed silly in Harrison's eyes and went right to gauche. I had two ugly Christmas sweater choices to go with a pair of black leggings and spike-heeled suede knee boots.

Taking the hanger from the hook, I held up the first one in front of me. A cartoon image of Santa riding a uni-corn with flowing red mane and a green and white striped horn embellished the front of the black sweater. Santa rode bareback and hoisted a brown sack of toys over his shoulder. White sequins dotted the front of the sweater and winked in the lights to give the illusion of Santa fly-ing through a night sky. A goofy concept that made for a truly ugly Christmas sweater.

The second sweater, bright green, boasted small red poinsettia blooms that spelled out Merry Christmas across my chest and ran down the center of the sleeves. A large, full-bloom poinsettia plant was appliqued on the front of the sweater. The fabric that created the foil wrap-per around the pot was shiny silver. Both were something

I'd never buy or wear, but in the spirit of the season and the show, I chose the lesser of the two evils.

Slipping on the poinsettia sweater along with the rest of my wardrobe, I did a twirl in the mirror. My stylist gave me a thumbs up and handed me large poinsettia blossom earrings that I inserted in my ears as I walked out into the common area like a model on a catwalk. Skylar burst out laughing. With his hair and makeup complete, his cape had been removed to show a red sweater with T-Rexes wearing Santa hats and carrying bags of toys in their small hands. Their expressions were fierce. Cross-stitch-type lettering across his chest read, "Scary Christmas."

"Great sweater!" Skylar surveyed me. "We will be a pair today on film."

We erupted in laughter as Harrison stood up. His cape was removed and his sour expression from earlier had deepened.

"Ugly Christmas sweaters aren't fun or humorous. They're tacky and most of the time sacrilegious." Harrison lifted his arms, which disrupted the scene on his sweater. The bulky green knit had ice skating cartoonish reindeer with red pompom noses and glittery gold antlers. The landscape of evergreen trees grew into the arms of the sweater with a large tree on the left sleeve and a mountain on the right. It lived up to the name ugly.

"What was your other choice?"

"Other choice?" Harrison blinked his surprise.

Skylar chuckled. "We didn't get two choices. How unfai—"

Shannon burst through the door. Her frantic expression faded when she saw that I wasn't camera ready yet.

Without a good morning or hello or sorry I'm late, she ran into her dressing room. Our ugly sweaters didn't even give her pause. Had Victoria been right behind her?

"Wow!" Harrison said, after her door closed. "She looks like she's been through a tornado. Literally."

Skylar nodded.

Since I'd seen Shannon this morning, I wasn't surprised by her appearance. A comb still hadn't found its way through her hair.

Harrison stepped closer to me. "Did she tell you what was wrong when you spoke with her yesterday?"

"No. She ended up getting angry. She's tired of getting questioned about Kinzy's murder and marched out of the room." I kept my voice low.

"I can understand that." Skylar smoothed a hand over his hair while looking into the mirror. "Being a person of interest is unnerving."

"Agreed," Harrison said.

Of course, I knew the feeling too, yet Shannon had been edgy prior to Kinzy's untimely death.

My stylist waved me to my chair and caped me up. While he was working my hair into a braided bun on top of my head, Skylar took a seat while Harrison paced.

"I hate this sweater."

"It's not so bad," Skylar said. "Viewers will love it."

"Why doesn't this sweater fit? Who ordered my clothes? None of the costumes fit. Why is everyone so incompetent?" Shannon snapped out her questions loudly and rapid fire. Her poor stylist never had a chance to respond. "I can't wear this one either." This time I heard tears in her voice. "They're both too tight. Find something else."

Her stylist stalked out of the room. "There isn't anything else. Choose one."

Shannon followed. Anger, or frustration, had shaded her complexion a deep red. The sweater she wore stretched tight across her bust and waist, giving the animated elf knitted on the front an unsightly shape. "I can't wear this on camera. Why did you order the wrong size in everything?"

"I didn't. It's you." Her stylist gave her a once over.

"I'm tired of everyone insinuating . . ."

"Shannon." Harrison stepped between her and her stylist. "Would you like to try on my sweater? I find it ridiculous."

"What will you wear?" Shannon studied his sweater.

"The suit I wore to work." He gave his stylist a warning look not to argue this point.

"I'll try it. Anything is better than this. I can hardly move my arms and I think I'm chafed already." She sent her stylist a very pointed look.

Shannon and Harrison exited the room along with his stylist. Hers remained in the common area.

In minutes, she returned in the gaudy sweater, which hung like a potato sack on her, but was a major improvement over the previous one. Her stylist made no motion or suggestions to adjust the sweater to fit better, like rolling the sleeve cuffs or perhaps pinning in tucks, unseen to the camera, to make the garment more form fitting. She didn't seem to notice. She plopped down in her swivel chair. "Now, make my hair and face look pretty since I'm in this ugly old thing."

The room fell silent at her commanding tone.

Harrison reentered the room. He wore his navy suit

pants and a white button-down shirt with a tasteful necktie striped with small evergreen trees.

"This doesn't seem fair," Skylar teased.

"Ha! Wait until you see what my stylist decided to do. It foiled my plan to not wear an ugly Christmas sweater." Harrison pursed his lips, but only seemed agitated, not angry like Shannon. He leaned back and called through the door to his stylist, "I have your promise this won't ruin my Armani jacket, right?"

"None of this would be a problem if I'd have been measured correctly," Shannon interrupted.

"You were." Her stylist kept curling her hair.

She opened her mouth and I dived in with a new topic. "Let's talk about our Christmas traditions, past and present."

I'd grown so tired of the tension created by Shannon's anger or upset or whatever was wrong with her. She had obviously gained weight. How could she not know? Was she in denial? Or just not admitting it?

"I'll go first." Skylar picked up on my change of topic. "My mom throws the best Christmas parties!"

"I can imagine," I said. I'd been to many fancy parties and knew they paled in comparison to any soiree Skylar's socialite mother threw.

"They usually happen the week before Christmas. She imports all kinds of good food and treats. She gives everyone a color scheme to dress in, so they match the decorations in the house." He laughed. "The silver and gold year, we almost needed sunglasses to look at one another in the shiny lame or sequined fabrics."

Harrison smiled. "When I was a kid, I had an uncle who trimmed every inch of his yard with outdoor Christmas decorations. The items that weren't lit, like a wooden church, he spotlighted. You could see the glow for miles. It's a good thing his family were his neighbors."

I watched Shannon. Her expression grew wistful and the corners of her mouth almost curved into a smile.

"What about you, Courtney?" Skylar asked.

"Our big event was helping Dad with the hospital Christmas toy drive. My mom, Aunt Kelli, my cousin Caroline and I gathered and wrapped and tagged gifts through the month of December. On the twenty-fourth, my Grandma Archer came. We'd bake cookies and candies to leave out for Santa and enjoy on Christmas Day. She's who got me interested in cooking." Although the memory was happy, longing squeezed my heart. I really missed my parents and wanted to see them so badly. I'd spent other Christmases alone, so I knew Eric had been right. This feeling had something to do with the murders I'd witnessed and been involved in over the past few months, the reality of mortality.

"Is everything all right?" Harrison asked.

Pushing my longing aside, I smiled and said, "Yes. If I was home, I'd be helping Caroline kick off the toy drive. I feel bad; not only did I have to cut our Thanksgiving holiday short, but she's stuck doing all the start-up work for the event by herself."

"Ha!" Shannon huffed. "That's nothing compared to how this filming inconvenienced me."

Aghast that Shannon thought no one else had problems, I couldn't even think of a response except to ask what it was and if that was why she'd turned into a Scrooge.

A tense silence filled the room until Harrison's stylist entered. She flashed a sly smile to Harrison and held up his suit jacket. Rolling his eyes, he slipped his arms into the sleeves. She adjusted it for him. She'd taken the strand of battery-operated Christmas lights that had been strung around the full-length viewing mirror in the dressing room and outlined the front of the jacket. She'd used dark hem clips to hold the lights in place. Once the coat was on, she fiddled around the back of the jacket at the hem line and the LED lights winked to life, then started to blink off and on.

Harrison looked down at his clothing, then up at us. "Somehow I don't think this is better than an ugly Christmas sweater."

Shannon was just getting out of her chair when Victoria opened the door. "Good morn . . ."

Her words trailed off as she looked at Shannon, then Harrison. "What's going on? This is not what was listed on the wardrobe sheet for today." She looked toward the stylists.

"Change of plans. Just like the show did to us," Shannon said, and sauntered past her and out of the door.

Victoria pulled a face and pinned Shannon's stylist with a look. "Let me guess. Her sweaters didn't fit. Harrison gave up his." Her gaze went to Harrison's stylist. "And you had to improvise."

We all just nodded since Victoria had begun pacing in front of us like a general chewing out his troops. "Today's ugly sweater day, not decorated suit jacket day."

"Victoria, it's the best alternative. Shannon's sweaters just didn't fit. It happens."

Cocking a brow, Victoria said, "You're a good friend, Courtney. Shannon gained weight and failed to tell the show. None of her costumes fit. However, you're probably right. It's easier to make something too large fit.

She'll need some adjustments on the sweater she's wearing."

Shannon's stylist took off for the wardrobe room and emerged with a small plastic sewing case. He headed down the stairs without a word.

Victoria let out a large, dramatic sigh. "I suppose the wardrobe changes will have to do if we want to film today." She looked at Harrison's stylist. "The lights were an ingenious idea. We will have to rework the script to include a comment about your jacket." She hesitated while looking at Harrison. "I guess Brenden will know if the LED lights will be a problem on film. Let's go."

As we all filed past her, I heard her murmur, "I handle one problem and there's another." I wondered if that's how she felt when running her acquisitions company too.

Once downstairs, Victoria conferred with Brenden about the change while the sweater Shannon wore became more flattering to her figure via the magic of her stylist. Brenden walked over and assessed the transformation. He circled her and said, "We won't be able to film her from the back. I guess it will only affect filming during the judging."

Shannon made no comment. She acted like this was the norm on our set.

Brenden walked off to speak with the camera operators. After a few moments, he called for Skylar and me to take our place at the threshold of the faux gingerbread cottage, where they checked our lighting and angles while Victoria led the contestants onto the set.

I watched the crew test the contestants' audio and noticed everyone slipped on their apron except Marley. He wore the same clothing as earlier this morning in the resort. My mind ticked off at least three questions I'd ask him after we completed the interview.

"Marley, apron up. We're ready to start filming," Brenden said.

Instead of answering, Marley looked all around the area like he was looking for someone or something. If that reaction wasn't odd enough, he turned a complete circle and frowned.

My gaze found Shannon, whose back was to the contestants while her stylist continued to alter the sweater. When I looked back at Marley, he repeated the same motion.

"Is something wrong?" Brenden asked, walking to his kitchenette.

He looked at Brenden and shrugged, then lifted the apron from the counter and slipped it on while stretching his neck and looking around the room.

Today's aprons looked like Santa or elf suits. The pockets were mitten shaped. It'd be a shame if Shannon had to pull the line. They'd make a festive hostess or exchange gift.

"Ready?" Brenden looked to the crew and then to Skylar and me.

Our monitor flashed on, and I started off the show. "Welcome, bakers. Today is double elimination day."

Skylar hit his cue. "Two contestants will leave the kitchen after the final judging today, leaving three bakers to compete in the finale."

Tension settled in on a few faces. "With trays of candy at the ready, it's time to concentrate your baking skills on cookies," I said.

"Continuing with our past, present and future theme," Skylar said, "the first challenge is filled cookies."

"Bakers, you'll have three hours to complete this challenge." I looked at Skylar and smiled.

He turned to the camera. "Like your cookies, the judges are *filled* with excitement to see what you bake for them today."

Staring into the camera, I said, "The baking begins now."

"Great. Cut," Brenden said.

Skylar and I relaxed as the bakers rushed for the pantry. I noted none of the contestants looked confused like they had the day before when the candy challenge was announced.

Brenden approached us. "Give them fifteen minutes or so, then start interviewing."

"Any particular order?"

"No." Brenden walked over and conversed with Victoria.

Skylar and I hit the commissary table for a quick bite to eat. "I wonder where Quintin is today." I took a bite of a banana.

"I noticed that too." Skylar finished off a donut and took a sip of coffee. "Maybe he's working from his room, trying to get a new assistant director hired. I'm sure he'll be here soon. He's too much of a control freak to stay away too long."

"True."

We noticed our cameraman waiting on the edge of the set, finished our quickie breakfast and headed over to our stylists, who now also hovered around the wings of the set thanks to Victoria. Given the hair and makeup okay, we headed to the kitchen area.

"I'd like to save Marley for last."

"Sure." Skylar walked to the back of the room so we could start with Mya.

The camera light turned green and Skylar started the interview. "What kind of filled cookie are you making?"

Really it was a rhetorical question since Mya worked at peeling a pineapple. She looked up and smiled. "Pineapple and golden raisin filled butter cookies."

"Interesting. I don't know if I've ever had one," I said.

"I hope you get to try one. They're a family favorite and a tradition on our Christmas trays." Mya cut the pineapple into spears as we moved on to Carol.

Carol stirred a pot with one hand and used the other to fan herself with an oven mitt. "What are you baking?" I stretched my neck to see.

She lifted the spoon and a dark brown mixture dropped from it back into the pot. "Date-filled cookies. The cookie portion has oatmeal so even though cookies are simple carbs there is some nutrition."

"It smells wonderful," Skylar said. "Have you made them before?"

"Every other year for a cookie exchange." She lifted the spoon again and shook her head. "This should be getting thicker."

"We'll leave you to it." I motioned for our trio to go to Tim's area.

"Whoa!" Skylar exclaimed. "I smell more than sugar or fruit getting hot."

Tim let out a jovial laugh. "You bet you do! Rum pairs nicely with mincemeat and that's my filling."

"Wow! When we say past, you go way back. I haven't heard of anyone using mincemeat in a long time." I smiled even though the smell of rum burned my nostrils. I wondered how much booze he'd used.

"It will fill a sugar cookie base. I plan to crimp and score them like a mini pie. Should be festive, right?"

Skylar and I nodded in unison. I faced the camera. "So far, no duplicates. Let's move on and see if it stays that way." For some reason, I really thought we'd see more date-filled cookies.

"Brystol, what are you making?" I asked.

She stopped rolling her dark brown dough. "A gingerbread cookie with traditional cheesecake filling to replicate the flavor of a gingerbread cheesecake."

"Do you consider that a filled cookie from the past?" Skylar asked.

With rounded eyes, Brystol looked from me to Skylar. "Isn't gingerbread from the olden days?"

"Yes." I exchanged a looked with Skylar.

"I was talking about the cheesecake filling," he clarified.

Brystol heaved a sigh and flipped her hand through the air. "It's been around since ancient Greece. I'm good." She put her focus on rolling her dough. I hoped the judges agreed with her opinion of a cheesecake-filled cookie being a past treat.

Skylar and I stepped over to Marley. Right away I noticed he'd removed his apron. Looking around, I saw it wadded and stuffed into an empty bowl on his counter. Could this have been how he discarded the murder weapon and that's why I didn't remember seeing it anywhere?

He looked over his wire rims at us. "I'm making raisin-filled cookies." He held up a spoonful of thick gooey filling. "Turned out perfect."

"What's your cookie base?"

"Oatmeal. I'm cutting large squares and making

turnovers. If I have time, I'll drizzle them with a vanilla glaze. If I don't, sprinkled powdered sugar." Marley had stopped working to chat with us. I liked how he and Tim described the finished product. He dropped the spoon into the saucepan, noticed there was sticky batter on his fingers and looked around for something to wipe his hands on.

I took the opening. "You know, if you wore your apron, you could wipe that off."

In a raised voice, Marley said, "I don't endorse products, especially murder weapons." He looked in the direction of the cast chairs.

"What?" Shannon flew out of her chair.

Marley smirked. He'd gotten the reaction he'd wanted. "Yeah, you heard me. I'm not promoting a product used to murder someone," Marley said, louder.

Shannon marched over to the kitchen area.

I turned to the cameraman and was relieved to see that he'd lowered the camera.

"You put the apron on." Shannon perused the area, saw the apron and grabbed it out of the bowl. She shook it at him.

"No."

I didn't take my eyes off Shannon. She'd stomped around the kitchenette and stood inches from Marley. Rage splotched her face red. "Put. It. On." She pushed the apron at him.

Marley raised his arms and hands like he was being held up. "Nope."

The low growl Shannon made deep in her throat echoed off the high ceilings of the room. She shook out the apron, finding the neck band. She moved toward him.

I looked around. Was Brenden or Victoria going to

stop her? Should I? All the contestants stopped working to watch the scene play out.

"Shannon, don't," I said, seconds too late. She'd rushed forward with the intent to loop the apron over his head.

Marley stepped back and she stumbled forward, dropping the apron to catch hold of the counter edge so she didn't fall on her face.

"Stop!" Brenden called. He and Victoria hurried to the scene.

Shannon bent down and retrieved the apron. Holding it at arm's length, she shook it at Marley. "Put this on."

"No!" Marley bellowed. He turned and looked past our group. "See, I fear for my life. She intends on hurting my person."

We all turned to see to whom he was talking. My heart sank. Sheriff Perry, Drake and Pamela had heard the ruckus and rushed from the crime scene area to see what had happened.

"This isn't good." Carol looked around at her counterparts. "I heard that's how the assistant director died, strangled with the neck loop of an apron. She seems to know the technique." She pointed at Shannon.

"Well, Mya's safe. Mrs. Collins loves her fudge." Tim had drawn out the word "love" in a sarcastic tone.

Both comments kickstarted conversations from the rest of the contestants until the set buzzed with chatter and no one could really hear anything.

Brenden and Victoria quickly moved toward Sheriff Perry. I heard Brenden say, "I can explain."

Shannon jerked her head from side to side like she'd been caught red-handed. Her expression on top of her actions could implicate her in Kinzy's strangulation. I knew she hadn't planned to kill Marley; however, judging by some of the crew and contestant expressions, they thought otherwise.

"People. Settle down." Sheriff Perry's words were muffled by the low roar of voices.

"Plug your ears," Skylar warned me before placing his fingers in his mouth and sending out a signature whistle. The crowd quieted.

"That's better," Sheriff Perry said. "Now, I want everyone to remain quiet while we sort this out."

"What's to sort out?" A deep male voice cut through the silence. Leon Chapski stepped out of a darkened corner and to the edge of the kitchenette area. "This is why we're petitioning for a restraining order. My client, Marley Weaver, is afraid he's going to become Mrs. Collins's next murder victim."

CHAPTER FIFTEEN

Shannon's eyes widened. I expected a surge of anger. Instead she seemed to deflate. Her shoulders sagged. She started to lose height. That's when I realized her knees were buckling.

Hurrying around the kitchen counter as fast as my spiked heels allowed, I looped an arm around her waist and forced one of her hands to the Formica edge to help brace her body. I was certain Shannon hadn't considered how trying to force the apron onto Marley looked to the spectators.

My eyes met Sheriff Perry's. "He was egging her on."

"No, I wasn't." Marley crossed his arms over his chest. "You know she tried to assault me this morning in the resort hallway. You witnessed it."

I glared at Marley. He didn't back down.

Switching sides so I was in between Marley and Shannon, I tried to inch her away from him. Again, I looked at Sheriff Perry. "I stand by my last statement. He fussed about wearing an apron before." I stopped. Sadness swelled in my chest and threatened to moisten my eyes. Little had Kinzy known when she handled that set problem that less than a yard of fabric would end her life.

"Yes, he did." Victoria finally stepped into the fray. She gave me a sympathetic smile. "I believe what Courtney planned to say is Marley hasn't wanted to wear the apron from the start of filming before Kinzy was murdered."

I wished Quintin was here. He'd have shut down this confrontation with threats of breach of contract. I looked at Brenden. Sadness had washed over his features and I knew his thoughts, like mine, were on poor Kinzy.

Looking at Victoria, I said, "Didn't Quintin state it was in the contract that the contestants signed to wear Shannon's apron line on the show when we had this argument the first time?" Then I sent a pointed look at Leon. Dressed all in black, I knew how he'd been overlooked lurking around the shadows of the set.

"This isn't about the contract. This is about the fact that Mrs. Collins threatened bodily harm this morning by making fists in the hallway and just now, trying to strangle Mr. Weaver in the same manner she murdered Kinzy Hummel." Leon took a step forward, encompassed the room with his gaze and slowly spread his arms. "We all just witnessed it." He turned. "Including you, Sheriff Perry."

Leon's courtroom antics sparked a change in Victoria. She set her jaw and stomped over to him. Standing toe to toe, she said, "He wears the apron or he's in breach of contract. Shannon stays on the show in a judge capacity unless you can provide a copy of the restraining order. If or when the sheriff brings me that petition, that will determine if Mr. Weaver stays on the show because quite frankly, unless Sheriff Perry plans to arrest Shannon for murder, she keeps her job. Marley Weaver will be the one to leave the set."

I almost cheered. I loved that Victoria was a supporter of women's empowerment. I glanced at Shannon. She'd grown pale, yet sweat beaded her lip and hairline. "You okay?" I asked in a whisper.

Her eyes searched mine. "I think I'm in big trouble." She bit her lower lip.

I wasn't certain if she meant her health or the realization that she could be arrested for murder had just sank in.

"Wait."

We all turned to Marley.

"Does that mean I can't compete? I don't want to leave the show. I'm going to win the competition and open a bakery."

Victoria laughed and turned around. "You don't really think the network is going to make one of their stars leave the show if you file a restraining order, do you?"

Marley stared at her for a minute, then his light bulb moment changed his expression from confrontational to remorse. "I'll wear the apron." His mumble was barely audible.

"No." Leon's voice carried through the workshop and all eyes turned to him.

His gaze was lasered on Marley while he shook his head. "They can't do that."

Brenden finally came to life. He walked over and stood beside Victoria. "Haven't you seen contestants recuse themselves from the competition because it's too stressful? Let me tell you, it's not always stresses or a family emergency."

I'd seen that happen on competition shows. Yet I didn't know if Brenden was telling the truth or bluffing. Were those excuses used for the contestant to save face on camera?

"I'm not stressed. I want to stay on the show," Marley said. "My raisin filling turned out."

Victoria smiled at her son, patted his back, then said, "In addition, why are you still here?" There was no question who she was addressing since her eyes bore into Leon.

He never flinched. "Sheriff Perry won't let me leave."

Shannon regained some strength and found her normal posture. I released my hold around her waist and walked toward Leon. "Why is that? Are you the secondary beneficiary on Harold Hummel's estate? Are your courtroom antics on our set a smokescreen to throw the spotlight off you being a suspect in Kinzy's murder? After all, you'd have a lot to gain. . . ."

"Enough!" Sheriff Perry cut me off. "Everyone calm down and stop making accusations." Unfortunately, his gaze rested on me. "Mr. Chapski filed a claim earlier that a confrontation happened between Mrs. Collins and Mr. Weaver. After witnessing this, it's clear to me that it has."

The cold, hard look Leon pinned on me was unnerving. It also told me I might have hit on the truth. Had I inadvertently put myself in danger again? Getting on a murderer's bad side is not the thing to do. I'd learned that twice, the hard way. I looked around the room. Victoria gave me a wink and approving smile, which did nothing to soothe the feeling of dread that settled over me.

"Let's go." Sheriff Perry turned to Leon.

"Now I have two things to do. File a restraining order against Mrs. Collins and a defamation of character suit against Miss Archer." Leon made no motion to leave.

"I don't want to restrain anyone anymore," Marley said. "I want to bake my cookies. The filling came out perfect."

"Sheriff, we're filming a show. Please remove him from our set so we can continue. Once his legal documents are filed, we will deal with the fallout. Until then, an apron-clad Marley will bake, and Shannon will judge. And maybe, just maybe, you can find proof to back up Courtney's claim because it sounds very viable to me."

Victoria turned away from the men, wearing a sly smile. I couldn't help but think this was her boardroom demeanor while taking over a company.

My gaze flicked to Sheriff Perry, who cocked a brow at a retreating Victoria but refrained from saying anymore to her. He nodded at Drake. "You go back to the crime scene area. Pamela, stay here and keep an eye on Courtney and Shannon." He pulled on Leon's arm and both men left the set.

For a moment the set was flooded with sunlight as the wooden door opened and closed.

"We lost about thirty minutes," Brenden said. "Let's reset and start over. Shannon, are you okay? Can you continue? You're very pale." He walked over to her. "Why don't you sit down?"

"I'm really sorry." Marley picked up the apron from the counter. "I'll wear the apron even though I don't like endorsements. But you must promise to judge my cookies fairly. No favoring others."

Shannon gave him an incredulous look. "I don't favor others."

"Well, you did yesterday. Eating all of Mya's fudge."
Marley tied the apron strings.

"Her fudge was delicious."

I cringed at Shannon's answer and decided to inter-
vene. "Shannon, let's go get some breakfast." I pulled on
her arm until she finally stepped away from Marley's
kitchenette.

We didn't get far when he said, "We all know you thought
so. You ate a lot of it and she's still here, so you're showing favoritism."

What was wrong with him? Was he high?

Shannon tried to turn. I tugged her toward the catering
table.

"Marley," Harrison said. "There're two judges on this
show. I will admit it was apparent that Shannon liked
Mya's fudge, and who wouldn't because it was terrific."
Harrison rested his gaze and smile on Mya. "That's not
the reason Mya is still on the show. She's here because
her candy turned out well. Dylan left because none of his
candy turned out and you, sir, were a close second. My
advice is to focus on *your* baking if you want to stay on
the show and be assured that we're both judging fairly."

Pride filled my chest at Harrison's defense of Shannon. Although it was bumpy in the beginning of the first
season, the cast had become friends and respected colleagues, something the show had strived for from the
start.

Skylar and Harrison joined us at the commissary table.

Shannon wrapped Harrison in a hug. "Thank you.
Y'all are great friends." She placed a hand to her fore-
head and wrinkled her brow. She reached for my hand.
"Do I feel feverish?"

Was Shannon getting sick or was the shock of the scene that played out getting to her? Or was it something else entirely? I touched her forehead. "You're a little warm. It could be the sweater or lighting."

"Or a combination of everything," Skylar added.

"Maybe. I think I'd better have it checked out. I'm going to run to the nurse practitioner's office and have her check."

Pamela looked at me, then Shannon, trying to figure out what to do since Sheriff Perry left her with instructions to watch us both. When she caught my eye, I jerked my head toward Shannon. She picked up on my message. "I'll give you a lift to the resort."

Shannon waved her hand through the air before she grabbed a large donut. "Y'all don't have to trouble yourself. I'll be back shortly." Shannon started to back away from the group. "Tell Brenden." Shannon turned on her heel and ran from the building.

Hesitating, again Pamela turned to me.

"Go after her. I'll be right here. I promise." I knew Pamela had a UTV parked somewhere close and could easily catch Shannon on foot. Pamela left the room in the same manner Shannon had.

"I hope she catches up with her. I'm not sure Shannon should be left alone right now." Harrison stared at the door. "She does seem unstable."

"Shh," I hissed. "That sounds incriminating." The words had barely made it out of my mouth when the door opened.

Shannon and Pamela entered.

The women walked over to the table. Shannon smiled brightly. "I'm so happy Pamela came after me. Even in this bulky sweater, I wasn't dressed for the outdoors."

"What in the world? We thought you were seeking medical attention," Skylar said.

"It turned out I just needed some air." A sheepish look crept onto Shannon's face. "And, I hate to say this in a social setting, but I belched and felt better." She rolled her eyes.

The skeptical expression on Pamela's face matched my reaction to her explanation. Shannon's excuse was flimsy at best. Since when did excessive gas cause a fever?

"Time's up," Skylar and I said in unison.

All the contestants stepped away from their plated cookies. The scent of sugar, spice and warm fruit mingling together made my mouth water.

"Cut," Brenden said.

I breathed deep. "This is a great job perk."

Skylar laughed. "Only when the baking is working out."

"True." I chuckled a little. We'd endured some pungent scents of burnt foods too.

He and I moved over to Marley's kitchenette. Brenden had decided both of us would accompany the judges. I hadn't figured out if it was to keep Shannon in line or if we were all on film, we'd be out of trouble since all four of his cooking stars had been persons of interest in a murder at one time or another.

I'd been thinking about the murder and couldn't help but feel Leon was involved in some way. Although it backfired, he seemed to be in control of Marley refusing to wear the apron scene this morning. What other reason would bring him to the set?

How had he gone unnoticed? His dark clothing helped

him to blend into the shadows, yet there was enough lighting someone would've noticed a person standing or sitting by the wall or in a corner. He must have found a hiding place just waiting to pop out at the right time. Looking over my shoulder, I studied the area, trying to see where he'd taken cover. There were some boxes stored in the corner. Had he crouched down behind them? If so, how and where did he get in? Supposedly, the contestant entry was locked until needed. Security manned the main door, so he'd need to use those back entries. Had he come in through the loading zone area?

If he could sneak in and make a surprise entrance on our set, he could've done that two days ago and killed Kinzy. Surely there were security cameras on the loading dock doors. Had Sheriff Perry reviewed those tapes? Had he considered these questions? Had he interrogated Leon again today?

"Ready whenever you are."

Brenden's instructions pulled me back to the present. I made a mental note that during downtime this afternoon I'd research Marley and poke around the building to see if I could find where Leon had hidden in the shadows.

"I'll take the lead on this one." Harrison smiled at Shannon.

"No." She looked at Marley. "I can do it." She glanced toward the camera, saw the light was green and flashed a sugary smile. "What did you prepare for cookies from the past?"

The appearance of Marley's cookies and how he presented them surprised me. He'd had time to drizzle green-tinted icing over the tops of the turnover cookies, giving the cookie a holiday dressing. Arranging them on a Christmas-themed rectangle platter, he'd placed the cookies, folded side to the bottom, in a pyramid to form an evergreen tree shape.

"Excellent presentation." Shannon looked at Harrison.

"I agree. It was well thought out. It'd be a festive addition to a holiday table. Let's see how they taste." Harrison took the top cookie and broke it in half. He handed one half to Shannon.

To her credit, she didn't nibble off a bite. She ate the entire half, then gave herself a moment to savor the flavor before saying, "They're very good. The filling is perfect. The cookie dough is the right consistency. I think the icing made them too sweet since raisins are naturally sweet. Maybe think about using a little powdered sugar for color or a sprinkle of sanding sugar." She held up her hands. "That's just my preference. Harrison?" She kept her tone light and her smile friendly.

"The icing wasn't too sweet for me, but Shannon's suggestions are a viable alternative to this recipe. I loved the unique shape of your cookie. Great job."

"Thank you." Marley beamed, then looped his thumbs under the neckband of the apron and pulled it away from his body. His smile turned sly.

Shannon's smile faded and turned into a grim line.

Although I didn't understand his message, I knew it could mean trouble. Skylar caught the subtle action. He moved us to the next contestant when he said, "What did Carol prepare?"

Our group shifted over to the next kitchenette without any incident at Marley's station. Now if he only kept his mouth shut during the rest of the judging.

"Date-filled cookies with an oatmeal base." Like most women, Carol offered a sweet smile to Skylar.

Carol had stacked her cookies on a cut-glass plate.

"Nice presentation for a hearty cookie from the past. You did well on mounding the filling in the center of each cookie." Harrison inspected the plate and looked at Shannon.

"I noticed the nice seal you have on the cookies without the use of a kitchen tool." Shannon snagged a cookie from the plate and broke it into quarters, handing us each a bite.

"I used water to seal the edges."

"Chewy with a sweet filling." Harrison looked at the cookies again. "I'd say you'll get lots of compliments on your dates this holiday season."

"Hey, I get to say the corny lines." Skylar pulled a face at the camera.

"Good job," Shannon said. "I have no suggestions to make these better."

Our quartet moved to Tim. He had indeed shaped his cookies to look like small pies with decorative vent holes. He'd used sprinkling sugar over the top of his dough and placed each cookie in a Christmas-printed cupcake wrapper and tucked them in a decorative tin.

"Presentation is nice," Harrison said.

"You had some seepage." Shannon pointed to several cookies where the filling came through the vent hole. "I don't think your mincemeat was quite thick enough."

"Maybe." The corner of Tim's mouth turned into a frown.

Harrison chose a cookie and shared with Shannon. He nipped off a bite. I knew why. The scent of rum permeated the air around us. "You used too much rum. The flavor of the mincemeat is lost in it. Your filling was too loose, probably from the rum, and that's why it leaked out of your vents."

Shannon broke her half in half. "It also made your bottom dough soggy." She laid the pieces of her cookie on the countertop.

I fought a frown. Had she sampled it? I know she lifted it to her lips.

Harrison tsked. "Or underbaked." Harrison looked at Shannon then Tim. "I'm not sure which."

Tim's expression grew grim.

"Could you try to give us a treat without the use of alcohol or flavorings of alcohol?" Shannon asked.

"It's what I'm known for."

"True," Harrison said. "Yet it isn't really working in the challenges. I'll give you kudos for presentation and choosing mincemeat, but your challenges need to be edible."

Stepping back, Tim looked down, I thought more out of anger than disappointment. With two eliminations today, I'd say he was worried.

Brystol gave us a wide smile. She'd also used a decorative tin to display her challenge.

"Tell us how you made these." Shannon held up a bite-sized cookie. "They're rustic. I like that."

"I used a small cookie scoop, then pressed it down with my fingers. I put a small amount of cheesecake in the center and repeated with the dough." She sucked in her breath.

"Well, they're all about the same size, which is good for baking time." Harrison smiled at her. "I like that they're bite sized." He popped the cookie in his mouth. Skylar and I snagged one and followed suit, while Shannon bit hers in two and studied the filling.

I loved the creamy texture of the cheesecake and it paired well with the spicy gingerbread cookie. It did remind me of a baked cheesecake on a gingersnap crust. I hoped Harrison and Shannon agreed.

"You know," Shannon paused and licked her lips, "I wasn't sure how a cheesecake filling would hold up, but this is good." She held the cookie out for a cameraman to get a close shot, then showed Harrison.

He nodded. "It's superb. I'm not sure if cheesecake counts as a past . . ."

"Ancient Greece." Brystol smiled. "Cheesecake dates back to ancient Greece."

Shannon finished eating the second half of her cookie. "We'll fact-check that since gingerbread is a cookie from the past."

"Good job," Harrison said as we moved on to Mya.

As always, Mya's presentation was unique. She'd placed a real pineapple in the center of a white pedestal cake plate. Graham cracker crumbs were sprinkled around it. She'd found a cookie cutter in the shape of a pineapple and used edible food paint to color the front of the cookies. She'd placed the cookies around the edge of the plate or leaned up against the real fruit. The filling in the center of the cookie gave it girth, and with her placement on the cake plate you could see the dimension of the cookie.

"Well, I'm not sure about your presentation." Harrison's expression grew serious. "This is a Christmas competition."

"Christmas in Hawaii?" Mya smiled and raised her palms.

Shannon laughed. "Ingenuity."

I'd forgotten what a nice laugh Shannon had.

"Tell us about the cookies," Shannon encouraged as she handed a sample to each of us.

I hoped this didn't look like favoritism, but I'd been

curious about the pineapple-stuffed cookies since my interview with Skylar.

"This is a basic butter cookie dough with a pineapple and golden raisin filling. I don't know how old the recipe is, but my family has made them since I can remember."

Harrison kept taking bites of his cookie.

"Is your heritage Hawaiian?"

Mya nodded. "My great-great-grandmother."

"Your cookies are delicious," Shannon said. "And so unique."

"I agree. I do think your presentation is a stretch though." Harrison's expression held warning.

I hoped Mya picked up on it. She was doing well in the competition. It'd be a shame if her creative presentations were what sent her out of the kitchen. But the judges had to take everything into consideration and if the judging was close, something like this non-Christmas display could send her packing.

"Cut," Brenden said. "It's early, but Mother contacted the resort and they can have the commissary here and the contestants' lunch ready in thirty minutes. Since we lost time this morning, we'll have a long filming afternoon, possibly into the evening. We'll reconvene at one-thirty except for Harrison and Shannon. I need you back here by one to film your judges' discussion."

Victoria guided the contestants to their exit.

"Shannon, would you like to join me on the *Cooking with the Farmer's Daughter* set while I practice making rosettes for my segment of the network's Christmas special? I've never heard of this type of cookie. They are an Iverson Christmas tradition and Eric assures me they are yummy. He's making vegetable beef soup for our lunch. There's plenty." I hoped she'd say yes. Maybe in that setting, she'd tell me what was bothering her. Also, we might have a chance to discuss our new show.

"I'd like that! Where's Pamela? She can give us a ride to the resort." Shannon looked around and saw her sitting on the stairway. "I'll go get her."

I sent a quick text to Eric telling him we were on our way. He immediately returned the text that he was tied up in his suite on a Zoom conference call. He assured me that he had started the soup and it should be ready and told us to eat without him. He'd join us as soon as he could.

Pamela loaded us into her vehicle and took off toward the resort on the back path. "Would you like to join us for lunch?" I asked when she pulled up to the coffee shop door.

"I would, but it's not my lunchbreak yet. I told Sheriff Perry I was taking you two to the resort, but Drake wants me to do paperwork in our office. I'm just a text away so if something happens."

"Nothing's going to happen." I don't know if I was re-assuring Pamela or myself. I wasn't scared for my life, but it seemed at any moment a fight might break out with Shannon.

We all entered the resort. Pamela bid us goodbye and headed down the opposite hallway.

"I can show you the prototype of my knives."

"Oh! That'd be great!" Shannon smiled. "But first I have to do something. I'll see you later."

Shannon hurried away. Even though I knew where she'd lead me, I followed a safe distance behind her. She twisted through the resort until she reached a familiar main hallway. I stayed in the cross corridor and peeked around the corner. Shannon rapped on the door while twisting her head to check up and down the hallway. When her head pivoted in my direction, I pulled back and flattened myself against the wall in hopes she didn't see me. What I didn't expect was to catch movement a few feet down the hallway. I blinked. Marley crouched behind an overstuffed chair. I caught my breath. I'd been so focused on Shannon. I hadn't paid attention to my surroundings. Who was Marley following? Shannon or me?

CHAPTER SIXTEEN

I heard the click of a door closing and stepped into the hall knowing Shannon had entered the suite. "Marley!" I started to walk toward him. He shimmied out of his hiding place and took off on a run. I started after him, surprised at how fast a man of his age moved. Then again, my spiked-heeled boots weren't designed for running. He kept a good lead and when I reached the large lobby filled with skiers waiting for transport, I lost him.

Disappointed and out of breath, I went to the suite that housed my set. I took a seat on a counter stool and thought about Marley. What had he been up to? Was he following Shannon to harass her about the aprons again or take another victim? I hadn't ruled him out as Kinzy's killer. Like Leon, he seemed to maneuver through the resort and appear out of nowhere. Eric's tablet lay on the countertop. I seized the opportunity to do some online sleuthing on Marley and Leon.

Leon's sudden appearance this morning bothered me. Where had he been hiding and why? Was he returning to the scene of the crime like some serial killers do? Had he talked Marley into not wearing the apron and confronting Shannon? He'd tried to coach Marley during the scene. Had he put Marley up to filing a restraining order to drum up business or billable hours? Leon seemed like the shady attorneys my dad had dealt with in his career, ambulance chasers who talked his patients' parents into suing for malpractice when there wasn't any neglect on Dad's part. It ate up valuable office time and helped him make his decision to retire from his practice and work with Doctors Without Borders.

I sighed. I missed my parents so much. Maybe if they couldn't come home for Christmas, I could go there. I put off my research for a minute and logged into my email account. I preferred to text, yet I knew an email was better because of the time difference and given some of the remote locations, they had no cell phone service. This way, they could read and respond to the email in their downtime. I started with "I miss you," then launched into everything that had happened since we had arrived to film the Christmas special, including Shannon's sudden personality and weight change and my fear that perhaps it was marital problems. I ended my email with "I love you and hope to see you at Christmas." With family on my mind, I grabbed my phone and sent Caroline a text to check in on her and the toy drive kickoff. Eric entered the suite as I hit send. Once again, my research would have to wait.

"Hi." Eric came over and kissed my cheek.

My heart warmed. I turned my head. He read my signal. Our lips met. After a few lingering kisses that drove the problems of the world out of my mind, we came up for air.

"I waited to eat with you."

Eric smiled. "Well, I'm not a chef so if the soup doesn't turn out . . ."

"I'm sure it's great. What are these?" I picked up what looked to me like branding irons. "Something to make a design in grilled steak?"

Eric laughed. "No. Those are rosette irons. You dip them in the cookie batter, then the deep fryer."

"Oh." I looked at the irons. "They look like snowflakes and stars, not roses."

"Trust me, they're the correct utensil to use. I've printed out my Grandma's recipe." Eric looked around the room. "I thought you said Shannon was joining us."

"We arrived at the resort and she took off. She had something to do." I air-quoted the last two words.

"I see."

"She and Marley had another confrontation on set." I filled him in on what took place and who witnessed it and Leon's interceding. I left out that Marley had followed one of us.

"What was she thinking?"

I shook my head. "I have to find a way to break through to her. Get her to tell me what's wrong."

Eric went into the adjoining room and returned with a package of disposable bowls and plastic spoons. "It's just as well she's not here right now. I have some business to discuss with you about your knives."

My heart dipped. By the sound of his voice, I could tell there was a hiccup. I'd waited so long to get an endorsement deal that I wanted everything to go off without a hitch. "What? Is that what your Zoom meeting concerned?"

"Yes. Their marketing department wants to package and sell the knives individually in addition to the chef set." His eyes met mine.

"You know what I'm going to say."

He nodded. "Here me out. The marketing department says individual knifes sell better than sets. They used wedding registries as a good example. People always need paring and bread knives. Not everyone wants, or needs, a cleaver or boning knife."

I opened my mouth.

He held up a halting hand and continued, "They have sales statistics to prove this is the way to sell knives."

"Okay," I said. "I get that. Yet I want people, especially my viewers, to have a professional set of chef knives. If we sell them individually, it defeats the purpose. They may never get the set. Besides, if someone is serious about cooking, they do need boning knives and cleavers. My name is going on the product. They'll advertise on my show and in cooking magazines. I want to stick to the original plan, a knife set."

Eric released the steam on the electric pressure cooker. "If they don't sell well as a set, are you open to trying individual sales?" He popped the lid. Steam lifted the fragrant, mouthwatering scents of beef and vegetables.

My stomach growled. "I don't think you have to worry about spoiling the soup. It smells wonderful."

"Are you dodging my question?"

I'd wanted this endorsement for so long and I wanted it to be successful. "I'd be open to it if sales of the knife sets aren't what we hoped for in the first six months."

I thought of Shannon's aprons. They released with a holiday line and would turn to everyday prints. Now that one of them had been used in a murder, would she pull the entire line? Could the company sue her? After all, they had a lot of money invested in those aprons. Is that why she'd gotten so angry when Marley wouldn't wear one? Not that any of this was her fault.

Eric dished up two bowls of soup. "I'll take that back to the company. We'll have another meeting tomorrow." He placed a bowl of soup before me and handed me a spoon. "Thank you for being cooperative and entertaining the idea to offer them individually. It gives me leverage."

"I hope they agree." I stirred the steaming soup with my spoon. "If they insist on selling them individually and in a set, I won't veto it." Something was better than nothing.

Eric set his soup on the countertop and his body beside me. "I'll try my hardest to discourage it. They do know their business. They're a reputable cutlery company."

"I know."

I dug into my lunch. The protein and veggies perked me up. I'd eaten too many sweets this morning without a good protein-filled breakfast first. I smiled. Shannon had turned me on to eating a fortifying breakfast. Before the first show filmed, I seldom ate a morning meal.

A knock on the door interrupted my thoughts. "Y'all in there?"

Shannon!

I hurried to the door and let her in. She greeted me with a wide smile. "Something smells good."

"Eric made soup and it's delicious." I inflected happiness into my tone and hoped my face didn't show my surprise. Once again, the only way to describe Shannon's appearance was rumpled. Victoria and her stylist wouldn't be happy when she returned to the set. Some of the tucking in the sweater had come loose, making it bag on her left side. The front of her hair and makeup looked fine, but the back had flattened and parted where she obviously had a cowlick.

Shannon put on a mock frown. "Don't let that get out or he'll have a show of his own and we won't have a producer."

Eric laughed. "No chance of that happening. I'm a behind-the-scenes kind of guy. I'm finished, take a seat." Eric vacated his stool and ladled soup into a bowl for Shannon.

"Speaking of our show, have you found a new director?" I addressed my question to Eric while my gaze rested on Shannon, whose focus was gobbling her lunch.

"I put out some feelers and have three names. Before I present them to you, I'm going to research their work and resumes. I'll share the information with Rafe, who, by the way . . ."

"Rosette irons!" Shannon exclaimed and picked them up.

Eric and I exchanged a look over her head. It was apparent she wanted to change the subject like she'd done every time her husband was mentioned. My heart sank further than before when the thought of marital problems popped into my head. A sad thought, but what else could it be?

Pushing off the stool, Shannon said, "I love rosettes. Is that what you're making for your Christmas favorites segment?"

"Yes."

"Can I help you make a batch?"

"Sure." I stood. "Or you can make them, and I'll watch."

"You've never made rosettes?" Shannon quirked a brow. "I don't know if we can be friends." She started giggling.

Wherever she'd been, she was in a much better mood. New love could do that to a person. I shoved the notion to the back of my mind, deciding to stay in the present and enjoy my friend. "It gets worse. I don't remember ever eating them either."

"That will end today." Shannon lifted the printed recipe from the countertop.

Eric cleaned up the lunch mess while Shannon read his grandmother's recipe and I put a heavy pot filled with oil on the hot plate to heat as instructed by Shannon, who had taken the lead on this project. Sticking a thermometer into the pot so we'd know when the temperature was perfect for frying the cookies, I waited for my next task to be assigned.

"Same recipe my family uses." Shannon smiled at Eric and busied herself measuring the ingredients. I stuck close by her side, so I'd know what to do when I made them myself.

Before she started to mix the batter, I handed her one of two aprons. For a moment she hesitated, then took it, looped it around her neck and tied it on.

"Do you think you'll have to pull the line?" I asked, hoping it didn't set her off. Carefully, I slipped the neck band of my apron over my hair so not to ruin the bun, then secured the ties around my waist.

"I don't know. It may make them sell better . . . you

know people love the macabre." Shannon's tone stayed pleasant. "Right now, I'm trying not to think about my aprons sales but rather about our loss."

Her answer surprised me. Had sadness replaced her anger? "I know."

"Now, I still feel she might not have been the right choice for our show, but not to the point she should lose her life." Shannon's eyes met mine. "Sheriff Perry thinks I murdered her."

"We know that's not true." I gave her a quick hug before I checked the oil temperature. It was perfect so I put in the rosette irons to preheat as instructed in the recipe. "I'm sure he has other persons of interest besides you. I suspect Leon or Marley. Something is up with those two."

"I agree." Shannon stirred the ingredients, then laughed. "Boy, you told Leon off this morning." She stopped mixing. "And made a valid point. I think whoever murdered Kinzy's the next in line to inherit her grandfather's estate. I don't know how Marley would work into that though. He just seems like, well, an old hippie. Sometimes I wonder if he's living in the same reality as the rest of us. He blurts stuff out even after he's told to be quiet. *The American Baking Battle* needs better screening for our contestants."

"I agree. The estate issue makes the most sense to me." I didn't add anything about Marley. It felt good to be talking to Shannon. She seemed like her old self. I didn't want to rock the boat. I'd missed talking to my friend like this and if Eric wasn't in the room, I might have run my love life dilemma past her.

"I think you both need to stop with the theories."

I looked up to find Eric, eyes filled with concern, staring at me.

Shannon glanced his way. "It's okay for us to talk about the murder. Courtney needs to stop asking questions of the people she suspects. Although it has helped Sheriff Perry crack the case the last two times, so . . . scratch what I just said. I didn't murder Kinzy and I want my name removed from the list, so maybe you should poke around."

"Shannon!"

She looked at Eric and shrugged. "She seems to get further than Sheriff Perry." Her expression sobered. "What surprises me is Quintin's absence on the set. It's so unlike him. You don't think he did it and Sheriff Perry has him under house arrest in a suite or something?"

"I don't know." She made an interesting point though. The other murders didn't faze Quintin and his quest for a low bottom line. He knew Kinzy. Did that make the difference? The rest of us knew and worked with her too and we were expected to report to work each day. "Perhaps there's paperwork or something he has to complete since she died on the job."

"Good point," Eric said. "Because there is."

"Yeah, I suppose." Shannon looked up from her work. "The batter's ready. Is the oil?"

I checked again and gave her a thumbs up. Shannon lifted the preheated irons, dipped them into the batter until they were coated and stuck them into the oil. "You have to hold them like this." When the cookie released from the iron, she used the iron to lift it out of the oil, placing it on a paper towel. She blotted the iron and started the process over. It looked easy enough. The delicate batter made a light and airy cookie she dusted with powdered sugar. While I took my turn making some, Shannon broke a cookie in two and gave me a bite. Eric devoured the other cookie.

"Oh my gravy, Eric. I see why they're a favorite. They're delicious."

"They're good covered in sugar and cinnamon too." Shannon finished her half.

The chime of Eric's phone interrupted our snack.

"Finally," Eric said. He held his phone screen out so we could see. "Rafe answered my texts."

Shannon's expression changed. Anger blazed hot in her baby blues while the corners of her mouth pulled into a frown. "What does he want?" she asked with disgust. "Well?" she snapped when Eric didn't answer right away.

"He's been stuck in a two-day blizzard in a cabin in Colorado." Eric made a statement but said it like a question.

"Oh! Is he okay?" Concern replaced the anger and aggravation on her face and in her tone.

"Yes. He says he's fine. He's trying to get a flight out of Denver. The airlines are behind." Eric tapped an answer with his thumbs and stared at his phone until it chimed with a response. He nodded. "Rafe sends his love."

Shannon rolled her eyes. She turned her attention to the cookies. Eric raised his brows at me. I totally agreed. The last few minutes of conversation were weird. First, she seemed appalled Rafe wanted something, then genuinely concerned for his safety, then she snapped right back into annoyance. It broke my heart to think they had relationship trouble. Had they separated?

She continued to make rosettes until all the batter was

used. "All done." She removed the last two cookies from the hot oil and shook the shaker of powdered sugar over them.

"Courtney, how many of those did you cook?"

"Two." I knew I didn't need to answer; Eric's question was rhetorical. "I promise I will make a practice batch all by myself before we tape."

He snagged another cookie while I turned off the heating element and set the pot of oil on a trivet to cool. Then I stuck the hot irons into the sink, so no one brushed against them and got burnt.

"Since we're all here, shall we talk about the kitchen design of your new set?" Eric leaned against the end of the counter.

"Sure. I'd like a window even if it's faux, with a kitchen table and chair. That way if Courtney and I need to have discussions about the food, we can sit down."

"I like that idea. Since my kitchen is all white on my set, I'd like wood cupboards," I said.

"Not dark though," Shannon added.

"Maybe light oak or pecan?" Eric asked. He grabbed his tablet and started jotting down notes.

"We need a full sink right behind the stovetop so transporting water is easy," Shannon said.

"Right, there's nothing worse than trying to drain steaming pasta so your makeup doesn't melt. I don't want appliances stored on the countertop either unless we're using them for the episode." I watched Eric tap the screen of the tablet. "I think having the refrigerator look like the wood of the cabinets would be nice."

"Yes. And the table and chair should be a separate set area. That's where we could pull out reader email or mail to try their suggestion for our next episode." Shannon's voice held the excitement it had when we came up with this idea.

"Perfect. We could name that segment 'coffee klatch' or something along those lines."

Shannon smiled and nodded at my suggestion.

"Okay! Finally, I have something to work with. I will have the set designers draw something up and investigate the expense. I'll copy Rafe on all of it."

"Should we toast to this with a cup of coffee from Castle Grounds?" I asked at the same time my phone rang. My parents! It had to be them. Everyone else I knew texted to communicate. I pulled my phone from my pocket and furrowed my brow. It wasn't my parents. It was Brenden.

"Hello, Brenden."

"Courtney," Victoria snapped. "Do you know where Shannon is?"

"Yes, she's right here. Would you like to speak with her?"

"No. Tell her to get to the judging set now. She's fifteen minutes late. We need to shoot her and Harrison discussing today's challenges." The call ended.

I looked up at Shannon, who had to have heard the entire conversation because Victoria was shouting.

Wide-eyed, she pulled off the apron. "Whoops, I forgot."

The door to the suite clicked closed and I stared at it. "She's always late to the set."

Eric came up behind me and wrapped me in a hug. "You're right. Something's going on. Rafe's text said more than I told you."

"Really?" I wiggled free from his embrace. "About Shannon or the situation or what?"

"The situation. He asked me if Shannon was okay. He received a call from Sheriff Perry and didn't want to return it until he knew what was going on here."

Sadness filled my heart. "That's a question a husband should ask a wife, not a business manager asking a producer."

"You may be right about marital problems. You'd think Shannon would've called Rafe right away."

"Unless she has a boyfriend onsite."

Eric cringed.

"Think about it. How does it feel to be in love? Happy, giddy. She took off for an appointment and came back elated." I leveled Eric with a sad-that-I-might-be-right look.

"True, but it doesn't explain her anger or her sadness. You've pointed out both of those emotions."

"The anger could be from the show taking her away from her personal time, and why she keeps sneaking out for a rendezvous. She has made comments that the rushed filming interfered with something. The sadness could be a result from her marriage breaking up?" I asked.

We stared at one another in silence for a few minutes.

"I don't want to believe any of that," Eric said.

"Me, either." I hoped and prayed it wasn't another man. I knew whatever Shannon and Rafe's issues were, I'd find the answer behind the hotel room door. How could I find out who was staying in the room? "Shall we go get that coffee?"

Before Eric could answer, the suite unlocked, and the door cracked open. "Hello?"

"Come in, Pamela."

She entered the room and flashed a wide smile at Eric. "Courtney invited me to lunch. Am I too late?"

"Not at all." Was now the time Eric and I should be honest with Pamela about our relationship?

Eric removed a bowl from the packaging. "Just enough left for another bowl and it's still warm." He handed it over to Pamela. "We also have dessert."

"Thank you." Pamela looked at us. "I always feel like I'm interrupting something. Other than work," she added in haste.

"Well, to be honest." I glanced at Eric, who gave me a slight nod. "Eric and I are taking our work relationship to a personal level."

"Oh." Pamela blinked a few times and dropped her gaze to the bowl of soup. She shoveled a few bites into her mouth. After a few minutes, she muttered, "Great." Then she looked up and gave us a genuine smile. "That's great. Congratulations. I hope it all works out. Is it a secret?"

"Kind of." Eric pinned me with a look. "For right now," I added. "We want to be comfortable and secure in our relationship before the world finds out."

"I understand." Pamela finished the soup and took a cookie. "Relationships are hard. You're in the public eye so . . . it makes sense."

"I feel like we should apologize. If you felt led on or . . ."

"No, no, no," Pamela interrupted Eric. "An apology isn't necessary. I do enjoy your company, Eric, but really, I'm happy for you. I'll keep your secret."

"Thank you. We were about to head to the coffee shop. Would you join us?" I asked.

"I'd love to. Then I'll take you back to the set. The rosettes are very good."

"Have another. Shannon made them." I gave credit where credit was due. "You just missed her. She was late and headed to the meditation room."

Pamela wrinkled her brow. "Are you sure she was heading back to the judging set?"

Concern grew in my chest. Had Sheriff Perry arrested her? Had she met up with Marley and argued again? "We thought that was where she was going. She was already fifteen minutes late."

Pamela heaved a sigh. "Never mind."

"Out with it." I'll admit it—my voice tone was commanding.

"I don't like to gossip." She stopped, then looked contrite. "I just saw her and her husband laughing and hugging, then they went into a hotel suite."

"On the first floor?" I asked.

Pamela nodded. "By the look on your face, it seems that wasn't her husband, was it?"

CHAPTER SEVENTEEN

Pamela dropped me off at the workshop with five minutes to spare. I wondered if Shannon had blown off her job responsibilities or made it to the judging shoot. Victoria answered the questions in my mind when she met me at the door.

"Thanks to Shannon, we'll be filming into the wee hours of the morning. Didn't you tell her to report to the meditation room?"

"I did." I didn't offer up the information Pamela shared.

"She showed up thirty minutes after I spoke with you. I meant for you to send her right away."

"I did." I held my hands palms up.

She pursed her lips. "Your set is probably a five-minute walk at the most to the meditation room. She couldn't have gotten lost. I told Brenden to have a talk with her."

Victoria paused to take a breath. She looked frazzled this afternoon, which surprised me. Her clothing and hair were still immaculate; however, her posture slumped, and stress lined the planes of her face. You'd think with her powerful profession, she'd have cool and confident projection down to an art even if she didn't feel that way on the inside, although in her day-to-day job she probably relied on a team of people rather than take on all the tasks herself.

She blew out a breath. "Anyway, Brenden sent me back here to start this filming since he's tied up at the resort. Please join Skylar in front of the counters to kick off the second challenge of the day." She stalked off toward the contestant entry.

I joined Skylar. Our stylists straightened, powdered and smoothed us. After they left, Skylar said, "I know Christmas is a stressful time and can bring out the bad side of some people, but it's ridiculous on this set."

"What do you mean?"

"Victoria's hot. I heard her chewing out Brenden in the resort hallway because he puts up with too much from his stars and staff. She kept saying, 'You must take control.'"

"That explains her long-day comment."

"Well," Skylar looked around, then finished, "if filming runs long, her attitude isn't going to make it pleasant."

"She's just helping out. In all fairness, she came here to see her son, not work with him."

"True, yet this is starting to feel like the filming of the first season."

I laughed. "Yep. We managed to bond last filming. What happened to that big happy family? What happened to a drama-free set?" I asked.

"That's how they sold it to me too." Skylar laughed. "Here they come."

We watched the contestants file in and apron up, including Marley. He smiled and finger waved to us.

"Good afternoon . . . everyone." Skylar greeted the contestants, then, in a loud whisper meant for all to hear, he said out of the corner of his mouth, "I'm not going to be accused of playing favorites."

I giggled. Marley pointed at Skylar like he was in trouble, then a smile stretched across his face. The rest of the contestants hollered greetings or silly comments, or waved, and even Victoria grinned. Maybe we just needed to interject some fun while on set. The trauma of murder, especially when it hit so close to home, did affect everyone, including the contestants.

"I'm just going to say action like we did when we filmed the opening by the fireplace. Okay?"

Skylar and I nodded. We really didn't need a signal or countdown if the camera was on; we could handle the kickoff.

"Action."

The monitor took a moment to light up. Then I started by saying, "The second challenge of the day involves multiple cookie dough."

"Present-day palates want more than just one flavor when they bite into their holiday treats." Skylar flashed a smile into the camera.

"In addition, colorful cookies create eye appeal on your serving tray."

I'd barely said my line when Skylar said, "So does a variety of shapes." He'd hit his line a bit too soon.

I allowed a slight pause. "You have two hours to complete this challenge." In my mind I ticked off the time it'd take us to finish shooting for the day. Victoria had been stretching the workday length. It should be early evening when we finished. "Wow us with your checkerboards, pinwheels or whatever shape you come up with."

"Just remember the cookies have to taste good and be at least two different flavors of dough."

Brystol, Carol and Mya's faces pinched with stress. Tim exuded the same confidence as always. Marley wasn't paying attention.

In duet, Skylar and I said, "The baking begins now."

"Cut. Great!" Victoria waved us off and focused on the camera capturing the frantic kitchen scene.

"Should we tell her I goofed and reshoot?" Skylar asked.

"I'm sure Brenden will view it when he gets back. We can always do a retake then."

Skylar nodded and walked straight to the commissary table and began to chat with the catering staff.

I went over to my chair and took a load off. I heard the door open and close, so I glanced over my shoulder. Brenden walked over to me, and to my surprise, sat down.

"How are you doing?" His face and tone told me it wasn't a polite question about my health. It was a sincere inquiry because I'd stumbled upon another dead body and this time, I knew the victim.

"Trouble sleeping like every time. I know it will pass." My eyes teared up. Brenden noticed and squeezed my hand. "Is there any update from Sheriff Perry?"

Victoria joined us before he answered.

"Thanks for taking the lead over here, Mom. I don't know what I'd do without you."

She smirked. "Isn't that the truth?"

"Mom!" Brenden sounded like a teenager scolding an embarrassing parent, then he laughed. So did Victoria.

"To answer your question," Brenden turned toward me, "I've received no updates. They'd probably tell Quintin anyway."

"Speaking of Quintin, where's he? He's pretty hands on, or was during the last filming."

"He's working in his suite. I understand there's a lot of paperwork to file with the network's attorneys and he's making arrangements to have Kinzy's body returned home." His voice hitched twice.

It was my turn to comfort. I squeezed his hand. "I realize that would fall under Quintin's job duties, but if her boyfriend is onsite, why isn't he doing it?"

"Boyfriend?" Brenden frowned. "I don't think she had one, let alone one onsite." When Brenden looked to Victoria like she'd know, I did too, and found it surprising she rolled her eyes and pursed her lips.

Brenden hung his head at her response. Had she thought he'd asked a stupid question, or did she feel Quintin should be on set chipping in like she was to get the show filmed?

"How would I know about her love life?" Victoria snapped out the question.

"Sorry, Mother, I don't know why I did that." Brenden looked up.

"Because you're overworked. Quintin should be on set doing his job."

"Legal paperwork takes a while." Brenden stood. "Let's go see how the bakers are doing. "I'm having Skylar interview the contestants. Courtney, if there's something you need to do, feel free."

There was. "Thanks, I'll be over here when you need me."

I watched mother and son walk away, glad neither asked about my boyfriend remark. Sheriff Perry didn't say it was colleague-to-colleague privileges, but I didn't want to explain why he told me either.

Even though I'd planned to research Leon and Marley, I decided to enter Kinzy's name with "boyfriend." I pulled out my phone and thumbed the words into a search engine, knowing it was a long shot and I'd get multiple pages of unrelated stuff, which I did. After perusing two pages of nonsense, I tried the heading marked "photos." Several hundred pictures came up, which included banners for our show and pictures of some contestants.

What else could I use to narrow this down? I decided to add her title to the search words. Most of the same pages popped up. I guess I'd been hoping for a social media page or something. In a last-ditch effort, I included the network name. Fewer site options appeared. I clicked on the photo tab.

The first photo was Kinzy's professional headshot for the network. Sadness swelled my chest and I blinked the mist from my eyes. Who and why would anyone murder this gorgeous young woman? I ran my fingers over the picture and made a mental vow, I'd do all I could to help Sheriff Perry solve this murder.

With renewed vigor, I scanned the photos. Someone had shared a throwback Thursday photo of her in a cheerleading uniform. I clicked on the social media page and perused it a moment. It appeared to be a classmate. I clicked back to the main search and scanned the pictures. One looked like a fancy party. I knitted my brows thinking I saw Quintin. I tapped on the picture to enlarge the thumbnail photo.

My breath caught in my throat. I'd been right. It was Quintin in the photo. Dressed in a black tux, he stood in a group conversing. I recognized other executives affiliated with the network. The picture had a website attached to it, so I clicked the link. It was a charity organization event. They had posted lots of pictures. In some of the pictures Quintin held a woman's hand. Her back always seemed to be to the camera and I wondered what his date would look like. By the way her hair was styled in a classic updo and the gorgeous gold gown she wore, I'd bet she was a stunner.

Not sure why Kinzy's name would bring up this picture, I continued to peruse the two hundred pictures posted. I kept my eye out not only for Kinzy, but also the woman in the gold dress since my curiosity was piqued. Surely the photographer had caught a photo of her face. I kept sliding my finger to the left and scrolling through the photos. I'd found such a good rhythm that I flipped past the photo I'd been searching for. Once my brain caught up with my index finger, I swiped right and gasped.

Looking around to make certain no one had heard me, I widened the picture on the screen. The woman, standing beside and holding hands with Quintin, smiled at the camera while he gazed down at her, face beaming with love.

The woman wearing the golden gown with her hair in a classic French twist was certainly a stunner. She was also Kinzy.

* * *

"I'm just too hot!" Shannon pulled on the neckline of the ugly Christmas sweater.

"That's because you're constantly late and hurrying," Victoria snapped. She stood with her arms crossed and a sour expression adhered to her face while Shannon's stylist tried everything to blot and stop the perspiration from trickling down Shannon's cheeks.

Shannon glared at Victoria. "It. Is. Hot. In. Here."

"You're the only one who thinks so. The air conditioning is set to sixty-five degrees because of the oven use."

Brenden guided over a crew member, who carried a fan. "Let's see if this helps. We can't film you this way."

"If I step outside, it may help."

Shannon started to leave. Victoria caught her arm. "Oh, no you don't. You're not going to disappear for an hour again."

"Bring her a chair and a cold drink," Brenden addressed two crew members. "Mother, why don't you have the cameramen check the shots."

Begrudgingly, Victoria left the group.

I'd accompany the judges. We'd been set to go when Shannon had what appeared to be a hot flash, which she was way too young for, so it had to be something else. Had I been assuming marital problems when perhaps she had a health issue? Or had Victoria nailed it? All of Shannon's hurrying to get to set and still arriving late might have caught up with her.

I felt badly for Shannon, yet I didn't want the filming to run past seven, so I hoped sitting and resting would take care of the issue.

When I'd discovered the picture of Kinzy and Quintin, things clicked into place. Quintin wasn't just mourning a coworker like the rest of us; he'd lost his love. On top of shock and grieving, he must be angry that someone murdered her. Dealing with all those emotions is what kept him from the set.

I'd entertained the idea that Sheriff Perry had placed him under house arrest, then disregarded it since no one had notified us the case was closed. I'd sent Eric a text about the information I'd found and suggested we invite Quintin for drinks or dinner or both. I wanted to express my sympathy and let him know he wasn't alone. Isolation wasn't good for his mental health.

Eric complied with my request, texted back that Quintin accepted our offer, then warned me to stop poking around the murder. Eric didn't know Quintin was relying on me to help find Kinzy's killer, and now I was more determined than ever to figure out who was responsible for her death. If Quintin asked, I'd address the few updates I had concerning the case.

"Thank you, Brenden. I feel so much better." Shannon handed an empty water bottle to Brenden. "Do you think you can position the fan somewhere on set to cool things down?"

"I'll try." Brenden found a crew member. They conversed and the crew member moved the fan.

By that time, Shannon's stylist had perfected her makeup.

"Are we ready to start?" My tone was anxious. I wanted to get the rest of this day over so I could talk to Quintin.

Shannon pulled a face. "Not you too."

"Sorry. I'm just tired of long filming days."

My apology and excuse placated her. Shannon smiled and stood. "I think I'm good to go."

Brenden noticed our movement, came over and hurried us to the set. When Harrison joined us, we started with Brystol.

"No cheesecake?" Harrison studied her arrangement.

She'd made pinwheel cookies and tucked them into a large glass sleigh-shaped candy dish. "No." Her lips curled into a nervous smile.

"It's good to leave your comfort zone," Shannon said. She and Harrison slipped out a cookie and studied it before taking a bite.

"Yum! Peanut butter, chocolate and vanilla." Shannon nipped off more of the cookie.

"Always a great combo," Harrison said. "You did what we asked. The only flaw is your pinwheels aren't quite even." He pointed to an area where the peanut butter dough was thicker than the chocolate and vanilla, making the pinwheel curve misshapen.

We moved to Mya and found a trio of dough.

"Italian Neapolitans. I haven't seen them in a long time."

"It's my great-grandmother's recipe."

Mya had placed red and green paper doilies on a cut-glass tray and stacked the rectangular cookies in a pyramid.

"They're a little flat, like they ran."

Mya sighed. "They're a refrigerator cookie and I don't think they chilled long enough."

"Or it's too hot in here." Shannon cranked her neck and pinned Victoria with a look.

"The taste is there though. It's a good recipe and a festive cookie."

Harrison's comment pulled Shannon back to the present task.

"I agree."

Tim was up next. I couldn't smell booze but wondered if there was some type of flavoring in his cookies. He'd been warned. Had he heeded it? He also served a tri-dough cookie, only in a circular shape.

"Spumoni?" Shannon looked at the cookies displayed in a single layer on a deep green plate.

"Yes." Tim smiled wide. "Chocolate, cherry and pistachio."

"How'd you get them into this shape?" Shannon asked.

"I rolled small balls of each dough and placed them with sides touching. When they cook, they meld together like clover leaf rolls." Tim pointed at the different colored dough on his cookies while he explained.

Shannon watched Harrison try the cookies.

"Wow!" Harrison exclaimed, and not in a yummy way. "What's in the chocolate?" He then ate the rest of the cookie.

Shannon made a yuck face. "Liqueur. Did you use chocolate liqueur?" She nibbled at the pistachio part of the sweet.

Anger smoldered in Tim's eyes. He puckered his lips.

"It's too strong," Harrison said, tone pointed. "We asked you to make something without alcohol."

"I don't think the flavor is too strong."

"But you have to think of your guests or customers or whoever you're going to serve the cookies to," Harrison countered.

"Maybe you used too much?" Shannon asked. I knew she didn't really expect an answer because she continued. "It's a shame because the other two doughs are very good." She laid the chocolate portion of her cookie on the counter.

Neither judge gave Tim time to respond. They moved over to Carol.

"Your pinwheels are perfect." Harrison turned to the cameraman. "Get a close up. The dough-to-dough ratio is perfect. A great addition to a Christmas tray. How do they taste?"

Carol let out a nervous laugh. "Well, I think they taste terrific." She pushed the silver tray with the cookies lying in precise rows toward the judges.

I joined them in taking a cookie.

"Harrison summed up the appearance of your cookie. I'm going to tell you that the chocolate and vanilla taste is there. It's just everything anyone would want in a pin-wheel cookie," Shannon said.

"Well done." Harrison nodded to Carol.

A happy smile and flush lit up her face.

"Oh, my!" Shannon looked at the cookies Marley displayed in individual plastic bags tied with ribbon and tucked into a wicker serving basket. She lifted it up so the cameraman could get a close shot. "Nice."

Marley pushed up his glasses. "I'm a cookie baker by trade."

I wanted to giggle.

Harrison covered well. "Yes, you are." He slipped the ribbon off his bag and took out the cookie. The dough was a mosaic of chocolate, green and white, cut in the shape of a lancet church window. "Obviously, you dropped small pieces of your dough and rolled them to-gether."

"I did. They're chocolate mint crèmes. Hand cut."

"Perfect for the holidays!" Shannon chewed a bite. Her eyes lit up. "Courtney, try one. Marley, you've outdone yourself."

"I agree." Harrison finished off his cookie. "I like the unique way that you melded your dough. And kudos for the hand cutting. You kept the same size and shape for all of the cookies."

"That's a wrap," Brenden hollered.

Shannon looked at Brenden. "It's a shame that the bakers can't try one another's creations." She snagged another cookie from Marley's plate and bit into it.

He puffed out his chest, then looked at the other contestants with a proud smile.

I waited for someone else to scream favoritism. They didn't have time. Victoria directed the bakers to a table full of snacks and beverages for a short break while their kitchens were reset for the final challenge.

Brenden gathered all four of us to the gingerbread house to mark lighting and camera angles. Relief washed through me that Shannon wouldn't be able to slip away and hold up filming.

About twenty minutes later, we kicked off the third challenge of the day, cookies of the future. The bakers groaned when they learned the show felt holiday cookies of the future would be gluten free and they only had ninety minutes to prepare the challenge. Due to the short time given to complete the challenge, interviews weren't conducted. Cameras caught their every move trying to beat the clock.

Victoria made sure Shannon stayed in the area by calling a briefing meeting for the cast of the show, which consisted of what the remaining filming day held for us. Her meeting lasted right up until I had to stand in front of the camera and call time.

Skylar and I took a break while Shannon and Harrison judged the challenge and decided who'd leave the kitchen. Now we stood with toes to tape, waiting for Brenden's closed fist.

"This is always the hardest part of our day," Skylar said.

The bakers stood in a straight line in front of the first set of kitchen counters. Most shifted their weight from foot to foot.

"True. We'll start with the good news, baker of the day. The judges loved the lemon goody gluten-free butter cookies."

Marley took a step forward. Did he think he was supposed to? Brenden frantically waved him back. It didn't work. "Keep rolling. Marley step back in line," Brenden said.

"But they called my name."

"They didn't. They said the name of the cookie. When they do say your name, you don't step forward."

Marley frowned and took a step backward.

The filming interruption broke my momentum. I found my place on the monitor and continued, "Marley is the baker of the day." I took an unscripted pause in the event Marley stepped forward again. He didn't, so I continued, "Tim, you didn't listen to the judges and burnt the flavor of two of your cookies with booze. The third challenge, flourless fudge cookies, were underbaked. I'm sorry, Tim, you're leaving the kitchen."

His reaction didn't surprise me. Disgruntlement shone on his face. He turned on his heel and stomped toward the contestant door, ignoring the condolences of the other bakers.

Skylar took over and I was glad. "The next contestant to leave the competition tried hard, but just missed the mark on the third challenge. The gluten-free sugar cookies came out so hard, dunking them in milk didn't help."

Carol sniffled and looked down.

"The second elimination today is . . ." After a short pause to build tension for viewers, Skylar said, "Carol."

Unlike Tim, Carol stayed for hugs. She and Marley had a moment. He chucked her under the chin. Whatever he'd told her made her smile.

Which made me smile. Perhaps Skylar and I hadn't been fair saying these contestants liked drama.

"Cut! Shannon and Harrison, you'll be transported to the meditation room to film the judging sequence. Everyone else is free to go."

I breathed a sigh of relief. Due to Victoria tightening the filming day, mostly by keeping Shannon in her sights and busy, we wrapped with enough time for me to freshen up before meeting Eric and Quintin for dinner.

Turning to head up to wardrobe, I saw Sheriff Perry and Drake standing by the door. I walked over. "Is there an update on Kinzy's murder?" I asked Sheriff Perry.

"Not yet." He looked past me. "Mrs. Collins, you need to come with me."

Shannon stopped several feet away from us. "What for?"

"Come with me and find out."

Nothing in Sheriff Perry's tone sounded threatening,

but Shannon freaked out. She started spewing out how he should be looking for the murderer and leaving innocent people like her alone.

He listened quietly for a few minutes. When she called him "the fuzz," he quickly moved over to where she stood, drew the metal handcuffs from his belt and said, "Do you want me to arrest you in front of your colleagues?"

CHAPTER EIGHTEEN

Shannon stared stupefied at Sheriff Perry. His question stopped her rant.

It didn't escape me that Shannon had the motive, opportunity and disposition to kill Kinzy. Despite those facts, I knew in my gut Shannon wasn't a killer. "There's no way Shannon murdered Kinzy." The words were out of my mouth before I could stop them. I marched over to him.

"Butt out of my investigation." Sheriff Perry turned to Shannon. "I have a few questions for you."

Her mouth opened. No words came out.

Clearly, she was in shock and needed an advocate. I turned to the few crew members who remained on set and said, "Nothing to see here." Skylar, Harrison and Brenden snapped into action, making sure no more prying eyes witnessed the altercation.

"What proof do you have that you're arresting her for the murder of Kinzy Hummel?"

"Who said I was arresting her for murder?"

My turn to stare stupefied at Sheriff Perry.

He smirked. "If I arrest her, it will be for disorderly conduct. Which I've heard she's been doing since she arrived at the resort."

"Yep, we've gotten lots of complaints." Drake swaggered over. "After her and Marley's outburst this morning."

I leveled him with a look. "Really?"

"Afraid so."

I sent up a quick prayer no one had filmed the confrontation and posted it to social media.

Shannon found her voice. "But we made up. I judged him fairly. He's still in the competition. Did that sleazy attorney file a restraining order?"

"I'll answer all of those questions back at my office." Sheriff Perry turned to Drake. "I can take it from here." Sheriff Perry held a palm out for Shannon to walk in front of him. Without complaint, she complied.

"I'm going too."

Sheriff Perry dropped his hand and turned blocking my exit. "Stay out of this."

I frowned. "No. I saw most of this morning's confrontation. I might remember something that'd help you." My explanation did nothing to change his stern expression. I tried another tactic. "I'm done for the day and need a ride back to the resort."

He appeared to be weighing his options. "At least if you're with me, I'll know you're staying out of trouble," Sheriff Perry said, teeth gritted. "You can come."

I begged for a minute to run upstairs and get my coat.

It took a tad bit longer because I was done with this ugly Christmas sweater. I quick-changed into my own clothes. When I made it downstairs, Sheriff Perry and Shannon were nowhere to be seen. Had Sheriff Perry bamboozled me?

Victoria, Brenden and Harrison walked toward me, bundled in their outerwear.

"Can I catch a ride with you? I think I was left."

"No, they're outside waiting," Victoria said. "We've decided to grab a quick dinner while Sheriff Perry interrogates Shannon, again. Then we'll film." Victoria sighed and turned to Brenden. "I guess we won't be skiing tonight either."

I heard her disappointment. My heart twisted. Her visit had started out as a vacation from her high-pressure job.

As soon as we exited, I saw that Shannon sat on the back bench seat of the UTV Sheriff Perry drove. I climbed into the passenger seat. I had a few questions of my own for the good constable.

As soon as I latched my safety belt, he hit the gas.

"Do you know Quintin was Kinzy's boyfriend?"

Sheriff Perry glanced at me for a second and cocked his brow. "You know I do."

"What?" Shannon snapped. She leaned forward and poked her head between the bucket seats. "That explains why he hasn't been on the set. Why didn't you tell me this?" Anger edged her tone.

I turned to look her in the eyes. "I just stumbled upon it."

"Oh." She settled back into her seat.

"Eric and I are having dinner with him tonight."

"I wish I could come. I have an appointment." She leaned forward again. "How long is this going to take? I still have to film the judging segment and I need to be done by seven."

"I don't know. It all depends on you," Sheriff Perry said.

"So, a couple of minutes? I've told you everything I know, which is nothing. You're treating me like a criminal instead of a law-abiding citizen."

I turned my head and my eyes widened. I'd heard this tone of Shannon's before. She was getting ready to tear into him. Thank goodness, the resort was in sight.

"I didn't murder Kinzy. Sure, I didn't like what she said about my weight and I stuck up for myself, but I didn't strangle her." Shannon scoffed. "Especially with an apron from my line. You know," she poked a finger in Sheriff Perry's bicep, "that's extra income for me. Why would I kill someone with my own product? Murder isn't good for sales."

Sheriff Perry jerked his arm away from her prodding finger. "Some people start businesses to lose money and have a tax write-off."

"You think I did that? You have some nerve!"

After Sheriff Perry guided the UTV to a stop on a cement slab, he turned in his seat. "The one you least expect to snap, does."

Narrowing her eyes, Shannon pulled her lips into a side pucker.

"Let's go." Sheriff Perry slid out of the vehicle and waited for Shannon and me to follow his lead. Which I did faster than Shannon. I'd never considered that maybe Shannon, or someone, wanted this line of aprons to fail. Had she run into a snag with the company that made them, like I seemed to with the knife company? Had they forced her into accepting a shoddy product or something that wasn't her original vision? Maybe she didn't care if the aprons had to be pulled? Is this what Sheriff Perry planned to question her about? Had she gotten caught up in unfair labor practices in another country? Is that where Rafe really was? A situation like this could cause a person to stress eat, which could explain her weight gain. Could it be possible her appointments were with a representative from the manufacturing company? If that were the case though, why would she always look like she'd been in a tussle when she exited the hotel suite?

"Courtney?"

Hearing my name stopped my hypothesizing. Shannon had exited the vehicle and stood before me. "Yes?"

"I asked if you'd come with me."

I didn't respond immediately. If I went with Shannon, I'd miss dinner with Eric and Quintin. Although this dinner was to help comfort Quintin in his time of loss, I might glean information that'd help me figure out who killed Kinzy. Shannon had stood by me when I was a person of interest and we weren't even friends then. Maybe if the questioning didn't last too long, I could do both.

"I will."

"You won't." Sheriff Perry hitched a thumb at the entrance to the coffee shop.

"I want her there," Shannon commanded.

"I don't care." Sheriff Perry held the door for us to walk through.

"If you have questions about the aprons, I should be there. After all, I'm the one who found Kinzy. I know the print of the apron, how it was wrapped around her neck and, in my opinion, staged to show the tag declaring Shannon's name."

Shannon groaned.

"Stop talking about that in public." Sheriff Perry surveyed our surroundings.

I did too. Not a soul in sight. The shuttle taking skiers must be on its rounds to and from the lift.

"I have your statement on that," he continued. "These questions are for Shannon and no one said anything about the questions pertaining to the aprons."

"But . . ."

"Enough." He used his hand as a stop sign. "You're not a part of the investigative team. You keep your mouth shut and your nose out of my investigation. Drake sent Pamela on an errand and I can't be in two places at once. It's up to you to keep yourself safe." He grasped Shannon's arm and led her through the coffee shop seating. She looked over her shoulder. The pleading look she threw my way broke my heart, yet I didn't follow. Between his voice tone and body language, I knew Sheriff Perry had reached his breaking point on patience with one or both of us. I also had gotten the feeling these questions might pertain to the incident this morning and not the murder.

Already fifteen minutes late to dinner, I mouthed "sorry" and headed in the opposite direction, fully intending on texting her later.

I glanced at the humungous wreath attached to the brick chimney on the fireplace. Green and red ribbon wound through white deco mesh. A plaque of the word "Joy" written in red and outlined in green hung diagonally through the center hole.

Sighing, I realized that so far this Christmas season was anything but joy filled. I walked to the lobby and took the hallway that led to the steakhouse.

By the time I arrived at the entrance, melancholy filled me. I thought of Caroline all alone and knee deep in the toy drive kickoff. Sure, it was a lot of work, but it was fun too. We shared laughter and excitement as donations and funds rolled in. We remembered our own visits from Santa and how our wish lists mimicked each other's. We agreed our parents gave us the best gift of all, the aware-ness that some children's Christmases were dim, not bright, and that we could help put cheer into their holi-days. I missed the charity work, Caroline and my parents. I checked my phone for a response to my email or my text. There was none.

In the few moments it took to strangle the life from Kinzy, someone had changed Quintin and her family's holiday from merry to grieving. My longings were noth-ing compared to his loss and what he'd been going through alone.

I gave the hostess my party's name. She directed me to the back booth, where Quintin and Eric sat in silence studying the menu. I scooted in beside Eric.

Quintin laid the menu on the table. He looked at me. "Hello, Courtney."

His features, drawn with grief, brought moisture to my eyes. I reached across the table and clasped his hand. "I'm sorry for your loss."

Momentary surprise crossed his eyes before he dropped his gaze to the black linen tablecloth. "Thank you." He squeezed my hand then withdrew it.

"My sympathies."

Quintin looked back up at Eric's soft words. "Thank you." He turned his gaze to me. "If anyone could figure out Kinzy and I were in love, I'd knew it be you. Do you know," he sniffled, "if there's any progress in the case?"

I gave my head a quick shake.

The waitress approached our table and set down three glasses of wine: white for Eric, a blush for Quintin and a burgundy for me. Like my morning coffee, Eric knew my wine preference too. The thought brought a slight smile to my lips and comfort to my heart.

"How's filming going?" Quintin sipped his wine.

"Long and tension filled. Nothing different than the first day." I cringed as soon as the words left my mouth. A lot had changed since the first day, especially for Quintin.

"It's okay. I know you're talking about the show."

"How are you doing?"

"It's hard." He blew out his breath and twisted the glass stem between his index finger and thumb. "So many things to take care of on a business and personal level. And I don't feel like doing any of it."

"I could help you on the business side."

Pride filled my heart at Eric's offer.

"I might take you up on that. Thank you."

The waitress interrupted our conversation. We placed our order and a few minutes of silence ensued. I hated to add to Quintin's burdens, yet I'd read his signal yesterday; he wanted me to help solve Kinzy's murder. In order to do that, I needed some information from him.

"Do you mind answering some questions for me?"

He shook his head.

"Has Sheriff Perry sequestered you in the resort as a person of interest?"

"I guess. He told me that I can't leave. Are there others?"

"Officially, I know of one. Leon Chapski. He's not happy about it either."

Quintin snorted. "Good."

"Do you think he had anything to do with her death?"

Quintin raised his brows. "He'd threatened her more than once. Even while Harold was alive."

"Why?"

"The ranch. He lives there, you know."

I nodded. "Do you know if he was next in line to inherit Harold's estate?"

"Not for sure, no."

"How does he play into their family dynamics?" Should I tell Quintin that I knew Leon was Kinzy's godfather? Did he know?

"He was her father's best friend. They were inseparable from kindergarten until their college years, then their interests changed. According to Kinzy, Harold called Leon his second son."

"How do you mean their interests changed?"

"Leon followed in Harold's footsteps and became an attorney."

"Kinzy's dad didn't?"

"No. He met her mother and their dreams lay with the stage and film."

"Actors?" It might explain why Kinzy and her grandfather didn't get along.

"Yes. They'd been touring with a Broadway stage production when . . ." his voice trailed off.

"They were in a fatal car accident. Harold didn't want Kinzy to become a director. He felt she was following in her parents' footsteps." I stated what I felt was the obvious rather than ask him.

He nodded. "He wanted her to stay in Montana and work for his firm in some capacity."

My thoughts went back to the will and how I could find a copy. I doubted Kinzy had one since she'd vehemently told Leon she'd wanted nothing to do with her inheritance. I sipped my wine.

Quintin sniffled. "I'm not trying to make Leon out to be the killer. After all, Shannon did threaten her too."

Our eyes met.

"Shannon has gained weight and Kinzy was within the scope of her job in her warnings." Quintin's lips pulled into a deep frown. "Brenden will never broach the subject so I'm asking you to do it."

"Do what?"

"Ask her why she's in denial about this weight gain. Her weight isn't the issue. The too-small wardrobe is. Costuming is expensive. She should've told us and not been so defensive."

I decided not to point out that Kinzy hadn't handled the situation correctly either. "You don't think Shannon killed Kinzy, do you?"

"I don't know what to think. She left the wedding-themed filming as the sweet Southern belle we hired and came back a shrew that needs to be tamed." Anger laced his tone.

"A change of attitude doesn't make a person a kill . . ."

"Quintin," Eric interrupted me, "how long had you and Kinzy dated?"

For a moment, love softened his features, then the sadness returned. "We'd known each other in passing for quite a while before we hired her for the show. In between the first season and the second, she did some fill-in work for an assistant director on another show who was off for medical reasons. I was present on the set and we just clicked. Soon we were eating lunches together then dinner or catching a movie. We decided to date exclusively just before filming of the wedding show began." He took a sip of wine. "Brenden promoted her to assistant director, not me. Of course, I had to sign off on the promotion, but I didn't initiate it."

Involuntarily, I knitted my brow.

"I told you because it was important to Kinzy that people didn't think she'd slept her way to the top. It's one of the reasons we kept our relationship on the down low. She wanted to be a respected director. I wanted that for her. As a matter of fact, she was so excited to get your offer," Quintin's eyes focused on Eric, "to direct the summer replacement show. She knew it was her big break. Contrary to what Shannon may think, she was thrilled to be working with established stars. It's all she talked about on the plane. Nonstop, just like our first-class flight." He chuckled. "She didn't drop names, but she was so excited running ideas past me and hoping you'd like them. I'm sure those seated around us didn't appreciate her chattering."

"We were just as excited to work with her."

"That's right," Eric added.

The conversation died while the waitress set our food down. Quintin ate a few bites of his steak while Eric and I doctored our burgers with condiments.

"Courtney, how did you figure out Kinzy and I were a couple? We were very careful to keep the relationship concealed."

"I found a picture on the internet. You were at some type of awards banquet."

"Aw, yes, she looked so beautiful that night." Quintin dropped his fork and his head. Silent sobs bounced his shoulders. He swiped at his face with his napkin, then looked up. His eyes locked to mine.

"She was young, beautiful, sweet, talented and on the

verge of success. Who would do something like this to her and why?"

I blinked back tears. "I don't know." I intended to find out though.

Alone in my suite, I sorted out my jumbled thoughts.

During dinner I'd forgotten about Sheriff Perry interviewing Shannon. Had he found out what he wanted? Had it pertained to the murder or her scene with Marley in the hallway? I knew Shannon didn't kill Kinzy even if Quintin entertained doubts.

Something was wrong in Shannon's life and I believed it was personal. I'd thought so since the first day of filming. The murder and the murder weapon just escalated her problems to a higher level. Eric didn't want to believe it was a marital problem. I didn't either, yet Shannon was a romantic with matchmaker tenancies and not once had she shown that side of herself during this filming. She never stayed on set long enough to talk to anyone. She spent all her free time, and some of her work time, sneaking off to appointments that I knew happened behind a hotel room door on the first floor of the resort. Was it another man? She acted like she didn't know Rafe's whereabouts but did show concern when Eric told her he'd been stranded in a snowstorm.

Another thought niggled through my mind. Perhaps I was a little off base. Maybe they were having marital problems and it wasn't another man behind that door, but a marriage counselor. It would explain her wrinkled clothes, if she'd been lying down talking. Could Pamela find that out for me? Would she?

Quintin managed to finish his dinner after he broke down. I was glad. He needed the sustenance to give him strength through this ordeal. My heart ached for him. When he spoke about Kinzy, there was no mistaking the love in his heart. He'd shared their plans for their future. With her chance to direct our show, she was resigning from *The American Baking Battle* after the Christmas special wrapped. They'd been excited to take their relationship public and he'd planned to propose over the holidays. How sad their happy future had been cut short by the cruel act of murder.

I sighed. Both couples' situations had similarities to Eric and my relationship. Like Shannon and Rafe, we'd been together a long time and worked together. Our livelihood and relationship went hand in hand. If one failed, the other might too. We paralleled Quintin and Kinzy falling in love on the job and then trying to keep our personal feelings secret.

The one thing I learned during the filming of all three baking competitions is that time on earth is fleeting. Eric and I needed to figure out what we were doing wrong. Were we simply trying too hard? Instead of aiming for a typical first date, should we have stuck to the tried and true? Did we need to try new things to breathe life into our relationship?

My gut said no. We had favorite restaurants and museums in Chicago. Places we enjoyed and had fun. Why were we switching it up? Why were we trying to find stories from our pasts to share? I thought a minute. The answer hit me. We were trying to fall in love. Trying to capture giddy attraction instead of recognizing love had softly entered our hearts through friendship and respect. I needed to tell Eric I was wrong to suggest we date other people. We needed to grab our happiness while we could. I didn't want to be with anyone else and I wanted the world to know we were a couple.

The thought brought Kinzy to mind. I'd ruled out Shannon as a person of interest. Quintin's story about Leon filled in some blanks and made me think there was a lot at stake if Leon had been the beneficiary of Harold's estate. If Kinzy had defied Harold, the same way her father had, and Leon maintained a familial relationship with Harold, he probably did deserve all or some of the inheritance. When it came right down to it, had blood been thicker than water? Or had Leon been left something and needed Kinzy to settle the estate so he could keep his home or the law firm running? People murdered for money.

Then there was Marley. I knew his generation felt strongly about things. Was he so against endorsing a product that he murdered someone? If so, why Kinzy? Why not Shannon? Was Kinzy just the person who'd been handy? Or was it because he saw her as an authoritative figure, "the man," who was making him do something against his principles? He was an enigma. First, he'd cause trouble, then he'd turn apologetic. He was spacey. Was it an act? Was he being passive aggressive for a reason? Had Leon influenced him to file a restraining order and Marley hadn't thought the consequences through? What was the connection between these two men? Marley had managed to sneak into the part of the resort that was off-limits to the contestants. Had he simply stumbled into the wrong area and met up with the wrong person in the hallway? Or was he following Shannon? Had he stalked and killed Kinzy? Was he now stalking and planning to murder Shannon?

A glance at the time on my phone told me it was too late for me to do anything tonight except formulate a plan of action for tomorrow. I had questions that needed answering. I didn't have the time to research first. I needed to ask the questions now, which included getting to the bottom of whatever was bothering Shannon.

If the filming day stayed on track, I'd insist Shannon eat lunch with me. This time I wouldn't let her turn the tables, even if it meant bringing up the hotel room.

In my free time tomorrow, there were three men I needed to talk to: Leon, Marley and Eric. Not necessarily in that order.

CHAPTER NINETEEN

I paused in the lobby entry of the coffee shop and surveyed the patrons. My eyes rested on Eric. I smiled. It was just like him to beat me to Castle Grounds and have my latte waiting. I'd texted him an hour ago to meet me for coffee because we needed to talk. All he'd answered was "okay."

He looked handsome in a dark green sweater and jeans. I caught his eye and waved.

I'd taken extra care with my appearance this morning even knowing my stylist would remove the makeup I'd just applied. I'd pulled on denim leggings, my knee-high boots and a black cashmere sweater. I accessorized with a filigree gold pin and earrings set in the shape of a Christmas tree. I'd tucked my straight tresses behind my ears. My smile widened at the surprise I had in store for Eric.

He stood when I approached the table. "Good morning."

I walked past the chair he'd slid out for me to sit on, stretched up on my tiptoes and planted a kiss on his lips, pressing long enough that the momentary shock wore off and he returned the affection. When the kiss ended, I giggled at the surprised and pleased look on his face.

"Am I . . ." he looked up and around the rafters of the room, "under mistletoe?"

"No." I smirked and took my seat. The aroma of hazelnut wafted from my coffee cup. "I made a decision last night."

Eric raised his brows and sat down.

"I was totally wrong about our relationship."

Confusion passed through his baby blues.

I reached for his hand. "I was wrong to think we'd developed false feelings for one another and needed to date other people. It's not true."

Joy spread across his features. He squeezed my hand. "Apology accepted."

Laughing I said, "I think you need to let me say I'm sorry because I am. I'm sorry I made such a ludicrous suggestion. In addition, I don't want to hide our relationship. I want people to know we love each other."

Eric drew back in his chair, never letting go of my hand. "I'm okay with this, but what brought on your change of heart?"

"Well," I used my free hand to take a sip of coffee, "Kinzy and Quintin's relationship. I totally understand her stance on making it as a director on her own terms. I don't have to do that. If it wasn't for you, I wouldn't have the career I have. I know this and as of last night, I don't care what other people think or say to us about our relationship. Life's too short. We can't waste a moment. We have to grab our happiness while we can."

Leaning forward, Eric said, "Did you say you loved me?"

I hoped the same elation shining on his face also showed on mine. "I said we loved each other, so yes, I did." I laughed then stared directly into his eyes. I lowered my voice. "I love you, Eric Iverson."

A wide smile stretched across his face. "I love you too. And that's the first of many times I plan to tell you."

"Good." I leaned toward him. He followed my cue and we kissed, a light, spontaneous, love-filled kiss.

"Does this mean, we're trying dates again?" Eric leaned back in his chair and grinned.

"No. I think that was our problem. We were trying to fall in love. We're past that." I copied Shannon's favorite gesture and flipped my hand through the air. "Love found its way into our hearts through mutual respect and friendship during our day-to-day lives. Don't you think?"

We both took sips of our coffee while Eric contemplated my question. "I do think so. We have so much in common and love what we do for a living, and it just crept up on us." He smiled even wider than before.

"I'm totally okay with comfortable love. A person who cares about me so much they know my every need." I lifted my coffee cup as exhibit number one, then took a sip.

"Me too. This is the best Christmas gift you ever gave me."

"Hey," I mocked hurt. "You said the same thing about the fitness tracker I gave you two years ago."

"Well, it was true then and now. Both gifts are keeping my heart healthy and happy."

Delight warmed every fiber of my being. It wasn't the

flirty banter of giddy attraction. It was more like comfy contentment. I was okay with that.

Eric lifted his cup. "To us!"

I tipped my coffee against his and we enjoyed a sip while holding hands. I glanced up at the wreath over the fireplace. This time I felt the joy of the season. I wasn't with Caroline for the toy drive kickoff, but I'd be there during the middle and then the race to the finish. There'd be plenty of time for fun and laughter. We were on day four of a projected seven-day filming schedule. Even with the murder investigation, we'd kept to task and would probably wrap in a day or two. There was no doubt in my mind we had Victoria to thank for keeping us on track.

"So, I want to be clear."

I pulled my gaze back to Eric.

"We're going public with our relationship."

"Yes."

"I can tell my family, my friends, my mailman, the front desk personnel . . ."

"Everyone!" I interrupted Eric, then laughed.

"And you are too?"

"Yes. I'll tell my parents first." I frowned a little. "I'd like to tell them in person. I wish they'd answer my email."

"They will. I'm sure they're in a remote area or haven't had the time."

"I know, I know. Sometimes a week passes before they can tend to their personal business. If they can't make it home for Christmas, maybe we can set up a Skype or Zoom meeting when they have internet access and we can tell them together that we're a couple."

Eric nodded.

"Worst-case scenario, I'll send them a text. I don't want their schedule to hold you up from telling your . . . mailman."

We shared a laugh and then sat in silence, gazes locked, holding hands, living in the moment while the sounds of the coffee shop faded to white noise. For a while it felt like the world revolved around us and our happiness.

Then I heard a familiar voice ask, "Do what?"

I scowled. I'd know that voice anywhere. I craned my neck to the left and didn't see him. I twisted it to the right, then to the far right. My eyes confirmed the voice. Marley. He and Leon sat at a table for two in a secluded corner of the coffee shop. "What's he doing here?"

"Who?"

I'd said the words out loud without really realizing it.

Knowing it'd ruin the mood, I turned back to Eric and said, "Marley." I jerked my head in the direction where they sat. "This is the third time I've seen him out of his authorized area." The show keeps the contestants sequestered in another wing of Coal Castle Resort and under surveillance to thwart cheating attempts. I wiggled in my chair, antsy to get up and walk over there. I needed to speak with both, and what better time than when they were together.

"Courtney," Eric said, lecture tone in place.

I turned to him. "It's against the rules that he's here." The words rushed out of me.

"Then report him to Pamela or Drake."

Taken aback, I blinked. That's the first time Eric said Drake in a normal everyday tone. I guessed since he'd gotten the girl, he'd dropped his animosity toward Drake. "I think I will." I pulled my phone from my purse and noticed a text from an unknown number. Thinking it might be my parents, I forgot about turning in Marley and tapped the message.

Disappointment cut through me. "I think a new director is trying to get ahold of you." I held out my phone.

Eric read the message. "We received her resume. Why would she contact you?"

"I know her from my charity work."

"Don't answer it." Eric stood. "I'll go back to my room and contact her. She needs to deal with me and Rafe."

"Did she make the cut?"

"I haven't reviewed the resumes in depth, just a quick perusal. It's the first thing on my to-do list. The posting didn't say who'd star in the show. She must watch your show to know I'm your producer. Any opinions you'd like to share?"

"She's okay to work with at charity events. As for her directing skills for a cooking show, I have no idea. She doesn't have to follow my show to know you're my producer. You know her too from the same events. Tall, strawberry blond hair and works for one of the local television stations in Chicago shooting commercials for small hometown businesses. She directed those humorous car lot commercials."

"Aw! I know who she is. Okay, then, if you want to answer the text feel free. Be very noncommittal though."

"I'll say it was good to hear from you and Eric will be in contact."

"Perfect." Eric bent down and gave me a longish and delightful goodbye kiss. It made me wish we could spend the day together at one of the resort amenities. If the show wrapped ahead of schedule, would Eric be up for staying at the resort for the remaining days we'd booked? I enjoyed his retreating view, then checked the time on my phone. I had fifteen minutes until I needed to report to wardrobe. I'd use this time wisely. Finishing off my latte, I stood, intending to throw my cup in a trash can near where Marley and Leon sat. It'd give me the opening I needed to start a conversation with them.

I turned and found the table empty. My shoulders slumped. I'd lost my chance with Leon. When would I get another chance to speak to him? Talking to Marley wasn't a problem. I'd see him a little later this morning.

My phone jingled. Hope caught in my heart, then deflated fast when I saw it was from Pamela and not my parents. I typed a response and headed toward the main lobby exit where she'd told me she'd be waiting. I walked out of the resort, looked around for a police or security vehicle and finally saw her frantic wave through the windshield of a half-ton pickup.

I crawled into the cab. "Good morning."

"Good morning. Sorry, I'm running late this morning. My flight." She stopped, stared straight ahead and clutched the wheel. "Anyway, sorry I'm picking you up in my rental. I didn't have time to clock in and grab a security UTV." She pulled away from the circular drive and turned toward the service road.

Petite Pamela behind the wheel of a half-ton pickup struck me as funny, yet she drove it like a pro.

"No apology necessary. This is much warmer." I looked out the side window and wondered about Pamela's slip of the lip. Did the errand Drake send her on have something to do with Kinzy's murder? Exactly where had Pamela gone and why?

I'd hurried my stylist along with the excuse that I was famished. I didn't tell him the real reason: I wanted to be on set when the contestants entered so I could speak with Marley. Pro that he is, he managed to get me ready to go in under thirty minutes.

Since it was the finale, our wardrobe was formal and tasteful. I wore creased black slacks and a black sweater with glittery gold thread woven into the cable knit. My two-tone pumps sported gold shiny leather over the pointed toes and slender heels while black patent leather rounded out the rest of the shoe. To keep with the theme, a gold sequined headband held my hair away from my face, showing off my own earrings that my stylist declared more perfect than the jewelry he'd picked out. My brooch didn't make the cut to appear on camera.

I left the makeup area while the other stars of the show were in their dressing rooms and stepped down to the main set. I was hungry so I snagged a protein bar and glass of juice before heading to the kitchenettes.

The crew had restaged the area overnight. All three kitchenettes were front and center. I read the name placards, then planted myself in front of Marley's counter. I wasn't missing my chance to talk to him again. I ate my breakfast and braced for a confrontation with Marley.

The side door clicked opened with Victoria in the lead. In a turquoise sweater and turquoise and tan plaid skirt with matching plaid heels, you'd think she was a star of the show. Brystol, Mya and Marley followed behind her.

"Good morning, Courtney. Have you seen Brenden?"

"Not yet."

Victoria drew her lips into a frown, then walked to the wings of the set while pulling out her phone.

Lucky for me, the crew attached Marley's microphone first, then pulled both the women to the side to work on their audio. His workspace was the center counter and with the gals tied up with the sound crew, we'd have a semi-private conversation.

"Marley."

He flashed me a wary look. "Courtney."

"Mind if I ask you a couple of questions?"

"I do, so don't. I'm not going to answer anyway."

I pursed my lips and studied him, then I said, "Maybe I should talk to Drake about how you keep showing up in the off-limits areas of the resort."

He dropped his chin to his chest.

"That's right. I saw you with Leon in the coffee shop this morning. How do you slip out of the sequestered area?"

He looked up. "Not telling. Next question."

"Does Leon help you?"

He shook his head.

I wasn't getting very far. I cast a glance at Brystol and Mya and gauged I still had a few minutes to play cat and mouse. "How do you know Leon?"

"Old friend."

I considered his answer. Marley had at least twenty years on Leon. Not that age mattered in friendships, yet I wasn't buying his answer. "So you're from Montana?" If he said no, I'd catch him in a lie and could move on from there.

"No. Don't you read our bios? I'm from California. I went to Berkeley." His voice filled with pride when he stated his alma mater.

"You graduated from Berkeley?"

He chuckled. "I didn't say that."

"Is that where you met Leon?"

"No."

My line of questioning was getting me nowhere. Another look in the direction of the sound crew told me I was running out of time. I cut to the chase. "How are you and Leon old friends? Leon lived his entire life in Montana. You, in California." I wasn't certain Leon spent his entire life in Big Sky Country. I was sure it was something Marley didn't know either.

I was correct. Marley's eyes widened with the realization he was caught in a lie. "I said that wrong. We're not friends, more like business associates."

"You're a retired attorney?"

"No."

"Judge?"

His eyes darted from side to side. "No."

I knew he was trying to think of a story to support another lie. I didn't give him a chance. I leaned over the countertop and whispered, "Did you work with Leon to kill Kinzy so he could inherit her grandfather's estate?"

"No!"

I didn't look around to see if Marley's raised voice drew any attention. My surprise question rattled him, so I forged ahead. Keeping my gaze locked to his, I said, "I think you did. That's why you insisted on not wearing Shannon's apron. You needed to throw it away so you or Leon could pick it up and use it to kill Kinzy, then frame Shannon so Leon could inherit Harold's estate." I managed to get the words out around the lump of grief in my throat at the thought I might have stated the truth.

Bug-eyed, Marley's face turned bright red. He broke eye contact and pivoted his head. Then whispered, "Come with me." He walked to the chiller and refrigerator area.

I followed.

With hands to his hips, he pinned me with a look. "None of what you said is true. I didn't even know Kinzy until I arrived at the resort. I'm only telling you this because you're making trouble where there is none. I spent my life protesting the unjustness in society. I was very good at it and eventually earned a living as a paid protestor. That's how I know Leon. He hired me to make trouble for an oil pipeline company in his state."

The pipeline State Representative Harold Hummel supported.

"When Leon saw me at the competition, he hired me to make trouble for Kinzy. I don't care if I wear a Shannon Collins apron on camera. It was the only thing I could think of to add to Kinzy's problems the first day of filming." He drew a breath. "Now, Leon wants me to keep badgering Shannon about the aprons."

"Why?" I'd failed to do a search on Leon and Shannon to see if there was some sort of connection.

"I don't know." He held his palms out in surrender. "Truly don't know. He told me to continue to raise a stink about those aprons and I did. I want to open my own cookie shop. He offered me a significant amount of money. When he pushed for a restraining order and Victoria told me I'd be released from the competition, I decided I was done making trouble. No more following Shannon to start a confrontation. That's what I was telling him this morning. I want to win the competition. I have a good chance, right?"

"At winning?" His question threw me off my game. "I don't know." I put us back on track when I asked, "If you told Leon you were done creating trouble, why were you with him in the coffee shop this morning?"

"Breaking our partnership."

"Marley, you said you were in Montana to protest an oil pipeline and that you didn't know Kinzy. Is that true?"

With exaggeration, Marley nodded his head. "I knew Harold though. He was a horrible man. He only cared about money. If Kinzy took after her grandfather, she got what she deserved."

I gasped.

"Contestants take your places." Victoria's command stopped our conversation. Marley hurried to his kitchenette.

I walked over to the faux gingerbread house, wishing Victoria hadn't interrupted us. I wanted to set the record straight. Kinzy was a good person. Yet most of what I'd read about Harold painted the same picture. Was a criminal hiding under the public façade? Or did Marley think anyone who didn't share his views and opinions was a horrible person? Had Marley protested on Harold's land and been arrested? No matter what Harold did, Marley's comment against Kinzy was uncalled for and cruel.

I watched the crew set the camera angles and lighting with the contestants for the new stage setup. I reached into my pocket for my phone to text Sheriff Perry. I came out empty-handed. I'd been in such a hurry to catch Marley, I'd left my phone in the wardrobe room. I needed to contact Sheriff Perry and update him on Marley's admission of being a paid protestor hired by Leon in the past and present. Perhaps he already knew about the past?

I replayed my conversation with Marley. He'd insisted he didn't murder Kinzy and I believed him. However, I wondered if he was an unknowing pawn in a murder plan staged by Leon. Had Leon hired Marley to disrupt the set to deflect away from him? Had he hidden on set, like the day he appeared out of nowhere, snagged the discarded apron and laid in wait for the perfect time to kill Kinzy?

As soon as we kicked off the first challenge, I'd go upstairs and grab my phone so I could alert Sheriff Perry about Marley's admission, then focus my research efforts on finding out more about Leon and his environmental work. Had he paid others to protest? Did Harold know about this side of him? Was he so passionate about the environment that he wanted Harold's ranch and the only way to get it was to murder Kinzy?

CHAPTER TWENTY

"My goodness." The sound of Victoria's voice ended my rumination. I caught her in my sights and followed her movement since her words came out in a disgusted huff. She'd been looking skyward toward the stairs to the second floor. The sour expression covering her features left no room for doubt in my mind. Shannon was headed to the set decked out in an outfit a size or more too small.

She grabbed Brenden by the sleeve of his sweatshirt and dragged him to the wings of the set just behind me. His style swung to the opposite of his mother. He wore T-shirts and jeans in the summer months. Sweatshirts rotated into the winter season.

I perked up my ears.

"Did you see Shannon? You need to say something to

her about her weight." I didn't need to see Victoria's face. Unhappiness came through loud and clear in her tone.

Brenden heaved a sigh. "I saw. Her stylist texted me, so I'd be aware."

"Are you going to talk to her?"

"It's a sensitive subject and she seems upset."

"Then talk to her manager."

"I tried. He isn't returning my calls."

I frowned. Brenden had whined like a small child.

"Well, take her aside and talk to her. Maybe the gift shop has something appropriate for her to wear."

"That's a good idea." I heard clothes rustle and knew Brenden had taken out his phone.

I'd never been in the gift shop of the resort. Did they sell clothing appropriate for the show? Curious, I chanced a look toward the cast chairs. No one was there so I turned toward the commissary table and found all three having breakfast. Shannon had piled her plate with breakfast potatoes and muffins.

I studied her red velour dress, a long-sleeved shift with a scooped neckline. It clung to her torso in areas where it shouldn't and stretched tight across her back. I cringed. How could it be fixed?

"What should I tell her to look for, Mother?"

"Tell her there's a lovely black brocade shawl in the gift shop that could be draped around her in some way."

Brenden repeated her words.

"Tell her to make a triangle fold and tie or pin it around Shannon to cover up the tightness on top."

"I'm sure she'll figure it out, Mother. It's her job." He must have ended the call.

"Talk to *her*. Viewers are going to notice. You have enough problems with murders always happening while you're filming. You don't need one of your stars setting your show up for poor ratings too."

Aghast that Victoria thought a woman gaining weight could cancel an entire show, I turned around. Brenden wore a stricken expression while Victoria threw a disgusted stare toward Shannon. When she looked back at her son, she wrapped an arm around him. "Oh, Brenden, I'm sorry. It's not your show's fault people get murdered, but it does seem the show provides the methods of murder."

"Maybe I should talk to Quintin." Brenden sniffled. "There's been too much murder. Maybe we should end the show with this special."

"No!" Victoria squeezed tighter. "You're doing a fantastic job. Shannon's weight gain is just a setback. You need to be firm with her about keeping the show apprised of things like this or losing the weight. As for the murders, Quintin should move the show to an undisclosed location."

Brenden nodded and gave his mother a hug. "Thanks, Mom. You're right. I'm so glad you're here. You're a comfort to me. Not to mention a tremendous help taking over for Kinzy."

Although I didn't share Victoria or Brenden's views, their family interaction reignited my longing to see my own parents. I wished they'd answer my email.

"Places, everyone." Brenden clapped his hands.

Skylar joined me in the gingerbread house doorframe. We watched Brenden count us down. At his fist Skylar said, "Bakers, this is it. One of you will walk away the winner of *The American Baking Battle Christmas Edition*. Today, we're putting your baking skills to the test. Your challenges are cakes from the past, present and future."

"Of course, as you've probably guessed by now, the cake from the past is fruitcake." I couldn't help but think Tim would've excelled at this round of competition with a rum-infused loaf. "You have two hours to complete this challenge."

In sync, Skylar and I said, "The baking begins now."

The bakers scurried to the pantry. When the camera light turned red, Skylar and I moved from our mark. "What a horrible challenge." Skylar shivered.

I laughed. "That's pretty much the consensus on fruitcake. They knew this challenge. It'll be interesting to see what they bake."

"You'll get to know that in about ten minutes," Brenden said. "Interviews will be short. Harrison and Shannon, come with me to film a judging discussion."

During this downtime, I ran upstairs and grabbed my phone. Of course, when I didn't have it, I'd received an email from my parents. Hope fluttered through my heart. I opened the application and speed-read my parents' short response. Disappointment replaced my expectance. They made no promises about coming home for Christmas. They expressed their concern about another murder happening at the resort and affiliated with the show and asked if I was safe. Then they signed off with love. Under that was a P.S. message from my dad asking if Shannon was pregnant.

I reread his notation. I'd never considered pregnancy. She'd never talked about starting a family. Was Shannon going to have a baby? Many of her symptoms matched pregnancy: weight gain, hunger and moodiness. Was she in her first trimester and not wanting to make an announcement until later? Excitement wound through me at the thought of Shannon having a baby. How fun would that be? Then I considered the other changes in her character, her anger especially at Rafe and her sneaking around. Had she not wanted a baby at this time in her life and was mad because Rafe did? Or did the baby belong . . . No, I wasn't going there. Shannon was not that type of a person. I'd earmarked today as the day I'd get to the bottom of a few things. I'd been making progress, and at lunchtime I'd cross talking to Shannon off my list.

Knowing I was needed back on set, I wobbled down the stairs on my heels, found Skylar and got set to interview the three remaining contestants.

"I have to admit," Skylar smiled at me while the sound people attached our microphones, "it smells great in here."

"It does."

We approached Mya first. Her batter sat at the ready while she chopped dried apricots and walnuts. Tubs of candied fruit sat to the side of her cutting board.

"Tell us about your fruitcake."

She glanced up. "It's an apricot walnut fruitcake with candied fruits and it's alcohol free." She used a scraper to pick up the fruit and nuts. Dropping them into the batter, she went to work on the candied fruit. "Sorry, I need to keep working. My recipe bakes for an hour. I need to get the cake into the oven, so it cools a little before I slice into it."

We took her hint and moved on to Marley. He had piles of red and green candied cherries chopped on a cutting board. He worked on measuring out the ingredients for the batter.

"You have some interesting ingredients here." Skylar pointed to the small bowls holding the flavorings, sugar, flour and shredded coconut.

"Do I smell rum?" I asked.

Marley smiled. "And brandy. My fruitcake has a tropical flair." He lifted a can of pineapple juice.

"Interesting. This sure isn't your grandma's fruitcake," I said into the camera.

"Yes, it is."

I turned to Marley, who wore a confused expression at my adlibbed comment.

I felt sure Brenden would edit out his response but decided to give him more to work with. I smiled, then looked back into the camera. "I stand corrected. This *is* your grandma's fruitcake!"

Stepping over to Brystol's kitchenette, Skylar exaggerated an inhale. "I smell citrus."

Brystol smiled. "I'm making an orange brandy fruitcake. It has the regular candied cherries along with golden raisins."

"No cheesecake?" I asked.

"There's cream cheese in the batter." Brystol winked at us.

Which made a great place to stop the interview. Skylar and I took our seats and watched the contestants ready their fruitcake for baking. Marley used a loaf pan. Mya and Brystol chose the traditional round shape. Mya selected a removable-core angel food cake pan, while Brystol went with individual-serving bundtlette bakeware. Once their fruitcakes went into the oven, they started preparing their area for cooling and plating.

"Skylar, would you do me a favor?"

He looked at me. "Anything."

"Would you corral Harrison and eat lunch down here or somewhere other than our dressing room area?"

"Why?"

"I want to talk to Shannon. I'm going to insist that she eat lunch with me in our makeup room so I can get to the bottom of what is bothering her, then see about getting her off Sheriff Perry's radar."

"I can do that. Good luck."

"Thanks." I knew I'd need it. The last time she turned the tables on me. This time I planned to ask what was wrong and if she hedged instead of answering, I'd use my ace in the hole: I'd ask her about the hotel room.

"Whoa! I feel ganged up on." Marley made a production of looking at us individually. Brenden had scripted the first judging with Harrison and Shannon only. Skylar and I wanted in on the action because, believe it or not, we wanted to try their fruitcake, which smelled delectable. After laughing hysterically and telling us that we were the only two people in this century who admitted to wanting to taste fruitcake, Brenden allowed us to tag along.

The stylist did wonders for Shannon's wardrobe snafu with the brocade scarf. She folded it on the diagonal before draping it over her shoulders at an angle. The tie-over in front was pinned with a large silver wreath-shaped brooch right over her bust line. The scarf covered her back and the long-fringed ties played peekaboo with the snug torso areas.

Marley had plated his unadorned loaf on a cutting board. Placing the loaf on a diagonal, he'd put a brandy snifter filled with dried fruits and wide-flaked coconut on the corner of the board. He'd tied a festive ribbon around the stem of the snifter.

"Nice presentation," Harrison said.

"I agree. It's simple and people can tell the fruitcake is spiked and what the ingredients are inside." Shannon twisted the board so the camera could get a better view.

"Thank you." Marley smiled. "Shall I do the honors?" He lifted the knife and sliced off the end of the loaf to reveal a jeweled confection with a soggy middle. "Uh-oh." Marley cut another slice, frowned and lifted the knife to make another cut. Did he think the other end was cooked?

"Just cut the slice into quarters," Harrison instructed.

We all took a bite except Shannon. She broke hers in half and lifted it to her lips and nipped at the crusted edge of the alcohol-infused sample. That action supported Dad's question. I thought a minute. I'd yet to see her imbibe over the past few days. She'd drank apple cider at the opening party and water at dinner. I chewed my bite while considering the pregnancy theory. I loved the flavor, which gave a new meaning to fruitcake. Had he left it in the oven maybe ten minutes longer, it would've been perfection. Shannon and Harrison's judging mirrored my thoughts.

Stepping to our right, we perused Brystol's display. She'd set the individual fruitcakes on red dessert plates. The red and green candied cherries peeked through the light-colored confection. She'd dusted the top with powdered sugar and used mint and dried cranberries to create a faux holly berry garnish.

"This is a beautiful way to serve your fruitcake," Shannon said.

"Indeed." Harrison passed out utensils, then lifted a plate so we could fork off a bite.

I watched Shannon. She pressed the tines to the crumbs left behind by the rest of us.

"The hint of brandy brings out the other flavors." Harrison looked to Shannon.

She put her fork back down. "The texture is perfect. Good job," she drawled.

Hmmm . . . had she tasted the crumbles? She must have. The fork tines were clean. Was anyone noticing this but me? I tried to think back to her judging Tim's challenges. I just couldn't remember if she took much of a bite, if any.

We waited for the cameraman to swing around to Mya's counter. Her fruitcake sat atop a cut-glass cake plate. She'd decorated the top with dried apricots and walnut halves in an eye-pleasing manner.

Shannon did the honors cutting into it. She sliced a piece and quartered it. She ate her quarter in one bite. Her eyes lit up. She covered her mouth while she chewed and spoke. "This is delicious."

Marley snorted.

Was it poor sportsmanship or had he noticed her nibbles? Is that why he called her an unfair judge? My heart sank a little. If it was, he wasn't wrong.

Harrison drew his brows together and cast a look over his shoulder at Marley. Then he smiled, and said, "It's light, airy, fruity and delectable." He popped the rest of his quarter into his mouth.

For me, his description nailed it.

Shannon took another slice.

"Hey!" Marley exclaimed. "That's not fair!"

I turned. He looked at Brenden and pointed to Shannon.

"Cut!" Brenden hollered.

Shannon said, "I'm not playing favorites. I just enjoy that it doesn't have booze in it."

I quirked a brow. Had Shannon confided in Harrison? Is that why he suggested no liquor in Tim's challenges?

Marley opened his mouth.

Harrison shut it for him by saying, "Your fruitcake was undercooked."

"We're breaking for an early and longer lunch. We'll reconvene at one to kick off the present-day Christmas cake."

I moved fast to thwart Shannon's great-escape-artist skills.

"Will you have lunch with me in the makeup room?" I cast a glance to see if the commissary table had been reset for lunch. It had.

Shannon bit at her bottom lip then smiled and said, "Sure."

The resort had prepared a Christmas feast for our cast

and crew. I loaded my plate with turkey breast, stuffing, cranberries and a pecan pie bar. Shannon ended up with two plates, one for hot food smothered in gravy, the other for cold food, which included a roll and two pumpkin bars.

In order not to spill our food or fall in our heels, we gingerly staired up to the makeup room.

"Well, look at this!" I held the door for Shannon. Sitting smack dab in the middle of the room, in the way no less, were our table and chairs.

"Merry Christmas to us!" Shannon set her hot plate down and waved her hand in the air. "I almost didn't make it. The food is hot."

We chatted about shopping and the ornate Christmas decorations around the resort while we ate. When we were ready for dessert, I made us coffee from our coffee maker, then slid my chair closer to Shannon.

"Is something wrong?" She took my hand. Concern filled her eyes and for the second time since we arrived, I felt like I was talking to the friend I knew.

"You tell me." I stared into her eyes. They misted.

"What do you mean? The murder? I didn't kill Kinzy." She released her grip.

I captured her hand. "Not the murder. I know you didn't kill Kinzy. I mean, what's going on with you?"

She frowned. "Nothing."

"Shannon, that's not true. You're moody, angry, sneaking off and coming out of strange hotel rooms."

She gasped.

I nodded so she'd know I knew it was true. "And you've hardly mentioned Rafe."

A single tear trickled down her cheek.

My own eyes welled. "Are you pregnant?" I blurted out.

She closed her eyes and squeezed my hand. Tears ran down her cheeks. She whispered, "I wish." I grabbed a napkin with my free hand and pressed it into hers. She swiped at her face. "Oh, Courtney." She opened her eyes and sniffled. "I'm such a failure."

"What?"

"I want to be pregnant."

I shook my head. "I don't understand."

She cleared her throat while she wiped her eyes. "We've been trying to get pregnant for over a year. It's not working."

"Oh, Shannon, I'm so sorry."

Her expression crumbled into heartbreaking sadness. Tears cut a path through her makeup on their downstream journey.

I gave her a few moments. "Is it due to the stress of the show?" She had indicated during the filming of the wedding show that the stress wasn't good for her body. At the time when I'd questioned her, she'd blown me off.

Sniffling, then regaining composure, she said, "I don't think it's helping, but we were trying before we ever filmed the first season of *The American Baking Battle*. We've been to doctors and it's me, not Rafe." She wiped the fresh tears from her eyes.

Since she brought up Rafe, I took the opening. "Is this causing marital problems?"

She sighed. "It wasn't until Quintin called with this rush production."

"Why would that cause a problem?"

"Bad timing. We were in the middle of an in vitro procedure with my doctor."

Which explained her weight gain.

"Rafe wanted me to decline the show. I didn't want to."

"Why? Did you think Quintin wouldn't understand?"

"No. Since the filming of the last competition, my life's a series of doctor appointments and disappointment. I thought work would take my mind off our fertility issues. Rafe and my doctor said I couldn't stop mid-treatment. I didn't see that as a problem. I planned to have medical personnel onsite to monitor my temps and give me daily shots." Shannon's lips trembled.

"Is that where the problem started?"

"Yes. Rafe and I had a huge fight. He insisted the in vitro was expensive enough without paying additional medical personnel to be here. Our insurance wouldn't cover it. As my manager, then as my husband, he pleaded with me to decline, saying Quintin could get a guest judge. I argued this would be great promotion for my aprons." She stopped talking and swallowed hard. "Then Kinzy was murdered with one." She pulled her hand free of mine and rubbed her temples. "I've made such a mess. I don't know what to do. Rafe told me he needed space and went to visit a friend, obviously by what Eric said, his college roommate who lives in Colorado."

I took a bracing sip of my coffee. "You didn't know where he went?"

She shook her head. "I haven't talked to him since he stormed out of the house with his suitcase in hand."

"I think the first thing you need to do is speak to Rafe." I didn't tell her that I knew he was en route to the resort. "Are the medical personnel in the first-floor hotel room?"

Shannon nodded.

"Is that why you're late, sneak away and come back rumpled?"

"Yes." Shannon studied her hands.

"Is that where you were going when the security camera took your picture?"

"Yes."

"Have you told Sheriff Perry any of this?"

"No." Shannon lifted her chin. Her eyes found mine.

"You need to. This is your alibi for Kinzy's murder."

"And maybe the restraining order nonsense. Yesterday, Sheriff Perry told me Leon was filing the restraining order. I couldn't tell him that the hormones they're giving me are affecting my mood." She looked at her empty plate. "And my appetite and weight. I feel like such a failure."

"You aren't. Many people face fertility problems. You should've told Quintin and the rest of us. We're your friends. We'll support you no matter what."

A slight twinkle shone from her eyes. "Thank you for understanding."

"You're going to be surprised. Everyone is going to understand. They would've from the start. Promise me you'll call Rafe and then go talk to Sheriff Perry."

"I promise. I'm going right now." Shannon fished her phone out of her nearby purse and walked toward the doorway.

"Shannon."

She looked over her shoulder.

"You'll be a great mom."

A broad smile creased her face. "Thank you," she said, and walked out the door.

I sipped my coffee and tried a bite of my pecan pie bar,

happy to know that by the end of the day Shannon would no longer be a person of interest in the murder of Kinzy Hummel. Mentally, I checked Shannon off my list of people to talk to. I was down to one, Leon Chapski. Checking the time on my phone, I saw that I still had an hour before we'd start filming again.

I drained my coffee, threw our lunch trash away and set out to confront Leon.

CHAPTER TWENTY-ONE

Turns out, Leon was harder to find than I thought he'd be. Since it was lunchtime, I tried all the restaurants and the coffee shop. I headed to the basement to check the resort's lounge, The Queen's Sacrifice, even though I thought it opened around five in the afternoon. I'd been right. Although I didn't check the nearby bowling alley, I searched the gym and pool area to no avail. As a last resort, I asked the front desk to ring his room—no answer.

Almost out of time and of ideas where to find him, I plopped down into a comfy lobby chair. Where could he be? Had he left the premises without checking out?

"Courtney, there you are!" Pamela sounded relieved. Had she thought I was in danger? "Victoria wants you back on set. Didn't you see your text?"

I pulled out my phone. "Sorry, I missed it." I'd also

missed one from Caroline that said, "Toy drive is going well thanks to *The American Baking Battle's* big donation. Miss you." I glanced at the time. It was later than I thought. "Do you have a vehicle?"

Pamela pulled keys out of her pocket. "A security van; let's go."

I followed her out of the main doors and toward the maintenance vehicle lot. Once inside the comfort of a security van, I ran a thought past Pamela. "Did Sheriff Perry clear Leon from the suspect list and allow him to leave?" It was possible the front desk hadn't updated their records.

"To my knowledge, Sheriff Perry hasn't removed anyone from the person of interest list."

Contemplating her answer, I stared out of the side window at the snow-capped Pocono Mountain range. Was Pamela's information up to date? Once Shannon told Sheriff Perry the truth and he verified her alibi, he'd cross her name from the list. In my mind, it would take one quick phone call to the medical personnel in the first-floor hotel suite to verify her story.

"However, I do know something you'll be interested in."

I gave Pamela my full attention.

"I'm only telling you this because you put yourself in unsafe situations."

"Not you too?"

She cast a sidelong glance at me, then rolled her eyes. "Leon's missing."

"What?"

"His firm called the resort. It's been almost twenty-four hours since they've heard from him, which is out of character. They're worried he became a second murder victim. The resort reported it to Sheriff Perry. We've been looking for him all morning."

Pamela pulled into a parking spot marked "Facilities" close to the back entrance. "Again, I could lose my job, but I like you and you have an uncanny ability of getting into danger's path and I can't be on set to guard you until Leon is found."

Hmmm . . . I wondered what kind of game he was playing. "Why are they so concerned?"

"I guess he's very hands-on running the firm and," she hesitated, "he's second in line to inherit Harold Hummel's estate—his vast estate, which I understand will give the firm a large infusion of money, but if Leon is dead, the estate will be tied up in probate."

My hunch was right about the will. "I saw him this morning. He was fine then." Why wasn't Leon answering calls?

"Really? Where?"

"The coffee shop. He and Marley sat in a secluded corner. . . ." My voice trailed off.

"Thanks for the intel. I'll let Sheriff Perry know. We'll probably need to talk to Marley."

I slipped out of the van and headed toward the back door. Pamela burned rubber turning the vehicle around.

I cut a maze through the corridor, past the restrooms and faux janitor's closet, just in time for my stylist to fix my flaws while I thought about what Pamela said. I didn't have time to poke around the shadowed wings of the set, but I'd keep those areas in my sights. Had Marley sneaked Leon onto the set somehow? Was he hiding somewhere in the workshop again, ready to pounce out with another accusation against Shannon, or lying in wait for another victim? Which I didn't plan to be me!

Perhaps Marley knew or said too much in telling me he'd been paid to make trouble for Shannon, then Kinzy, and Leon planned to do him harm. Pamela's knowledge of Leon being the next in line to inherit Harold's estate confirmed in my mind that Leon killed Kinzy. Fear sent a shiver through me, raising the hair on my arms and the back of my neck.

I sent a quick text to Pamela asking her to remind Drake and Sheriff Perry of Leon's acumen for hiding on set and asked them to send someone to check it out. Her reply was a thumbs up.

"Places." Brenden clapped his hands.

Skylar and I started to walk to the gingerbread house.

"No." Victoria waved us over. "We're filming in front of the contestants."

Once in our places, a final camera and lighting angle was checked, Brenden counted us down.

"Bakers, you'll have four hours to bake and decorate a Christmas cake that represents present-day themes."

I picked up where Skylar stopped. "We have a Christmas surprise for you!" A crew member brought out brightly wrapped boxes. "Unwrap your gifts and see what you get to incorporate into the decoration of your cake."

With doubt-filled faces, they opened the boxes.

"I can do this!" Mya squealed and lifted a pinecone.

Marley frowned and lifted out a reindeer. Brystol looked stumped for a moment at a snowman.

With merriment in our voices, Skylar and I said, "The baking begins now."

"Cut."

We backed away from the action so the cameras could catch the frantic start.

"Harrison and Shannon, if she comes back to the set, are doing the interviews. You're free for a few hours," Brenden said, then walked away.

"I think I'll go take a nap!" Skylar saluted with a wave and left.

I surveyed the room and didn't see any extra security. Should I walk around the perimeter of the set?

My phone pinged with a text. I retrieved it from the seat of my set chair. The message was from Pamela saying security would come and look around. I answered by reminding her not to forget the janitor's closet, which was an entry to the tunnel system. I received another thumbs up.

While I had my phone out, I sent a quick text to Eric apprising him of the Shannon situation. Then I took a seat, intending on staying here, where I felt safe, and watching the baking action.

My phone jingled. I read Eric's reply. He, like me, was relieved to hear Shannon had confessed her troubles. He'd heard from Rafe, who was on the last leg of his trip to the resort. He then reminded me that when I had downtime, I should head to my set and practice the rosettes since we'd be filming tomorrow morning.

So much for relaxing. When I replied that I'd go to the set now, he answered that he was tied up with the director resumes and would get to the set as soon as he could. I stepped up to wardrobe with caution. Pamela's warning had spooked me. I trusted the security detail in the building, yet I remembered what it was like to be attacked by a mad killer too.

Once inside I saw that the stylists, or someone else, had rearranged the room so the table was in the opposite corner as before and closer to the coffeepot. In record time, I changed into my own clothing and scurried down the stairs to the main floor.

Apprehensive, I wondered if I should walk to the resort. After all, I'd deemed Leon the killer and his location was unknown. I sought out Brenden. "Do you know if anyone is shuttling over to the resort?"

"I am." Victoria stood. "I have some business calls to return. Can I offer you a lift?"

"Yes, please." I smiled.

"I'm glad you have a jacket." Victoria lifted a black wool cape and swung it over her shoulders. "The only thing available was a multi-passenger cart."

We walked outside and accessed the vehicle. "It surprises me you know how to drive one of these."

Victoria let out a hearty laugh. "It's an oversized golf cart and I'm an avid golfer."

She turned onto the path that looped around the resort and ended at the main entrance.

"Thank you for the lift. I have to tell you I didn't really want to walk back to the resort alone."

"Why?"

My turn to let out a laugh, a nervous one. "Well, I heard Leon is missing and I think he's the murderer." As soon as the words came out, I realized I'd spoken out of turn. Again. "That's not common knowledge," I hastily added. "Please just be aware of your surroundings."

"Thank you, I will. Since you've brought the subject up. I'm intrigued by your amateur sleuthing. I'd think after being attacked by not one but two murderers, you'd shy away from danger instead of running toward it."

Why did everyone always say that? "I wasn't trying to find danger. I wanted to clear my name, and my friends' names. It's unnerving being under the suspect of the law."

She smiled. "A pure heart then?"

"I don't know, maybe."

"So, you think Leon murdered Kinzy, not Shannon or Quintin?"

I turned my head so she wouldn't see my frown. No one had ever said Quintin was under suspicion. Then I realized that she was new to this process and just had just thrown out random names. "Neither. Shannon has an alibi." I was confident by now Sheriff Perry removed her name from the person-of-interest list.

"Really? I'm glad to hear that." She grinned and cast a glance my way. "I enjoy Shannon's show and I'm looking forward to your joint venture. Have you considered Brenden for a director?"

"He's too seasoned for a summer replacement program with no guarantee of renewal." I managed to cover my surprise at her admission of being Shannon's fan since I'd overheard her conversation with Brenden about Shannon's weight. Then again, a fan would want their favorite to look their best and keep their job, so maybe she did have Shannon's best interest at heart. It didn't faze me she was only a fan of Shannon. Citified Victoria wasn't in my programming demographic.

"Does Quintin have an alibi for the murder too?" Victoria asked.

"I don't know. I guess I never suspected him. Do you?"

"Oh, just a thought since his absence on the set may be house arrest." She laughed and continued, "Under surveillance or something. You're stuck on Leon, huh?"

"I am." My thoughts settled on him. Suddenly another conversation popped into my mind: Leon and Kinzy's argument on the day she was killed. He'd told her settling the estate was more important than her directing job, not her assistant directing job. Had he misspoken or did he mean Shannon and my show? If it was our show, that was a secret. The only way he'd know about that was if he was on the same flight as Quintin and Kinzy and overheard them talking.

Sheriff Perry might think this was a stretch, but I didn't. I'd learned my lesson about not telling him information that might be vital to the investigation. I pulled out my phone and tapped out a text to Sheriff Perry, copying Drake and Pamela.

"What was that all about?" Victoria stretched her neck to look at my phone.

"Our conversation helped me remember something that might be key to the case."

"Really, what would that be?"

"I asked Sheriff Perry to check the flight list of passengers on the plane with Quin . . ." I stopped, catching myself before giving away any more of my friend's secrets. I cleared my throat, "Kinzy."

"Why did you do that?" Victoria snapped out the question. "Sheriff Perry has asked you repeatedly to stay out of his investigations. I get that you're a naturally curious person, but you get in his way, and quite frankly, undermine his authority. I was just having a fun little conversation with you to pass the time on the ride and you took it too far."

She huffed then stopped the cart with a jerk. My body

snapped forward then back. Thank goodness for safety belts.

She turned a horrified look on me. "You do realize that these murders and your name associated with them could cause the show cancellation?" She turned, exited the vehicle and stomped passed the valet attendant. "Brenden just can't catch a break." She was still ranting, although I couldn't make out the words, when she entered the resort.

I swallowed hard. Talk about being on the wrong side of an angry mama bear!

The Cooking with the Farmer's Daughter suite was empty when I entered. Flipping on the lights, I saw facilities had decorated the room. The large Father Christmas with his reindeer stood centered in front of the counter. The long shots zooming in and out would capture their festiveness. Fir and holly boughs edged the front and side of the counter. Clusters of pinecones and holly hung on green velvet ribbons from the drop-ceiling tile tracks in varying lengths. The decorations, plus the red and black plaid holiday sweatshirt I planned to wear, should give the segment a country Christmas vibe.

I stood for a moment in the solitude of the room. Had Leon been found? Could he be in our suite? I had flicked on all the lights. There were no shadowy corners in this room. I quickly stepped over to the door that adjoined the second suite and locked it. Leon would've had to steal a security key from Sheriff Perry, Drake, Pamela or Eric to get into the suite. The thought eased my mind. For good measure, I texted Eric my whereabouts. He responded he'd be at least another forty-five minutes. He'd left his tablet on the counter. I woke it up, entered the password and found his music app. I chose the station that played contemporary Christmas music and turned the speaker volume up.

I danced over to an apron laying on my counter. It was from Shannon's holiday line but clashed with the set decorations. The print was blue with aluminum Christmas trees. I still needed to ask if wardrobe had the apron from Shannon's line with either reindeer or snow-covered evergreens for use on the baking competition and if I could borrow one.

Slipping the neck strap over my head, I paused for a moment and thought of Kinzy. Had the information I sent to Sheriff Perry helped his case? Had he taken it seriously? I wrapped the apron around me and bowed the ties, then put my focus on the task at hand and not the murder investigation.

I really wanted the cookies to turn out. Eric loved them. Although they'd never replace the ones his grandmother made, maybe they'd become one of our traditions. I smiled. We'd created happy couple memories without knowing it, like going to the opening day of the Christkindl market and rewatching *Jingle All the Way* while sipping hot chocolate and eating popcorn. Or maybe Eric had known, and I hadn't? I knew now and planned to add making rosette cookies to our holiday traditions.

Giving the recipe a thorough read through, I started with the first step, heating the oil. I filled a heavy stockpot with vegetable oil and put it on the electric hot plate. I clipped a cooking thermometer to the side of the pan, making sure it didn't touch the bottom and give me a false read. After I lined a cookie sheet with paper towels and cookie racks, I grabbed the recipe and whipped up the batter. I checked the oil temp. It wasn't quite hot enough. I stuck the rosette irons in to preheat. Impatient to get started, I watched the thermometer gauge, which didn't seem to move.

When the door handle rattled, I jumped. My heartbeat revved. I waited. If it was Eric, security or Sheriff Perry they'd use their key entry. It rattled again. I drew a shaky breath and grabbed my cell phone.

Hard rapping shook the door. "Courtney? Courtney? Are you in there?"

Panic sounded in Victoria's tone. Had something happened on set?

"Yes," I hollered running toward the door. "I'm coming." I opened the door a crack, confirmed it was her, and then widened the entry. "Is something wrong?"

A sheepish expression crossed her features. "No. Sorry, I didn't expect the door to be locked. With your history, I thought maybe . . ."

Her voice trailed off. I appreciated her concern. "I'm locked in at all times. It's a security measure."

"Am I interrupting you and Eric?"

"No. Eric's working in his suite. I'm practicing a recipe for filming tomorrow."

Victoria grinned. "May I come in? I'd like to apologize."

I stepped aside and she entered the room.

"I won't stay long," Victoria said walking over to a stool.

I joined her, standing at the corner of the counter.

"I feel so badly about how I walked away from you. My tone and actions were rude. I apologize. Of course, you aren't trying to sabotage the show with your nosing around. It's your livelihood too."

I stared at Victoria. Did she realize she just gave me a backhanded apology?

"Brenden's finally successful. I just don't want anything or anyone messing that up like Kinzy planned to."

Scrunching my face, I said, "Kinzy wasn't messing anything up. She was an asset to Brenden."

Victoria pinned me with a look that told me she thought I was being naïve. "Kinzy was after Brenden's job."

"No, she wasn't."

"Courtney, I know for a fact she was. I overheard her talking to Quintin." She stood and stepped closer to me.

Had Kinzy slipped and mentioned something in the resort? Had Victoria caught a snippet of a private conversation in a restaurant? "No, you're mistaken. Eric hired Kinzy as the director for Shannon and my new show."

In an instant, rage settled into Victoria's features. She squared her shoulders. Was this about protecting Brenden or being told she was mistaken?

Our eyes met.

Her lips curled into a satisfied smile. "I'm a mother. I'd do anything to protect my child. Anything."

The baking timer in my brain buzzed. My eyes widened. I'd locked myself into a room with a killer. "You strangled Kinzy."

"I had to. Brenden had finally made it in his career with a hit television show. I was no longer the laughing-stock in my social circles because my son was artsy instead of business minded. I couldn't let a woman who'd slept her way to the top take it away from him." She closed the already small gap between us.

I took a long step backward. "You were on the plane with Quintin and Kinzy."

"Yes, I was. She and Quintin sat behind me. Of course, I didn't know who they were until she went on and on about *The American Baking Battle* and her new directing job while engaging in lovey-dovey banter." She snorted. "I hate unqualified women who sleep their way to the top. I learned the business from the bottom up to earn my appointment as CEO."

"But Kinzy wasn't doing that. Eric offered her the director's job, not Quintin."

"I know that now." Victoria snapped. "But it's too late. You texted that buffoon of a sheriff. He'll find my name on the first-class passenger list. I'll be under suspicion for murder. I've thought about it and you're going to have to pay for that."

Before I could defend Sheriff Perry, or buy more time, Victoria lunged forward. I turned and started to run around the counter. Her long arm darted out and caught my apron tie. She held fast to the fabric and tugged. My forward momentum untied the back bow. The fabric flapped loose of my body. The only thing holding it on was the neck band. The same part of the apron that cut off Kinzy's airflow.

I tried to rip it from my neck while I continued to move. It caught on my earring. Victoria tugged and twisted, sliding the apron around to my back. The fabric snapped off my earring. The band slid down my neck and choked me. Victoria pulled hard. I pushed my fingers under the fabric to relieve the tightness.

Victoria seized the opportunity. She rammed into me full force. I released my hold on the neckband to stop myself from face planting on the counter. The edge hit me mid-torso, knocking the wind out of me. I gasped a big breath.

Before I could move, Victoria spun me around, pinning one hand behind my back. I pounded her with my free fist. She had a height and weight advantage and used her body as leverage to hold me against the counter. The hard-plastic pinecones in the Christmas garland bit into my back. She started twisting the apron band.

What should I do? Force my fist under the strangling fabric or continue to use it to beat her? I decided to go for her eye with my thumb, but only managed to scratch her nose with my nails. She let out a yelp. A red welt appeared, but she continued to twist the fabric with a vengeance. Evil distorted her features.

I needed to buy time. "Victoria, don't do this. Think of what it will do to Brenden's career when you're caught." My words croaked out.

She laughed. "I won't be caught. There isn't any way they can tie me to Kinzy or your murder."

The twisting fabric bit into my skin at the back of my neck. I swung my fist through the air as hard as I could several times, hoping to connect with a vital area to make Victoria back off. She managed to dodge most of them. "You know I switched the name cards the first day to make Kinzy look incompetent. I planned to continue with those types of pranks until Brenden fired her. Then she overstepped her authority. With me of all people. I knew the only thing to do was eliminate her. She was a stronger personality than Brenden. Pair that with her big-shot lover and it'd be a cinch for her to step into his director job."

Victoria spoke as fast as she twisted. I savored each breath I could still take.

"I grabbed Marley's discarded apron when no one was looking. So many hands had touched it, it'd be hard to get a good fingerprint reading. I scooted it across the floor with my foot for good measure, hoping to pick up dust, dirt and various hair samples. Then instead of leaving, I hid in the janitor's closet. Which I found out was an entry to the tunnel system, making it easy to escape."

The tightening fabric now pinched the circumference of the skin around my neck. I gasped and swallowed as much air as I could to ward off the lightheadedness from the lack of oxygen. I had to get away. I had to think now while I could.

Had it been forty-five minutes yet? Was Eric on his way? Evil or madness distorted Victoria's features. She pressed into me. The arm pinned behind me was numb. My head swam. In dizzying double, the lights floated over my head. I needed air. I tried to inhale deep through my mouth and nose. The aroma of overly hot oil assaulted my nostrils just before my breath coughed out of me.

I couldn't let her twist the strap any tighter. In a last-ditch effort, with what little strength I had left, I kicked my right foot in a side-to-side motion, hoping to knock her off her feet. It worked. She staggered, losing some of her footing. She stopped twisting the fabric while she re-covered, which was just long enough for me to reach be-hind and to the side with my free hand. Heat radiated from the hot plate and kettle, helping me gauge the distance. I caught my pinkie on the side of the hot pan and instinctively pulled it back.

A guttural growl cut through the room. Victoria straddled my legs and leaned forward, bending my body backward and lifting my feet from the ground. I kicked and thrashed them, occasionally hitting some part of her lower body. I knew this position gave her better leverage to finish me off. Her eyes, intent with concentration on the matter at hand—killing me—didn't seem to notice what my free hand was doing.

I found the heat source again and carefully searched for the handle of the rosette iron. My fingers brushed it. Greedily, I tried to suck in air. Very little made it through to my lungs. My head swirled. My limbs weakened. My world started to darken. I knew before long I'd be out. With everything I had, I flipped my fingers around. It only took two times before I grasped the handle. Fighting to keep my eyes open and my brain conscious for just a few more seconds, I whipped the hot iron through the air, hoping to catch her hand.

I heard the sizzle, then Victoria's bloodcurdling scream echoed through the room. I knew I'd hit my mark. She released her hold on the apron and fell away from me. Dropping the rosette iron, I coughed and choked and managed to loosen the fabric enough to get some air into my lungs. Weak-kneed, I staggered for the door at the same time the lock beeped.

Help had arrived! I started to lose consciousness. I dropped to my knees.

"Courtney!" Pamela hollered as she followed Sheriff Perry into the room. She wrapped an arm around me for support and with nimble fingers untwisted the band from my neck.

"I guess it wasn't you who screamed." Sheriff Perry holstered his gun and stepped around me. I leaned against Pamela for support and watched Sheriff Perry. He hovered over Victoria, who'd slumped to the floor holding on to her right cheek. He pulled her hand away and whistled before saying, "That's going to leave a mark."

CHAPTER TWENTY-TWO

Eric rushed to my side when Shannon and I entered the Grand Ballroom and slipped his arm around me. I leaned into his strength and support. It'd been a harrowing forty-eight hours for all of us. As protective as Eric had been since the incident, you'd think I was the only person affected.

I'd never lost consciousness. My total air supply hadn't been cut off so once the fabric had been loosened, I could breathe normally. The whole ordeal left wardrobe with another costume problem: how to cover up the bruises and red marks on my neck. Luckily, the gift shop had another brocade scarf. My stylist wound it, not too tightly, around my neck so we could finish filming the segment. The resort's gift shop had a turtleneck I'd worn to film the rosette segment of the network special.

Covering up my narrow-escape wounds was the easy

fix. Brenden had a mental breakdown when he learned his mother had killed Kinzy over a misunderstanding on her part and then tried to end my life. Quintin, still bearing his own grief, scurried to find a replacement. Thanks to Eric, it didn't take long.

I lifted my face to the man I loved and smiled. He dipped his head and captured my lips in a quick kiss. "Isn't this better than being mad at me?" I asked.

His just-moments-ago sweet lips pulled into a grim line. He clenched his jaw. "Courtney, you have to stop putting yourself in danger. I love you and I don't want to lose you."

This seemed like his millionth warning. "No one suspected Victoria of murder until Sheriff Perry checked the flight list. I thought I was safe." I kept my tone nonconfrontational. I thought I made a valid point.

"That fact seems like a bit of a technicality to me. I'm just glad Sheriff Perry was coming to talk to you about your text."

"Okay, you two, this is a party," Shannon drawled. Rafe stood by the bar. She caught his eye and waved him over.

"Have I told you how proud I am of you?" My eyes searched Eric's face.

His wide smile cracked his stern veneer. "Once or twice."

"I'm so glad you had those director's resumes and Tina could make it." Shannon welcomed Rafe into the group by opening her arms. He stepped into her hug. When their embrace ended, she said, "It's bad enough we lost two filming days with only a few hours left to shoot the end of the baking competition. I just want to go home."

Rafe nodded a greeting to Eric and me. "What are we talking about?"

"Eric saving the day by suggesting Tina to direct the last half of the finale and handle all the editing." Pride filled my tone and heart.

"Speaking of Tina." Rafe looked around. "Is she attending the party?"

"I think so," Eric said.

I scanned the small crowd of cast, crew and contestants. My eyes rested on Drake and Pamela standing beside a cocktail table. Turns out the errand Pamela ran for Drake had nothing to do with the murder of Kinzy Hummel and everything to do with Nolan Security's next gig.

"I don't see her yet."

Eric's response pulled me back into the current conversation.

"Shall we make the offer tonight?" Rafe asked.

"Yes!" Shannon and I said at the same time, then laughed.

We'd both clicked with Tina and liked her directing style. A single mother with a real woman figure brought comfort to Shannon. I told Eric if Shannon was happy, I was. Just like that, we'd both became excited again for our joint venture and nailed down the design for the kitchen. Eric and Rafe were working on renting a studio close to Shannon's Texas home to film. We hoped the location wouldn't deter Tina from accepting the job offer.

"Hello."

I turned to see a man and woman standing behind me. The woman, flushed and beaming, stared at me, obviously starstruck. I flicked my eyes to the man. "Sheriff Perry?"

His expression morphed into a glower.

I laughed. "Sorry, you look different out of uniform."

He harrumphed.

"Oh, Milton, get over it." The woman patted his arm, then looked at me. "That always bothers him. I'm Kayla Perry, his wife."

I grasped the hand she stuck out. Petite like me, she kept her white hair in a spiky pixie and appeared to be a woman of her own mind. I liked her already.

"I'm a big fan of yours. I suppose Milt's told you that in all of your dealings."

My gaze flew back to his and I thought I saw a hint of fear. I laughed. "He hasn't, but in his defense, he's working and it's always under unfortunate circumstances."

"True." She sighed. "I don't know how you continue to work while murders happen all around you."

I had no answer, so I shrugged.

The applause of the party attendees drew our attention to the door. Marley pushed a cart with the cake that made him champion of *The American Baking Battle Christmas Edition,* his cake of the future, which he called his out-of-this-world cake. It was. He fashioned a Santa, sleigh and all eight reindeer out of modeling chocolate. They flew around a large circular cake covered with fondant that looked like the globe. He'd placed the confection on a rotating cake plate, so it looked like Santa circling the world on Christmas Eve.

Although Mya and Brystol made delicious cakes, they couldn't beat Marley in design or flavor. He literally made the challenge look like a piece of cake.

The clapping died down. Mya and Brystol moved from the crowd and helped Marley start to serve his cake.

Looking at Shannon and Harrison, I said, "I would never have guessed he'd take the top prize."

Harrison shrugged. "You never know."

The catering staff started to uncover the buffet chafing dishes.

"Is that prime rib?" Sheriff Perry asked. "Nice party!"

"It is. Sadly, Victoria planned a terrific party that neither she nor Brenden can attend," I said.

"It's too bad for Brenden." Sheriff Perry shook his head. "I hate to see innocent people get hurt."

"Me too." Involuntarily, I fingered the scarf around my neck.

"I didn't mean you," he said, tone pointed. "You nose around and get into trouble."

"Milton! What a thing to say!" Kayla admonished.

"Well, she does." Sheriff Perry turned his attention to his wife.

"I'll second that," Eric piped up.

I decided to change the subject. "Did Leon leave?" I asked, my gaze on Sheriff Perry.

"Yesterday. The coroner rushed the death certificate, which made him very happy."

Leon hadn't been missing or hiding. He'd booked two all-day skiing excursions with the resort. He didn't contact his office because he felt he needed some time off. After the restraining order incident, he'd done some soul searching and wondered when he'd become *that* kind of attorney. After Victoria's arrest, he'd apologized to Marley for using him as a pawn, putting him under suspicion for murder and almost messing up his chance to participate in the baking competition. Turns out Leon was co-executor with Kinzy. She only stood to inherit a tidy sum of money along with heirlooms, valuable jewelry and artwork. Harold had left Leon the land. Leon planned to turn it into a nature preserve to counter the oil pipeline Harold had supported.

"Enough police talk. Let's go get a drink and let Courtney enjoy her evening." Kayla looped her fingers through Sheriff Perry's hand and led him to the bar along the far wall.

"Merry Christmas!" Skylar approached our group. "I wanted to say hello and tell the ladies how ravishing they look tonight." He followed his compliment with a charming smile.

Shannon and I gave him our thanks and a hug.

"Hey, I want in on this!" Harrison joined us, turning our trio into a group hug. "I enjoy working with all of you. This was a tough filming to get through. It makes me wonder what the future will hold."

"Well," I broke our embrace, "Eric can shed some light on that."

"Do tell?" Harrison asked.

Our group circled around him. "Quintin's taking a six-month sabbatical. He's asked me to take over his producer responsibilities, one of which is the negotiation of more *American Baking Battle* seasons."

Surprise lit Harrison's face. "Does that include the *Children and Chef* livestreaming from the network's kitchen?"

Eric nodded.

Harrison turned to Shannon. "Great news."

"It is." She looked at Rafe, then her eyes searched the group. "We've decided I shouldn't take part in the project."

"What are you talking about?" Skylar asked.

"Harrison's talking about a livestreaming segment

Quintin developed for him and Shannon where two lucky children name the menu and get to cook the meal with a chef," Eric said. He furrowed his brow. "Is it because I'm taking the reins?"

"Oh, no!" Shannon waved a hand through the air. "We feel I need to take time off from extra job duties until I'm finished with in vitro."

"That's an excellent idea," Skylar said.

"I'll second it. You need to know that we'll support you through all of this." I gave Shannon an encouraging look.

"You bet," Harrison said. "No more hiding your sorrow."

"Okay." Shannon's blue eyes misted. "I'm so lucky to have friends like you."

"We're the lucky ones," Skylar said.

The mist turned to happy tears. One trickled down her cheek. She chuckled. "Darned hormones." Rafe gave her a squeeze. We all knew this time her emotions had nothing to do with in vitro shots.

"Do you know who will take your place?" Harrison asked.

Sniffling, Shannon swiped away her tears. "I'm looking at her." Shannon smiled my way.

"Of course!" Harrison smiled. He turned to Skylar. "Shall we go get everyone drinks for a Christmas toast?"

"Only soda for me," Shannon called after them. "I need to sit down. These shoes are killing me." Shannon looped her hand through Rafe's arm and nodded toward a table for eight.

"We'll be there in a minute," Eric called after them. "I need to speak with Courtney."

I studied Eric. "What's wrong?"

"Nothing. I have good news. The knife company agreed to sell the knives as a set first. They pushed the production date up, so you should have them available during both new shows."

I threw my arms around his neck. "That's wonderful! My Christmas couldn't get any better."

"Wouldn't your parents coming home make your Christmas better?"

A wide smile stretched across my face. "They are. I got a long email from them just before I came to the party. They'll arrive in Chicago a few days before Christmas and stay through the New Year. We can all finish the toy drive just like old times."

Eric hugged me, then clasped my hand and led me toward the Christmas tree.

"What are you doing? Shannon and Rafe are over there." I pointed.

"The mistletoe is over here. I want a kiss. Not the quick, we're in public type of kiss. A meaningful one, and mistletoe provides the perfect alibi."

Eric captured my lips before I could respond. I leaned in. He tightened his embrace and deepened his kiss. Joy filled my heart. All my Christmas wishes were coming true. It was truly a very merry Christmas.

Connect with U(s)

Visit us online at
KensingtonBooks.com
to read more from your favorite authors, see books
by series, view reading group guides, and more.

Join us on social media

for sneak peeks, chances to win books and prize packs,
and to share your thoughts with other readers.

facebook.com/kensingtonpublishing
twitter.com/kensingtonbooks

Tell us what you think!

To share your thoughts, submit a review,
or sign up for our eNewsletters, please visit:
KensingtonBooks.com/TellUs.